8140   GAL/C

GALLEYWOOD

Essex*Works.*
For a better quality of life

2 4 SEP 2010	2 4 MAR 2011	
1 – FEB 2011	– 4 DEC 2012	
1 0 AUG 2013 7 FEB 2014	– 4 APR 2015	
0 3 JAN 2012		
3 0 AUG 2013	30/1/24	
2·7 SEP 2013		
0 3 OCT 2013		
0 1 AUG 2014		

Please return this book on or before the date shown above. To renew go to www.essex.gov.uk/libraries, ring 0845 603 7628 or go to any Essex library.

il

GW00503734

'Well, well, what have we here?' Nick's voice was low, surprisingly cultured. His tone was teasing. **'A kiss from the prettiest woman here will be my prize.'**

Serena could smell him. Fresh sweat, laundered linen, something else deeply masculine she couldn't put a name to. Reluctantly she forced herself to hold his gaze, to counter his teasing smile with a haughty look of her own.

'Definitely the prettiest woman here. A kiss will be worth all the money in the winner's purse and more.' The words were whispered in her ear as he pushed back her bonnet, tilting her chin with a firm but gentle finger. He hesitated for a tantalising moment, then pulled her closer, confining the contact to his lips alone.

It was a teasing kiss, which lasted no more than a few seconds. His breath was warm and sweet. His lips were soft against her own.

'Get off me, you ruffian!' she said angrily, pushing him away. What had she been thinking?

The man who had taken such a liberty eyed her quizzically. 'Ruffian or not, you enjoyed that as much as I did, I'll wager...'

Born and educated in Scotland, **Marguerite Kaye** originally qualified as a lawyer but chose not to practise—a decision which was a relief both to her and the Scottish legal establishment. While carving out a successful career in IT, she occupied herself with her twin passions of studying history and reading, picking up a first-class honours and a Masters degree along the way.

The course of her life changed dramatically when she found her soul mate. After an idyllic year out, spent travelling round the Mediterranean, Marguerite decided to take the plunge and pursue her life-long ambition to write for a living—a dream she had cherished ever since winning a national poetry competition at the age of nine.

Just like one of her fictional heroines, Marguerite's fantasy has become reality. She has published history and travel articles, as well as short stories, but romances are her passion. Marguerite describes Georgette Heyer and Doris Day as her biggest early influences, and her partner as her inspiration.

When she is not writing, Marguerite enjoys cooking and hill walking. A confirmed Europhile, who spends much of the year in sunny climes, she returns regularly to the beautiful Highland scenery of her native Argyll, the place she still calls home.

Marguerite would love to hear from you. You can contact her on: Marguerite_Kaye@hotmail.co.uk

THE RAKE AND THE HEIRESS

Marguerite Kaye

First published in Great Britain 2010
Large Print edition 2010
Harlequin Mills & Boon Limited,
Eton House, 18-24 Paradise Road, Richmond, Surrey TW9 1SR

© Marguerite Kaye 2010

ISBN: 978 0 263 21157 3

Harlequin Mills & Boon policy is to use papers that are natural, renewable and recyclable products and made from wood grown in sustainable forests. The logging and manufacturing process conform to the legal environmental regulations of the country of origin.

Printed and bound in Great Britain
by CPI Antony Rowe, Chippenham, Wiltshire

THE RAKE AND
THE HEIRESS

*For A, who makes all things,
especially me, possible. Just love.*

A previous novel by Marguerite Kaye:

THE WICKED LORD RASENBY

Prologue

Paris—August 1815

The doctor closed the bedchamber door gently behind him and turned to the young woman waiting anxiously in the hallway. He noted with sadness that she was showing clear signs of strain following the trauma of the past few days. Her delicate beauty, while still intact, seemed fragile, as if frayed. The sparkle had gone from her cornflower-blue eyes, her creamy complexion was dull and ghostly pale, her blonde hair unkempt, confined carelessly under a bandeau. Despite his stern countenance and insistence on the timely settlement of bills, the doctor was a compassionate man at heart. He sighed deeply. At times like this he cursed his vocation.

The grave expression and resigned shake of his head told Serena all she needed to know. She fought to quell the tidal wave of despair that threatened to overwhelm her.

'You must keep him comfortable, Mademoiselle Cachet, that is all you can do for him now. I will return in the morning, but…' The doctor's shrug was all too eloquent. It was obvious he didn't expect Papa to survive the night.

Valiantly suppressing a sob—for what purpose would tears serve now?—Serena wearily forced herself upright from the support of the door frame she'd been leaning against. She tried to absorb the doctor's instructions, but his clear, calm words barely penetrated the fog enveloping her shocked mind. His voice seemed faint, as if it were coming from a far distant shore. Clean dressings and sleeping draughts would ease Papa's suffering, but not even a magic potion could save him now.

The doctor departed with an admonition to send for him if necessary, giving Serena a final comforting pat on the shoulder. As he opened the strong oak door at the foot of the stairwell which separated their living quarters from the gaming rooms, a sharp burst of drunken laughter pierced the air. With a steady supply of men returning from Waterloo the tables were always busy, but for once Serena cared naught. What use was a full purse without Papa to share its bounty?

Nothing mattered now save making the most of these last precious hours. Papa must see his daughter calm and loving, not tearful and dishevelled. Resolutely tucking a stray golden curl back under her bandeau, carefully straightening the neckline of her dress and taking a deep calming breath, Serena re-entered her father's bedchamber with a heavy heart.

Velvet hangings pulled shut over the leaded windows contained the stifling heat of the room and muffled all noise from the busy street below. A huge mirror above the marble fireplace reflected the rich rugs, the polished wood, the bright gilt and glowing silver fittings of the opulent furnishings. Reflected too, the snowy white pile of linen torn for bandages and the collection of vials and bottles atop the bedside table on which a decanter usually sat. On the floor a mound of bloodied dressings paid testament to Serena's hours of tender nursing. The scent of lavender water and laudanum lay heavy in the air.

Philip Cachet lay on a large tester bed, dwarfed by the mountains of pillows that had been arranged around his tall frame in an attempt to ease the flow of blood from his wound. *Why had he not simply handed over his purse?* For the hundredth time since Papa had staggered through the door clutching his chest, Serena cursed the cowardly footpad who had taken his valuables and now, it seemed, his life too. She was shocked to see how diminished her father looked, his shaven head bare and vulnerable without the wig he still insisted on wearing, despite it being out of fashion. His breath came in irregular, rasping sighs, and in the short time it had taken to confer with the doctor, his skin had assumed a waxen pallor.

Papa had been warned not to move lest the bleeding start again, but his eyes, the same vivid blue as her own, brightened when he saw her. As she closed the door softly, he raised his hand just a little from the silk counterpane in a frail gesture of welcome.

'*Ma belle*, at last. I have something of great

import to tell you, and it can wait no longer—I fear my time is almost come.' Ignoring her protestations, he gestured for Serena to come closer. 'No point in denial, *chérie*, I've lost too much blood. I need you to pay attention—you *must* listen.' A cough racked him. A small droplet of blood appeared at the side of his mouth. He wiped it away impatiently with a trembling hand.

Even now, Serena could see faint traces of the handsome man her father had been in his prime. The strong, regular features, the familiar charming smile that had extricated him from many a tricky situation. He was a gambler, and good enough to win—for the most part. For nigh on thirty years, Philip had supported first himself, then she and *Maman* too, by his sharp wits and his skill with the cards. Skills he had practised in countless gaming houses, in countless towns and cities across Europe.

Pulling a chair closer to the bedside, Serena sat down with a rustle of her silk skirts, gently stroking the delicate white hand lying unresponsive on the counterpane. His life was draining away in front of her eyes, yet she had to be strong. 'I'm here, Papa,' she whispered.

'*Mignonne*, I never meant to leave you like this. Your life was to have been very different. I'm sorry.'

'Don't be sorry, I wouldn't have had it any other way. We've had our share of fun, haven't we?' She smiled lovingly at him, the spark of humour in her eyes drawing the shadow of a response from his.

'Yes, but as you know only too well, at the end of any game there is always a reckoning.'

Serena muffled a sob with her handkerchief.

His fingers trembled in her hand. '*Ma fille*, you must be brave. Listen now, and don't interrupt, it's vitally important. Please don't judge me too harshly, for what I am about to tell you will shock you. It will also change your life for ever. *Écoute, petite*, I must go back to the beginning, thirty years ago…'

Chapter One

England—April 1816

Serena paused to catch her breath and admire the beautiful façade of the house. It was much grander and more imposing than she had expected, a classic Elizabethan country manor, the main body of the mellow brick building flanked by two elegant wings, which lent it a graceful symmetry. She had entered the grounds by a side gate, having decided, since it was such a pleasant morning, to walk the short distance from the village rather than take a carriage. It was very clement for the time of year and the spring bulbs were at their best. The grass by the side of the well-kept path was strewn with narcissi, banks of primroses and artfully placed clumps of iris just coming into bloom. The perfume of camellias and forsythia mingled with the fresh, damp smell of new-mown grass.

You must go to England, to Knightswood Hall, the home of my dear friend Nick Lytton. Papa's dying words to her—and amazingly, here she was, in the country of his birth, standing in the very grounds of his friend's home. It had been a wretched few months since her father's death, making ready for the move from Paris, but at least the sheer volume of things that needed to be done were a welcome distraction from the aching pain of his loss. Closing down the gaming salons had realised a surprising amount of money, more than enough to cover the expenses of the next few months and to establish her in comfort if things did not turn out as her father had hoped.

Serena had never been one to plan for the future, having been too much in the habit, of necessity, of living in the present. Of course what she wanted was her own home and her own family, but she wished for this in the vague way of one who had had, until now, little control over her own destiny. She had not met—or been allowed to meet—any man who came close to inhabiting her dreams. And as to a home! She had spent most of the last two years in Paris, and that was the longest she had ever been in one place.

Papa's revelations offered her wealth and position which, he vowed, would change her life completely. Change, she was ready to embrace, but the nature of it—in truth, she was not convinced that Papa's vision for her future was her own. *One step at a time*, she reminded herself. No point in jumping too far ahead. Today was just the beginning.

As she turned her mind to the interview that lay ahead, a cloud of butterflies seemed to take up residence in her stomach. The imposing bulk of the house only served to increase her apprehension. Nick Lytton was obviously a man of some standing. She countered the urge to turn tail and return to her lodgings by making a final check on her appearance. Her dress of lavender calico was cut in the French fashion, high in the waist and belling out towards her feet with rows of tiny ruffles edging the hem and the long sleeves. The shape became her tall figure, as did the three-quarter pelisse with its high collar. Her gold hair was dressed simply on top of her head, also in the latest French style, with small tendrils allowed to frame her cheekbones, the rest confined under a straw bonnet tied with a large lavender ribbon beneath her chin. The kid half-boots she wore were perhaps more suited to a stroll round a city square than the rough terrain of the countryside, but they had survived the walk without becoming too muddied, as had the deep frill on her fine lawn petticoat. She would do.

The path she had taken ran round the side of the house and disappeared towards some out-buildings, presumably the stables. She was about to follow the fork to the right leading to the imposing main entrance of the Hall, when a roar of voices diverted her. Another roar and a gust of laughter followed, too intriguing to be ignored. Lifting her petticoat clear of a small puddle, Serena moved cautiously towards the source of the commotion.

As she had surmised, the path took her to the stable yard, a square of earth surrounded on three sides by horse boxes and outhouses. The arched entrance way in which she stood formed the fourth side. In front of her were not horses, however, but an animated circle of people, men and boys mostly, with a scattering of women standing apart in the shelter of a doorway which presumably led to the kitchens.

In the centre of the circle two men, stripped to the waist, were boxing. The crowd roared encouragement and advice, many people excitedly betting on the outcome. The scent of horse and hay was overlaid by a fresher, richer aroma, of wet wool, sweat and mud. Over the noise of the crowd, Serena could hear the panting breath of the two fighters, the dull thwack of fist on flesh, the soft thud of stocking-clad feet on the hard earth. Though she had witnessed the occasional drink-fuelled scuffle before, she had never seen a mill. Drawn in by a mixture of curiosity and an unfamiliar *frisson* of excitement, she edged cautiously closer.

Both men wore buckskins and woollen stockings, their torsos stripped naked. The larger of the two was a fine specimen of manhood, with a bull-like neck, huge shoulders and hands as large as shovels, but even Serena's novice eye quickly saw that his weight and height hindered him. He was slow, his footwork stolid, and from the look of his left eye, which was closed and weeping, his opponent had already taken advantage of these shortcomings. He looked like a blacksmith, and in fact that is exactly what he was, his bulging biceps the product of long hours at the anvil.

It was the other combatant who captured Serena's attention. Compared to the giant he was slighter, built along sleeker, finer lines, although he was still a tall man and muscular too, without the brawn of the smithy. Most likely he was a coachman, for he exuded a certain air of superiority. His were muscles honed by exercise, not labour. It was, she thought, eyeing his body with unexpected relish, like watching a race horse matched with a shire.

The man held himself well, showing little sign of fatigue. His body, although glistening with sweat, was virtually unmarked. His buckskin-clad legs were long, and as he teased his opponent, dancing forwards and back, landing light punches, then dodging neatly aside, Serena watched entranced. The muscles on his back, his shoulders, his arms, clenched and rippled, tautened and relaxed. Her pulses quickened. She felt the stirring deep within her of a strange, unsettlingly raw emotion.

The sweat that glistened on the man's body accented his honed physique in the dappled sunlight. The control, the energy so economically expended, made her think of a coiled spring. A tiger ready to pounce, assured of dispatching his prey, but content to tease. The lumbering giant in front of him didn't have a prayer.

Around her, the murmuring crowd seemed to agree. 'Looks like Samuel's done for again.' 'Land 'im one for us, Sam, come on, boy!' But the encouragement was in vain. The blacksmith stumbled as a punch landed square and hard on his left shoulder. The crowd prevented him falling, pushing him back into the ring, but he was blown. He made a lunge for the coachman, a wild punch that caught only fresh air and threw him off balance into the bargain. He staggered forwards cursing, righting himself at the last minute.

The other man smiled, a sardonic smile that lit up his dark grey eyes, making Serena catch her breath. He was devilishly handsome, with his glossy black hair in disarray, those wicked grey eyes framed by heavy black brows, his perfectly sculpted mouth curled up in amusement.

The two combatants stood to for one last joust. They circled each other slowly, then Samuel lunged, taking his opponent by surprise for the first time and landing a powerful blow on his chest. The other man reeled, countering with a flurry of punches to Samuel's stomach, the blood from his bare knuckles smearing itself on to the blacksmith's skin, mingling with his sweat. Samuel bellowed in pain and turned to the side to shield himself, trying at the same time to use his hip to push the coachman away. It was a fatal mistake for he mistimed it, leaving his face exposed. A swift hard punch sent his head flying back, and a second under his jaw had him on the ground. It was over.

The crowd roared in approbation. Money changed hands. Samuel staggered to his feet. The victor stood, a triumphant smile adorning his face. His chest, covered in a fine matting of black hair that arrowed down to the top of his buckskin breeches, heaved as he regained his breath. He shook hands with Samuel, and when presented with the winner's purse, to Serena's surprise and the crowd's evident approval, handed it to his opponent.

'You deserve this more than I, Samuel, for you never know when you're beaten.' Laughter greeted this sally—they were obviously old rivals. Now Samuel was saying that in that case the victor deserved a prize too, and the crowd cheered. The coachman stood surveying the scene around him, shaking his head, denying the need for reward as he pulled a cambric shirt over his cooling body. That was when he spotted Serena.

She tried to turn away, but could find no passage through the circle of the crowd. A strong arm caught hers in an iron grip. 'Well, well, what have we here?' His voice was low, surprisingly cultured. His tone was teasing.

Serena coloured deeply, but remained where she was, transfixed by the look in those compelling grey eyes, restrained by his firm grip on her arm. The crowd waited silently, casting speculative looks towards her blushing countenance.

'A kiss from the prettiest woman here will be my prize,' the coachman announced.

He was standing directly in front of her. She could smell him. Fresh sweat, laundered linen, something else deeply masculine she couldn't put a name to. He was tall; she had to look up to meet his eyes. Reluctantly Serena forced herself to hold his gaze, to counter his teasing smile with a haughty look of her own.

His eyebrow quirked. 'Definitely the prettiest woman here. A kiss will be worth all the money in the winner's purse and more.' The words were for her only, whispered in her ear as he pushed back her bonnet, tilting her chin with a firm but gentle finger. As if in a trance Serena complied, her breathing shallow. He hesitated for a tantalising moment, then with a slight shrug pulled her closer, confining the contact to his lips alone.

It was a teasing kiss, like his teasing smile, which lasted no more than a few seconds. His breath was warm and sweet. His lips were soft against her own. The reserve of power she had sensed in the boxing ring was there too in his kiss, daring her to respond.

The crowd cheered lustily, bringing Serena to her senses, reminding her of the reason for her visit. 'Get off me, you ruffian!' she said angrily, pushing him away. *What had she been thinking?*

The coachman who had taken such a liberty in kissing her eyed her quizzically. 'Ruffian or not, you enjoyed that as much as me, I'll wager,' he said, quite unflustered by her temper. 'What are you doing here anyway? This is a private estate—have you lost your way?'

'Are you employed here?' Serena asked curtly.

'You could say I have the honour of serving the estate, yes.'

'Then I'm here to call on your master, Mr Lytton.'

'Well, you're not likely to find him round here, fraternising with tradesmen and servants and ruffians like me, now are you,' he answered with a grin.

Serena gritted her teeth. He was insufferable.

'If you care to call at the front door and present your card, I'm sure he'll be delighted to receive you.' Without a backward glance, the coachman turned on his heel and strode off.

Struggling to regain her rattled composure, Serena found her way back through the yard to the path that led to the main entrance. As she listened to the clang of the doorbell she put the episode firmly to the back of her mind, took a few calming breaths and tried to remember everything Papa had told her. Her heart fluttering with anticipation, she gave her name to the butler, following in his stately wake as he led her through what must have served as the great hall when the house was first built. It was an immense panelled space with a huge stone fireplace on one wall, the staircase leading to the upper floors at the far end. She was given no time to admire it, however, being ushered through a door in the panelling and deposited in a small sunny parlour, which faced on to the gardens at the front of the house. A fire crackled in the grate. A large arrangement of fresh spring flowers scented the room.

'Mr Lytton will join you shortly, madam.' The butler bowed and departed.

Serena pressed her tightly gloved hands together in an effort to stop them from shaking and took stock. It was a cosy room, stylish but comfortable and obviously well used. The warm colours of the soft furnishings, russet-and-gold patterned rugs and deep red upholstery, contrasted with the dark wood panelling that covered the walls, all the way from the wainscoting to a decorative rail just above head height.

How would the owner of this enchanting house receive her? It was bound to be an awkward meeting. Though there had apparently been some letters in the early days, her father and Nick Lytton had not met for nigh on thirty years. Serena was not looking forward to breaking the news that Papa had passed away.

Serena paced the room nervously, noticing the detailing on the wooden panelling for the first time. A frieze of roses was worked into the wood, connected by leaves, briars and little carved animals. *The last rose of summer left blooming alone.* The secret code that Papa had confided in her on that dreadful night when he died of his wounds. The words he had her repeat over and over so that Nick Lytton could be sure of her identity. The phrase had seemed strange, but now she could see it was apt.

What would he be like, this man who held the key to her future? Papa's age, obviously, and, it was clear from her surroundings, a man of wealth and status. A country squire run to fat, as men of that age were wont to do. Like as not he suffered also from the gout.

'Nicholas Lytton at your service, madam.'

Serena jumped. She had not heard him come in. The tone of the voice was deep. Cultured. Supremely confident. And horribly familiar. The charming smile she had been composing froze upon her face as she turned around.

He had bathed and changed after his exertions in the boxing ring, standing before her elegantly attired in a pair of biscuit-coloured knitted pantaloons and a tailcoat of green superfine cut close across shoulders which had no need of buckram wadding to emphasise their breadth. A clean white shirt and a cravat tied simply, with a striped silk waistcoat and gleaming Hessians, completed the outfit. Raising her head, she saw a strong jaw line, a mouth curved into what could be a smile, glossy black hair combed forwards on to high cheekbones. And those grey eyes.

Nicholas bowed and moved towards Serena, an arm outstretched in greeting. A pink flush tinged her skin, which had little to do with the heat of the fire crackling away at her back.

Amusement lurked as he watched her struggling to make sense of the situation, taking advantage of her confusion to usher her compliantly into a wing-backed chair beside the fire while he took the matching seat opposite. 'Coffee will be here any moment. You look as if you could do with some, Miss Cachet.'

He was relishing her embarrassment. Serena sat up straight in her chair, forcing her countenance into a look of cool composure completely at odds with the mixture of humiliation and fury she was feeling. 'Sir, you have already misled me once as to your identity. I beg you not to do so again.'

'I did not mislead you, madam. I said I had the honour of serving the estate and I do. I rather fancy it was you who jumped too quickly to the wrong conclusion. Perhaps your judgement was clouded by your all-too-obvious enjoyment of the base spectacle on offer?'

'There is no need to indulge in more jibes at my expense,' Serena said icily. 'I am here to meet Mr Nicholas Lytton on a matter of some import.'

'*As* I said, I *am* Nicholas Lytton.'

'But—you can't be! No, no, that's ridiculous.

The man I have business with is an old friend of my father's.'

'Ah. I expect you refer to *my* father.'

'Yes, that must be it. Of course, your father,' Serena said with enormous relief. 'May I speak with him?'

She leaned forwards eagerly. Her flushed cheeks blushed bright against the creamy smoothness of her skin. With her guinea-gold hair and cornflower-blue eyes framed by startlingly long dark lashes, she looked quite breathtakingly beautiful. Nicholas drank in the vision of loveliness she presented, regretfully shaking his head. 'I'm sorry, I'm afraid that will be quite impossible. He's dead these last ten years.'

'Dead!' Many times in the past few months she had pictured this scene, but this particular twist had never occurred to her. Serena sank back dejectedly in her chair. 'Dead. I did not expect— that is, I'm sorry, but it's rather a shock.'

What on earth was she to do now? Trying desperately to rally her thoughts, she took covert stock of the man opposite. She knew nothing of him save that he could box well and that he took outrageous liberties. Exactly the sort of man

Papa would have taken great care to keep well away from his daughter. Perhaps because their life was somewhat unconventional, her father had always been very protective, almost overly so. Naturally, she was banned from the gaming salons. Since their somewhat ambiguous position in society made it impossible for her to socialise in more respectable circles, however, the opportunities to meet men—eligible or otherwise—were few and far between. In fact, Nicholas Lytton was the first man to have kissed her, though she wasn't about to tell him that. He was insufferably arrogant enough as it was. Serena grappled for a solution to what appeared to be an insoluble problem. She was to trust no one save Nick Lytton. Yet Nick Lytton was dead. There seemed to be no way to avoid confiding in his son if she were not to leave empty-handed.

Still, instinct that had nothing at all to do with Papa's urge to secrecy and everything to do with Nicholas Lytton himself made her reticent. That fight. That kiss. The unexpected effect the man himself was having on her. The watchfulness that lurked there, despite the nonchalant way he sat in the chair. Recalling the scene in the stable yard, a heat swept through her, which had naught to do with embarrassment. Shocking though it was to admit it, she had enjoyed the sight of Nicholas Lytton semi-naked, his muscles rippling. When he kissed her, her first instinct had not been to draw back as propriety demanded, but to pull him close, to feel for herself the warm skin, the crisply curling hair, the cord-like muscles and sinew. She had never had such lustful thoughts before. Now was certainly not the time to have them again. Looking up, she became aware of his close scrutiny.

Giving herself a mental shake, Serena sat up straight and licked her lips nervously. A raised brow encouraged her to speak. 'Your father's death makes my errand more problematic, but it does not make it any the less urgent. I believe I must enlist your help.'

'Must? I sense a reluctance to confide, Miss Cachet. Don't you trust me?'

He was toying with her. 'Why? Would I be unwise to do so?'

'That you must decide for yourself, when you are better acquainted with me.'

'Sadly, I do not intend to spend long enough

in your company to become so,' Serena replied tartly. 'I am come to reclaim some papers, which my papa entrusted to yours. They are personal documents that he did not want to risk losing on the Continent. You must know that we led a—well, an itinerant life there.'

'You've just recently arrived in England then?'

'Yes, from France. This is my first visit.'

'Allow me to compliment you on your command of our language.'

'I am, in fact, English, Mr Lytton,' Serena said stiffly. 'My father was English, we always spoke that language at home. I can understand your being suspicious—my turning up here unannounced must give a strange appearance—but I assure you I am no fraud. Nor am I a French spy, if that is what you are worried about.'

'*Touché, mademoiselle.* I'm afraid you're doomed to disappointment, though, as I know nothing about your papers. I've been through all my father's effects long since. If they were here, I think they'd have turned up by now.'

'But they must be here! Are you sure he said nothing before he died—could he have perhaps lodged them with his lawyer?'

Nicholas frowned, puzzled by the earnest note in her voice. 'No, I would have been informed if he had.'

'You must remember something. Surely your father mentioned Papa's name at some point?'

Her desperation aroused Nicholas's curiosity. Whatever her tale, she had quite obviously not told him the whole of it. Her lovely face was fixed on him with such a look of entreaty as would melt all but the hardest of hearts. He could not but wonder what effect gratitude would have on her. 'Perhaps if you could tell me a little more, it may prompt my memory.'

'They are private papers, of no value to anyone else. My father's name is on them.'

Her very reluctance to expand was intriguing. 'Cachet?'

Serena bit her lip, more aware than ever of his too-penetrating grey eyes. Though he maintained his relaxed posture, she was under no illusions. Nicholas Lytton distrusted her, and she could not really blame him. 'Not Cachet, Stamppe.'

'Stamppe? Then Cachet is your married name? My apologies, I must have misread your card, *madame*.'

'I'm not married. My name is also Stamppe.'

'Yet your card says Cachet.'

'Yes, because—oh dear, this is most awkward.' Serena risked a fleeting glance up, caught her host's sardonic expression, and looked quickly down again. Nicholas Lytton was smiling sceptically. In her lap, her fingers twined and intertwined, weaving a complex pattern of their own devising, which all too clearly betrayed her discomfort. She clasped them together and forced herself to meet Nicholas's gaze properly. 'Cachet means seal. My real name is Stamppe, though I did not find that out until my father informed me of it on his deathbed. He had a whimsical sense of humour.'

At this, Nicholas gave a twisted smile. 'Amazing what facing mortality will do to a parent.'

'I beg your pardon?'

'I sympathise, *mademoiselle*, that is all, having had a similar experience. It must have come as a surprise.'

'A shock. Papa died very suddenly; he was the victim of a violent robbery. I find it difficult—I still find it hard to accept.' She paused to dab her eyes with a handkerchief plucked from her reticule.

'I'm sorry, I didn't mean to upset you,' Nicholas said more sympathetically. 'Do you have other family?'

'No. No one. At least—no. *Maman* died when I was ten, and since then it has always been just me and Papa. Now it is just me.'

'I find it hard to believe that someone so very lovely as you is wholly unencumbered. Are Frenchmen quite blind?'

'Perhaps it is just that I am quite choosy, Mr Lytton. We seem to have strayed some way from the point.'

'Ah, yes, the point. Your papers, which have lain unclaimed with my father for—how long?'

'Over twenty years.'

'And you have known about them all this time?'

Serena inspected her gloves. 'No. Only since…'

'Don't tell me, Papa told you about them on his deathbed.'

She laughed nervously. 'I know, it sounds like a fairy story.'

'Exactly like one.'

'I see you don't believe me.' *And no wonder,*

she thought, rising to leave. She would just have to face the lawyer without her documents. 'I won't waste any more of your time.'

Though he did not doubt that her papers, if they ever existed, were lost, Nicholas was not ready to allow Serena to leave just yet. He was bored beyond measure and she was quite the most beautiful creature he had clapped eyes on in a long time. With her air of assurance and her cultured voice she could pass for quality, but he was not fooled. No gently bred young woman came calling on a single gentleman unaccompanied. Of a certainty, none allowed themselves to be diverted from their call into watching a mill. The more he saw of her, the more certain he became that her gratitude would be worth earning.

'Don't be so hasty, *mademoiselle*, give me a moment to reflect. Your father's name—his real name—does sound familiar. Is there nothing else you can tell me that would help?' He was simply teasing her, drawing out her visit in order to while away the time, so her reply surprised him.

'The last rose of summer left blooming alone. I was to say those words so that your father

would not doubt my identity.' She smiled in reluctant response to Nicholas's crack of laughter. 'I know, it sounds even more like a fairy tale now.'

'Perhaps it's a clue,' Nicholas said, pointing to the panelling. He meant it as a joke, having no faith at all in his visitor's story, but Serena's reaction gave him pause.

'Of course,' she said excitedly, clapping her hands together. 'A hiding place. How clever of you to think of that.'

A long curl of hair the colour of ripe corn tangled with her lashes and lay charmingly on her cheek. Her vivid blue eyes sparkled like turquoise. She smiled at him quite without guile and he remembered the feel of her soft lips beneath his own. Delicious. She was really quite delicious and he was really very, very bored. 'Of course,' Nicholas agreed lightly, 'a clue. Why not? This house is Tudor, after all, it's absolutely strewn with roses. There are roses on the panelling in almost every room, to say nothing of the ones worked into the stone on the fireplaces, and even hidden away on some of the original furnishings. What's more, when it was built the family were Catholic. We've priest holes, secret passages, concealed doors, the whole kit and caboodle. It could take weeks to search it thoroughly.'

'Weeks!'

Chasing rainbows seasoned with a little light dalliance would pass the time most agreeably, he decided. He had planned to quit the Hall within the week for London or, depending on the news he was awaiting, the Continent. He could not bring himself to care which. Why not indulge the so-charming mademoiselle with some tapping on panels in the meantime? Such enforced intimacy was bound to bear fruit. Delicious, forbidden fruit. 'Perhaps just days, if you have someone to help you—someone who knows where to look,' he said with an innocent look.

'You mean you,' Serena said cautiously.

'Yes, who better? Though you should know that you'd be keeping company with a murderer.'

She could see from the tightening of his mouth and the frown that brought his heavy black brows together that he was no longer teasing her, yet she could not take him seriously. 'I hope you jest, Mr Lytton.'

'No jest, I assure you, although I am not quite a murderer yet. I fought a duel two weeks ago. A stupid thing, but I was in my cups, and my opponent was so very insulting I could not resist the challenge.'

'My papa was given to saying that it is better for gentlemen to fight it out fairly and in cold blood than to resort to what he called fisticuffs in the height of a quarrel.'

'A man of sense. That is exactly what we did. My opponent is a poor swordsman, whereas I am attributed somewhat better than average. I pinked him, a mere warning cut, a perfect lunge that caught his shoulder and disarmed him at the same time. Harry Angelo, my fencing master, would have approved, but my opponent, I am sorry to say, was merely angered. I turned away, assuming all was over. He picked up his sword and lunged at me. I had no option but to fight back, and, in being caught unawares, caused him an injury that may yet prove fatal. So here I am, rusticating and awaiting the outcome, ready to flee to the Continent from the hands of the law should he avenge himself upon me by dying, for duelling is become illegal now, you know. And so you see why I am quite happy to put myself at your disposal.'

The glint in his eye made her uncomfortable, for she could not help wondering what he might want in return. 'That is very kind, but I can't help thinking it would be an imposition. And in any case, it wouldn't be proper for me to spend time here alone with you.'

'Proper! No, indeed, I was very much hoping that it would be quite the opposite.'

Startled by his bluntness, Serena got hastily to her feet, blushing wildly. 'I fear my coming here unaccompanied has misled you as to my character.'

He remained quite annoyingly unflustered. 'That, and the way you kissed me.'

She wrestled with the fastening on her glove, and her flush deepened. 'Well, Mr Lytton, let me put you to rights. Even if I agreed to accept your help—which I have not done—and accepted the risk to my reputation which being here alone with you would engender, I am not the type of female to reward you with kisses.'

'Aren't you? Then I am to assume the kiss after the fight was out of character?' Nicholas took her wrist and dealt expertly with the recalcitrant button.

She tried to pull her hand away, but he held on to it. His fingers were warm through the soft leather of her glove. They were long and slender, the nails trimmed and neat. His knuckles were grazed and bruised from the fight. His touch seemed to flicker from her hand up her arm, raising goose bumps on her skin under the long sleeve of her dress. Nervously, Serena gazed up at him, her hand still lying compliant, knowing she should move, yet caught as before in a trance of awareness. His intentions were unmistakable. He was going to kiss her again. 'No,' Serena said in that curiously breathy voice that did not belong to her. 'I will not pay for your co-operation by allowing you to take liberties. You mistake me.'

'You would kiss a ruffian in a stable yard, but not a gentleman in a parlour,' he teased. 'I did not take anything from you that wasn't freely given, and I won't now.'

'Then let me go.'

'I will, just as soon as you persuade me you want me to, *mademoiselle*.'

That look of his again—it made her feel as if he could read her thoughts, which meant he would see all too plainly the war between ought and want going on her mind. *It was just a kiss, nothing more.* If he could treat it lightly, so surely could she.

'It's just a kiss, after all,' Nicholas whispered persuasively, echoing her thoughts so precisely she wondered if she had spoken out loud. 'A kiss to seal the beginning of our quest together.'

She opened her mouth to say no, but somehow the words did not come and he took it for an invitation. His lips were cool, exploring, gentle. Questioning. For a breathless moment she hesitated. His mouth stilled. Then she felt her free hand reach up of its own accord to stroke the silken hair at the back of his head. She opened her mouth like a flower to the sun. Softening her lips against his, she melted into his embrace, savouring the taste, the smell, the power. Lost in the newness, the strangeness of it all.

And then it was over. Nicholas took a step back. 'Enough for now, I think; any more would be a liberty. I *am* a gentleman, despite my earlier appearance, and I meant what I said, I will never take anything you do not want to give.'

Serena shook her head, resisting with difficulty the urge to touch her hand to her lips, for they were tingling. 'I have agreed to nothing.'

'Come, come, *mademoiselle*, you cannot possibly be thinking of leaving without these precious papers of yours. What are you afraid of?' Nicholas asked in a perturbingly confident voice. 'Is it perhaps yourself you don't trust?'

No, frankly, she didn't! He was a wolf in wolf's clothing from whom she should run as fast as she could. 'Don't flatter yourself,' Serena replied tartly, 'I have every confidence in my ability to resist your charms.'

'Then you'll allow me to help you?'

It was simple really. Without his help she could not claim her inheritance. She could seek out her father's lawyer, but unless she had the papers—it would be useless. She searched his face for reassurance. 'I have your promise that you will behave properly?'

'I have already given you one promise, *mademoiselle*. I see no need for another.'

They had reached an impasse, and he knew it! Serena fumed inwardly. 'Oh, very well,' she finally conceded rather ungraciously. 'With such a knowledgeable guide as yourself, it can't possibly take too long, after all.'

'Very sensible. Do you wish to start immediately?'

She tried to collect her senses, which by now were utterly scrambled, not least by her own shocking responses to being kissed. And not once but twice! 'Thank you, Mr Lytton, but, no, I have had quite enough excitement for one day,' Serena responded drily. 'I think it best that I return to my lodgings in the village for now. I'll come back in the morning, if that is acceptable to you?'

Nicholas grinned. 'My dear *mademoiselle*, I can think of little regarding you that wouldn't be most acceptable to me. Until morning, then.'

'Until morning, Mr Lytton.'

Chapter Two

Serena arrived at her rooms in the small village of High Knightswood, just over a mile's distance from the Hall, to find Madame LeClerc awaiting her. Madame was a Parisian *modiste* anxious to make her fortune in London. On hearing that Serena was leaving for England, she had offered to accompany her. 'To lend you countenance, *chérie*, as the *bon papa* would have wished. I want to set up my own establishment,' Madame LeClerc had gone on to explain. 'These wars have prevented the English ladies from enjoying the benefits of our French *couture*. Now that we are friends again, it is time for the rich *mesdames* to learn how to dress properly. Like yourself, *mademoiselle*,' she added obsequiously.

Serena had accepted Madame's offer gratefully, being well aware that Papa would not have expected her to travel unaccompanied. Sadly, she soon discovered that the price for Madame's companionship was significantly higher than the generous salary and lodgings the *modiste* had demanded. Madame lent her countenance, but her company was tedious in the extreme.

The journey on the packet steamer made Madame heartily sick. She continued to be sick the entire road to High Knightswood, punctuating bouts of nausea with trembling complaints of everything from the carriage springs to the state of the post roads and the dampness of the sheets at the post houses. She spoke very little English, obliging her employer to intervene when things became difficult. With a shudder, Serena recalled a particular episode involving Madame, the land lady of the Red Lion, and an unemptied chamber pot. Nor could Madame come to terms with the English climate. '*Il pleut à verse.* Rain, rain, rain,' she exclaimed every day, regardless of whether the weather was inclement or not.

As Serena divested herself of her bonnet and pelisse, Madame LeClerc subjected her to a lengthy diatribe on the subject of English food. 'I am sick to my stomach with the *rosbif*. All this meat and no sauces, I am starving.'

Eyeing Madame LeClerc's ample figure, hovering over her like a plump vulture, Serena found this last claim difficult to believe.

'*Look at this!* Just look, Mademoiselle Serena! This *débâcle* is intended to be our dinner. Please to tell me how I, a good Frenchwoman, am meant to eat this?' With a dramatic gesture, Madame indicated the serving dishes, which were set on the table.

Reluctantly, Serena lifted the covers. She had to acknowledge that their landlady's cooking was somewhat basic, but after the day she'd had, she was in no mood to sympathise. 'It's pigeon, *madame*, with peas, and perfectly edible. Eat it or not, I don't care, but please sit down, I have something to tell you.'

Serena served them both before embarking upon the tricky matter of informing Madame that they would of necessity be delayed in High Knightswood while she resolved a 'personal matter'. Madame, chomping her way steadily through two whole pigeons, distaste writ large on her face, listened in sullen silence. As soon as her plate was cleared, however, she launched into a bitter tirade.

'You promised me we would be headed straight for London. The Season has already started, I need to find my clientele now, before they have all their gowns. This delay will ruin me!' A plump white hand fluttered against her impressive bosom. Serena's companion was for some time loudly inconsolable.

The vague notion she had entertained, of asking Madame to accompany her on her visits to Knightswood Hall, faded from Serena's mind as the *modiste*'s anguish grew. She tried to imagine what Nicholas Lytton would make of her companion. Like as not he would send Madame below stairs if he did not send her packing. Serena would then be responsible for the inevitable fracas between Madame and Nicholas's chef, and no further forward in observing any of the proprieties.

She retired early to bed, but sleep eluded her. In the next chamber she could hear Madame LeClerc's rhythmic snoring all too clearly through the thin walls. Loud enough to rattle the windowpanes, Serena thought grumpily, plumping the bolster in a vain effort to get comfortable. It had been a trying day. The news of Nick Lytton's demise had been a shock, though she supposed it should not have been. She was annoyed at herself for having been so unprepared. His son's promise to help was a mixed blessing. Nicholas Lytton had made it quite clear he did not think her at all respectable.

Nicholas Lytton was a man who gave off danger signals as he entered a room. It would be foolish indeed to ignore them. He carried about him an edge of excitement, as if always on the verge of committing some wild act, about to trespass the safe confines of conduct just for the sport of it. It was this, Serena realised with a start, that drew her too him, rather than the more basic tug of physical attraction. She must be on her guard with him at all times. Despite her unorthodox life, her reputation was spotless. She could not afford to tarnish it now, though it would be a lie to say she was not tempted. A fact of which, unfortunately, Nicholas Lytton was all too well aware.

Perhaps after all she should induce Madame LeClerc to act as her protector. A particularly loud snore came from next door, making Serena giggle. Not even Nicholas Lytton would be tempted to overstep the mark in Madame's presence. But then he would simply get rid of her. Serena closed her eyes. She was going round in circles, far too tired to argue with herself any more. Surely Knightswood Hall was too remote from London for anyone to care what did—or did not—go on there?

As Serena finally dropped into slumber, Nicholas sat in splendid isolation in the small family dining room of Knightswood Hall, musing on the contentious topic of his father's will. The table had been cleared and the covers removed. In front of him lay the latest update on the situation from his man of business. Frances Eldon was not optimistic.

The butler placed a decanter of port and a jar of snuff on the table before feeding another log on to the fire and reassuring himself that the curtains were perfectly drawn. 'Will there be anything else, Mr Nicholas?'

'No, thank you. Tell my man not to wait up, I'll get myself to bed. Goodnight, Hughes.'

'Goodnight, sir.' The butler bowed and withdrew silently from the room.

Nicholas poured himself a small glass of port, idly swirling it around in the delicate crystal glass. His thoughts, like the wine, circled endlessly. He was tired, and no wonder—it had been a closer contest than usual with Samuel. They had been sparring partners since childhood. Ruefully, he examined his raw knuckles in the glow of the firelight. Hardly the hands of a gentleman. It was high time he stopped such foolishness. And yet—he never could resist a challenge.

But he was twenty-nine now, old enough to know better. In less than three months, as Frances Eldon so needlessly reminded him in his letter, Nicholas would be thirty. If they could not find a way to break the will before that date, his fortune would go to his cousin Jasper—unless Nicholas took Frances's advice and married.

He had always been so carelessly certain that his lawyers would find a way to overturn the fateful clause, but as the deadline approached and every legal avenue turned into a dead end the decision loomed over him like a menacing black cloud of doom. He should have instructed them sooner. *Dammit, there must be a way!*

Nicholas rose to stir the fire, carelessly throwing on another log, stepping back hastily as the sparks flew out on to the hearth rug. He was not going to be forced down a path of another's choosing. He would not be black-mailed into the bonds of matrimony, not even by his own dead father.

His parent had remarried late in life. Melissa was a malleable widgeon, a young woman content to play nursemaid to a man in failing health many years her senior. To the astonish-ment of all who knew him, Nick Lytton, after a lifetime of raking, settled contentedly into domestic bliss and became an advocate for the institution of marriage into the bargain. The present Nicholas Lytton sighed deeply. He should have seen it coming, after that last un-comfortable interview.

'I hear you've been causing a scandal again, my boy.' The chill which his father had caught while out hunting had taken hold of his lungs. It was obvious he had not long to live. Nicholas re-membered each breath his father took as a painfully sharp intake, a long drawn-out rattling exhale. What he couldn't remember now were the exact circumstances of the scandal the old man was so upset about. Some bit of muslin Nicholas had tried to pass off as one of the *ton* at a party, as he recalled. Yes, that was it, a bet, and he had lost when the lady told a rather warm story and had then been recognised by one of her previous protectors.

Before Melissa, his father would have laughed, but with his second marriage the old man had acquired a pompous righteousness. 'You've shamed our name once too often, my boy,' Nick Lytton wheezed.

'For pity's sake, Father,' Nicholas retorted, 'you talk as if I was a libertine. As you very well know, I am scrupulous about confining that sort of thing to the muslin company. As you used to,' he said pointedly. 'I never raise false expectations. I would have thought that was something more to be proud of than ashamed.'

His refusal to repent served only to bring down the full extent of his father's wrath on his head. Nick Lytton had stormed, ranted, cursed and finally, when his son showed no signs of remorse, resorted to threats. 'I'll see to it that you can't carry on this life for ever. You're turning into a damned loose fish, Nicholas, and by God I'll put a stop to it, you mark my words.'

The interview had ended then. Nicholas thought no more of it until after his father's death, when he was informed of the significant change to the terms of his will. He'd laughed and refused to take it too seriously. Until now.

Not even in his salad days had Nicholas come close to being in love, finding that passion faded all too quickly once sated. His dashing looks and flamboyant generosity made him a highly sought-after catch, but not once in all his years on the *ton* had any lady managed to stake a claim. He was far too careful for that, unlike some of his peers. Poor Caroline Lamb's latest attempt to avenge herself upon Byron, so it was rumoured, was a thinly disguised *roman à clef*. Nicholas shuddered at the very idea of encountering the spectre of a rejected lover hovering at a society party, never mind the iniquity of the details of any *affaire* being bandied about in the press.

No, he made a strict point of confining his

amours to women from a different sphere who understood the rules of the game perfectly well. Over the years he had been fortunate in his mistresses, all of whom combined beauty with experience. When he grew bored it was a simple thing to pay them off. No sulks. No pain. No regrets. Just a few trinkets, a generous sum, a goodbye. It suited him. It was how he had chosen to live his life, and he enjoyed it. He saw no reason to change.

Dammit to hell, he would not *change.* Nicholas consigned Frances Eldon's letter to the fire. When the lawyers had exhausted every possibility, then perhaps he would force himself to contemplate marriage. Right now he had better things to think about. Like the luscious Mademoiselle Serena Stamppe and her preposterous tale of hidden documents and long-lost friendship.

The friendship part could be true—his father had been wild in his youth. The wars with France favoured many a person wishing to hide their dirty laundry in the hustle-bustle of the Continent; no doubt that Serena's dear papa was one such. An adventurer of some sort, of a certainty. She was obviously an adventuress herself—she had given herself away with that remark of hers—what was it—*an itinerant life*.

Stamppe. The name was definitely familiar. He would write to Frances in the morning, tell him to crack the whip over the will, and get him to find out what he could about the lovely Serena and her father. Yawning, Nicholas placed the guard over the fire, snuffed out the candles, and headed wearily for his bed.

In the end, Serena decided not to introduce Madame LeClerc to Nicholas unless it became absolutely necessary—and she refused to allow herself to contemplate just what she meant by that. She made an early start the next morning, leaving her lodgings long before her companion surfaced for breakfast. On the assumption that the search would be dusty work, she wore a simple dress of printed cotton and sturdy half-boots of jean. A short woollen cloak protected her from the early chill of the English spring, and her hair was looped on top of her head, a bandeau of the same material as her dress holding it in place.

Charming was the epithet with which

Nicholas Lytton greeted her, himself simply attired in fitted buckskins that clung to his muscular legs, teemed with a dark blue waist-coat and plain dark coat. He clasped Serena's gloved hands between his for a brief moment on greeting, but made no further attempt to touch her. She could not make up her mind whether to be relieved or not.

They sat together in the small morning room over a pot of coffee, discussing how best to tackle the search using the only clue they had. 'I suppose it's safe to assume that the hiding place really is here,' Serena said. 'You don't have any other houses with rose panelling, do you?'

'No. And both the London house and the hunting box post-date the time you said your father gave mine his papers—over twenty years ago, do I have that right?'

Serena nodded. 'He told me he sent them not long after I was born.'

'Where was that?'

'*La Bourgogne*. Burgundy—it is where my mother comes from.'

'So that is where you would call home?'

'No, *Maman*'s family did not approve of the marriage. My parents would not talk about it. I don't think there's anywhere I'd call home, I've never stayed in one place long enough to put down roots.'

'Why not?'

She thought for a moment, her lips pursed, a small frown drawing her fair brows together. 'It's strange, but I've never really questioned why. Papa said it was expedient for his—his business interests, but I'm not sure that's wholly true. He just liked to travel. I've lived in some beautiful cities, Vienna, Rome, Strasbourg, and Paris of course, but I've always considered myself an outsider. We lived so much, my parents and I, in a little world of their making. I have any number of acquaintances, but I don't really have any friends of my own.'

'May one ask what precisely Papa's business interests were?'

'Oh, he dabbled in lots of things,' Serena said vaguely. 'He preferred me not to become involved in such matters.'

'Whatever your father was involved with, it must have been lucrative. I could not fail to notice the quality, and expense, of that delightful outfit you wore yesterday. Assuming, of course, it was your father who provided the funds.'

He was looking at her with that curling half-smile that made her pulses flutter and raised her hackles at the same time. 'You think I have a rich protector? A fat, elderly gentleman perhaps, on whom I bestow my affections in return for gifts?'

Nicholas felt a sudden and most unexpected pang of jealousy at the thought of anyone being in receipt of Serena's affections. His smile hardened.

'This is a ridiculous conversation,' Serena said, sensing the change in his mood. 'There are no skeletons in my closet, I assure you. Now, can we stop wasting time and start looking for my papers?'

Nicholas shrugged. 'Oh, very well. There are a number of secret panels and a couple of priest holes that I know of, we can start with those. You don't mind getting a little dusty, do you? Some of the places won't have been opened for years. At the very least I suspect we'll find a few spiders. Maybe even some rats.'

'I've encountered much worse, believe me.

I'm not fond of them, but they don't scare me. Papa taught me never to be missish; you needn't worry that I'll be fainting into your arms.' Serena looked up to see surprise writ on Nicholas's face, and raised her brows. 'Oh dear, were you *wishing* me to faint into your arms? I do beg your pardon. I suppose I could *pretend* to be afraid if you had your mind absolutely set on it?'

He laughed softly. 'No, thank you. If I wish to have you in my arms, my intrepid Mademoiselle Stamppe, I can think of easier ways of managing it.'

Serena rose from her seat, shaking out her petticoats. 'You take rather too much for granted, Mr Lytton.'

'We shall see,' was all he vouchsafed in return.

Three hours later they were both smudged with dirt, and Serena had a goodly amount of cobwebs trailing from her frilled petticoats, but of the papers they had found no trace.

In the first priest's hole located beneath a cupboard at the side of a fireplace carved with a number of Tudor roses there had been only some mice droppings.

The second priest's hole was a cunning little trapdoor in the upstairs drawing room operated by turning yet another rose in a nearby panel. When Nicholas lowered himself into it, he found a squashed shallow-crowned hat from a much earlier age. He emerged from the hiding place wearing it. Serena laughed, not so much at the absurd spectacle he presented—for the hat was much too big—but at the ring of dirt it left around his brow when he removed it. With the dusty halo and those gunmetal eyes he looked, she thought fancifully, like a dark angel. Or maybe a devil. She reached up to brush it away, drawing back immediately at his startled look. 'I'm sorry, you have—if you look in the mirror, you have dust on your hair.'

In the large formal dining—once more panelled with a design of roses—a concealed door lifted away to reveal a space built into a hollow column. 'My father was minded to keep his own papers here, until I informed him that the entire household, if not the whole country-side, knew of the place. After that he stuck to the rather more orthodox method of locking them in his desk.' Once more the space was empty.

In the master bedchamber, where Nicholas pulled back one of the window shutters to reveal yet another 'secret' space, a piece of paper fluttered to the ground. He handed it to Serena, smiling at the look of anticipation on her face as she opened it, bursting into infectious laughter when it turned out to be an account for three pairs of evening gloves and six ostrich feathers.

'This was my father's room. I can only assume it was a bill he didn't want my mother to see. Before he married my stepmother, my father was rather free with his favours.'

'Was he? Well, so was my father after my mother died—and before he married her, I presume.'

'Don't you find that shocking?'

'No, why should I? Papa was very much in love with *Maman*, and it was a long time after she died before he took an interest in any other woman. Why should I grudge him pleasant company?'

'What a very enlightened attitude.'

Nicholas's coolly ironic tone irked her. Remembering just in time, however, that it was not in her interests to quarrel with him, Serena took a calming breath before speaking. 'It's not enlightened, it's just—honest. Why pretend the world works one way when it is obvious to anyone who cares to look that it works in quite another? I don't mean that I approve of such choices, but to deny that they happen would be quite foolish.'

'Foolish, I agree, but it's what most of your sex claim to do none the less. And may I ask if Papa had the same enlightened attitude when it came to his daughter?'

'Of course not. It's different for a woman, as you very well know. I think you're making fun of me.'

'On the contrary, I must commend you for the candour of your outlook.'

Once again she struggled to contain the spark of temper his words ignited, for though he denied it she knew she was being deliberately riled. Biting back the riposte that sprang to her lips, Serena instead executed a mocking curtsy. 'You are too kind, sir. I would that I could commend you for the same.'

'Well done, *mademoiselle*. A hit, I acknowledge it.'

She was forced to laugh. 'Oh, for goodness' sake, please call me Serena. I can't bear to be on formal terms. In any case, it's absurd, to have been grovelling about amongst all this dirt and cobwebs and still to call each other Mr Lytton and Mademoiselle Stamppe, a name I find rather strange, even if it is my own.'

'I'm honoured. Serena is a beautiful name, and I'd be flattered if you'd call me Nicholas.'

'Papa named me for serenity, although I'm not sure he got it quite right. But thank you, Nicholas.'

She pronounced it in the French way, leaving off the last consonant, making awareness curl in the pit of his stomach. There was something inherently sensual about her, made more so because he could not make up his mind whether or not she intended it. *Nicholas.* It was like a caress.

'I take it you don't favour this room yourself,' Serena said, looking around her, oblivious of his stare. 'I'm not surprised, it's quite depressing.'

'I agree,' Nicholas replied, dragging his mind back to their conversation. 'To be honest, I've never been enamoured of the idea of taking over the room of a dead parent. Rather off-putting, I would imagine, especially if one had company. As if one was being watched at a time when one would particularly wish not to be observed.'

Serena gave a startled gasp. 'There was no need to be so blunt! I thought only that the room was oppressive. What you do—or don't do—in your own bedchamber is none of my business.'

'Not yet.' Giving her no time to respond to this challenge, Nicholas grasped Serena by the elbow and headed towards the door. 'That's the last of the hiding places I remember for the present. It has obviously escaped your notice, but it is long past noon, and I am ravenous. I asked Hughes to set out a luncheon for us downstairs, but before you sit down, my lovely Serena, you should know that you have smut on your nose, so I will direct you to a room where you can clean up, and I will see you as soon as you have done so. Don't keep me waiting lest I faint from hunger.'

Turning her by the shoulders, he pointed Serena in the direction of a doorway down the long corridor and strode effortlessly down the stairs towards the breakfast parlour.

After lunch they engaged in a few more hours of fruitless searching before Nicholas judged it time to call it a day. 'There's always tomorrow,' he said brightly. 'Rest assured I'll rack my brain for more ideas to occupy us then.'

'You don't sound overly disappointed by our lack of progress,' Serena said suspiciously. 'In fact, you sound quite pleased.'

Nicholas flashed her a seductive smile. 'The longer it takes, the more grateful you are liable to be.'

'As I said earlier, Mr Lytton, you take far too much for granted. Right now, what I would be most grateful for is the comfort of my bed. It's been a long and tiring day, I must return to my lodgings.'

'Then I insist you let me send a servant to accompany you. After all, we wouldn't want any aspersions to be cast on your reputation or intentions, now would we?'

'No, Mr Lytton,' Serena conceded with a smile, 'we most certainly would not.'

'If I never see another Tudor rose before I die I'll be happy.' Serena was perched precariously on a window seat in the formal dining room at Knightswood Hall the next day. 'My fingers are aching from tapping and prodding and poking at panelling. I'm beginning to think this is a wild goose chase.'

After hours of searching they were no further forward, but although she knew she should be concerned, she was finding it very hard to fret. Her father had created this situation, giving her no option but to keep company with a man whom she was almost certain was a rake. The world would surely damn her if it ever found out, but she would make sure it didn't, and in the meantime, provided the rake continued to behave, she was enjoying herself.

Nicholas smiled lazily up at Serena from the chair from which he had been watching, with relish, her attempts to reach a rose he had suggested—with no foundation whatsoever— looked particularly suspect. She had had to stretch, giving him a delightful view of her shapely ankles and a tantalising glimpse of her even more shapely rear as her dress was pulled tight. 'Poor Serena, don't give up yet, I'm sure I can think of lots more places to look.'

She turned round to face him, her hands on her hips. 'I'm sure you can. And I expect most of them will involve me clambering up on to something or crawling about on my hands and knees.'

He stood to assist her down from the window. 'It's your own fault for having such a very charming *derrière*.'

'A gentleman wouldn't have looked.'

'No, you're wrong about that. No man, gentleman or other, could have resisted looking, but a gentleman would have pretended he had not.'

'You told me *you* were a gentleman.'

'I lied.'

'You're impossible,' Serena said, trying desperately not to blush, for it only served to encourage him.

And you are adorable, Nicholas thought. A long tendril of hair had escaped its pins and curled down her back over the tender nape of her neck, giving her a charmingly dishevelled air. Not for the first time he found himself imagining what she would look like with all of the pins removed, her hair loosened and allowed to cascade down over her bare shoulders. It would brush teasingly over her breasts, causing the rosy buds of her nipples to stiffen and darken in delicious contrast to the creamy fullness of…

He dragged his eyes away. 'Let's go for a walk. We could both do with some fresh air.' He picked up his coat, which was draped over a chair at the head of the long oak table. Serena was delightful, charming, and fun to be with into the bargain. A very heady and alluring combination. The evidence of that was pressing insistently at the fabric of his breeches. Adjusting the ruffles on his shirt sleeves, he pulled his waistcoat straight. 'Come on, fetch your hat and shawl. It's much too nice a day to stay cooped up in here. A stroll in the gardens is what we need. You'll be relieved to know that it's too early for the roses to be in bloom.' Placing a hand firmly on the small of her back, he guided her from the room.

Outside, Serena raised her face towards the sun, luxuriating in the gentle caress of its warm rays on her skin. 'You're right…' she sighed contentedly '…this is a lovely idea. Where shall we go?'

'There's a pleasant walk down through the gardens to the trout stream at the bottom,' Nicholas replied. 'It's been dry for almost a week now, so the path shouldn't be too muddy.'

'I wish you'd tell Madame LeClerc so.

According to her, it has been raining non-stop since we arrived.'

'The good Madame—and how is her heroic snoring?'

Serena giggled. 'I don't know, thank goodness. I was so tired last night that I barely noticed. I should inform you, though, that her French sense of propriety is extremely offended at my spending so much time alone with you. She is for ever reminding me that my papa would strongly disapprove.'

'And would he?' Nicholas asked curiously.

'That's an impossible question since the only reason I am here with you in the first place is to do as he wishes. He would think our acquaintance—unwise.'

'Perhaps he would be right. Most fathers would think the same way about me, I've a dreadful reputation. After all, I've already kissed you twice—who knows what else I have planned for you?'

Serena stumbled. 'You said you would not take liberties.'

'I said I would not take anything that is not given freely. That's quite a different matter.'

'Oh.' She glanced up at him through her lashes. 'You know, I considered bringing Madame LeClerc here with me to ensure that nothing improper occurred between us.'

'Good God, I'm very glad you didn't. I suspect I'd have resorted to murder.'

'If I have to put up with her for much longer, I'll resort to murder myself. Her dresses may be charming, but her disposition is rather less so. I find her company tedious, and she finds our delay here beyond bearing. I can't wait to be rid of the woman.'

'When will that be?'

'When I get to London. Once I have Papa's papers, I'm to take them to his lawyer there in the city.'

'And then? Do you have plans?'

Serena frowned. 'I thought I did, now I'm not so sure. You'll think me fanciful, but I feel like— oh, I don't know—a ship. All my life I've been safely anchored in a harbour, or becalmed, or tethered to another vessel. And now I've been cut free I can go where I want, do whatever I want to do. I don't really want to make plans just yet. Don't laugh.'

'I'm not—far from it. I find the image of you unfurling your sails most distracting.'

She blushed at the intimacy of his tone, but ventured no reply. They were walking side by side along a small path lined with cherry trees, the blossom just beginning to come into flower. Serena's hand was tucked into Nicholas's arm, their paces matched, so perfectly in tune that neither had noticed.

The atmosphere over the last two days had been relaxed and lightly flirtatious. Until now, Nicholas had shown no sign of wishing to make more serious advances. Which was a good thing, Serena assured herself, and had indeed almost come to believe. Almost. Part of her was tempted to explore the attraction she felt between them, though it was a complication she could well do without. Every time he touched her, no matter how innocuous the circumstances—to hand her a book or her gloves, to seat her at the table or as now, to lend her an arm while they walked— a tiny shiver of awareness flickered inside her. Did he feel it too?

I find the image of you unfurling your sails most distracting. She wished she had not mentioned it, for now she found it distracting too. *Unfurling.* Why was it such a sensual word?

They continued strolling along the path, but their pace slowed. 'There's a seat by the stream and a pretty enough prospect from there over the fields,' Nicholas said, pointing ahead. 'We can rest there for a while in the sun, if you wish.'

There was indeed a charming view from the little wooden bench they made their way towards. 'It's lovely, really lovely,' Serena said delightedly. 'I wonder if my papa and yours spent time fishing here. He told me they knew each other as boys.'

'Did he? Then perhaps they did.' Though Nicholas thought it more likely that Serena's papa poached than fished, he decided not to disillusion her. 'I fish here myself sometimes. There's not much sport, trout and carp merely, and to be honest I haven't the patience for fly fishing. I haven't been here in an age—I'd almost forgotten how pleasant it is.' He wiped the bench with a large handkerchief. Serena sat obediently, but Nicholas continued to stand, gazing off into the distance.

'Don't you spend much time at the Hall?' she enquired.

'No, not really. I have a town house in London—that's where Georgiana, my half-sister, and her mother are at present. Georgie's seventeen now, and Melissa is launching her on to the unsuspecting world. She's a bit of a hoyden, Melissa is quite unable to control her, but she'll be a hit none the less, she's a pretty little thing with a handsome portion. Between my hunting box, visiting friends, and trips to the races at Newmarket, I'm lucky if I spend more than a month or so in a year down here.'

'That seems a shame. It's such a lovely place.'

'Well, the prospect is certainly breathtaking at the moment.'

He was not looking at the view. His meaning was unmistakable. Serena could think of no reply, only of what he would do next. She did not have to wait long.

'Stand up, Serena, I mean to kiss you.'

Somehow she was on her feet. *How did that happen?* He was pulling her close into the warmth of his body. His arm was looped round her waist. She could feel the heat from his fingers through the thin muslin of her dress. Now he was untying the strings of her bonnet with his other hand, tossing it carelessly on to the bench.

'I don't intend to let you,' she finally managed to say.

Nicholas raised a quizzical brow. 'I think you'll find that you do.' He moved closer, watching her all the while, his hold on her still loose, unrestraining, allowing her space and time to retreat. His fingers were on the nape of her neck now, gently exploring, stroking down to her collar bone, up to the shell of her ear. Her body hummed with anticipation, her nerves tingling, her skin, her whole being urging her towards him, as if invisible strings pulled her in, tangled her up, enmeshed the two of them together.

'Serena?' His voice was husky. His eyes, dark and disturbing, searched her face questioningly.

She hesitated as his fingers stilled their caress. His hold on her slackened. She knew she should resist, knew it with certainty.

Chapter Three

His lips were gentle, pulling her bottom lip between his own, moulding his mouth to hers, delicately flicking her mouth open with his tongue. Their bodies nestled, thigh to thigh, chest to chest. The buttons from his coat dug into her through the thin fabric of her dress. Still Nicholas teased, a determinedly slow onslaught on her mouth that licked and sipped and kissed with seemingly no intent but to tantalise.

She was suffused with a warm glow. A hotter flame flickered low in her abdomen, and yet she shivered too, goose bumps rising on her neck, her waist, her arms, everywhere their bodies touched. So different. So lovely. Unfurling.

His breath was warm on her cheek. She wanted to melt into him. To drink deeper of him. To feel more of him. Instinctively she returned his kiss, relishing the myriad of sensations flooding her senses, blocking out all thought, building so slowly from warmth to heat that she hardly registered the change in temperature, the intensifying ache becoming a need for more.

Nicholas's hold on her tightened. The pressure of his mouth increased. His tongue touched hers, or hers touched his, and everything changed. He pulled her so close that even through their clothing there could be no mistaking his arousal. His hand left her waist, trailing lower, gripping the soft flesh of her thigh, cupping and moulding the rounded flesh of her bottom. A throbbing pulse inside her responded to his hardness. Heat sparked.

His mouth became demanding. His tongue penetrated deep, tangling with hers, his lips no longer gentle, no longer sipping, but drinking, driving her towards a place hotter and wilder than any she had been before. She was trembling. Would have fallen were it not for the strength of his grip on her. 'Nicholas,' she said, though what she meant she had no idea. Her voice sounded ragged.

He released her abruptly, breathing heavily, his lids hooded over eyes that were almost black with desire. Serena slumped down on to the bench, her head swirling.

'If I'd known the response I'd get I would have waited until we were indoors,' Nicholas said with a grim attempt at humour, taken aback by the strength of passion that had erupted between them.

'You said you were going to kiss me, not ravish me,' Serena flashed in return, desperately struggling for a modicum of composure. *Just a kiss!* Well, now she knew there was no such thing!

Nicholas turned away, taking his time to adjust his disarrayed neckcloth, allowing himself to be distracted by this small task in order to give them both time to compose themselves. He had intended no more than a teasing kiss, something to test the waters. That they had plunged immediately into the depths was most unsettling.

Serena sat on the damp wood of the seat, wrestling with the tangled strings of her bonnet. Desire and heat warred with shame and guilt as she realised what she had done. *What must he think of her?* What was she to think of herself?

For even as she sat here, trying to compose herself, she was distracted by an unfulfilled yearning for more. She barely recognised herself. Perhaps she had become infected by Nicholas's spirit of recklessness.

But it was done now, and she could not regret it. She would put it down to experience—at least, she would at some point, when she was gone from here, somewhere far from this man's disturbing, bewildering presence. In the meantime the best thing she could do was protect her dignity. She was *damned* if she would let Nicholas Lytton see how easily his kisses overwhelmed her. Serena straightened her shawl and smoothed a wrinkle from her glove. 'We should go back.'

Nicholas ran a hand through his hair, smoothing it into something resembling its former stylish disorder and tried to decide what to do. Apologise? No need, surely—he had given her every chance to repulse him. He had done nothing wrong, yet still he felt he had. But then why was she sitting there, looking annoyingly calm, when he was on fire with need, and just moments before he could have sworn she was too. Baffled, he helped her to her feet.

'Thank you, Nicholas.'

Deliberately misunderstanding her meaning in an effort to rouse her out of her irritating self-possession, Nicholas bowed mockingly. 'It's more customary for the gentleman to thank the lady. It was a pleasure, I assure you.'

Serena blushed, and was annoyed at having done so. 'I trust you are suitably refreshed,' she said tartly.

'You're anxious to resume your search, I suppose. You know, Serena, the papers are just as likely to be lost as hidden.'

'I'm perfectly well aware that you don't believe in their existence,' she snapped. 'I am also perfectly well aware that I am simply a distraction for you. You're helping me because you are bored. You kissed me for the same reason. Why the sudden need for honesty—are you feeling guilty? You needn't, it was just a kiss, as you said. You need have no fear that it raised false expectations.'

'If we are to talk of false expectations, I think you have raised a few of your own! Dammit, Serena, you said it yourself, that wasn't a kiss, it was a ravishment.'

The implication made her temper soar, hot words pouring from her like lava from a volcano. 'There is no need to take your frustrations out on me, Nicholas. You had the good grace to comment yesterday on my enlightened attitude. Would that you had the same. Instead you are behaving all too typically of your sex, happy to blame mine for arousing your desires, equally happy to berate us when they are not fulfilled.'

His voice was steely. 'I think I am not the only one to be suffering from frustrated desire.'

They stood glaring at each other on the narrow track. Behind them the weak spring sunshine glittered, casting dappled shadows on the lush green verge. In the brief silence her temper abated as quickly as it had risen. 'You are quite right, I beg your pardon.'

Her simple acknowledgement took the wind from his sails. Nicholas lifted her hand to his lips. 'You are far more gracious than I. I accept your apology unreservedly, and offer my own in turn.'

She snatched her hand back. 'Forget it, there is nothing more to be said. Let us return to the Hall, shall we?'

Nicholas nodded in grudging agreement and, linking Serena's arm through his own, turned back on to the path and led them towards the house.

In London, Mr Mathew Stamppe entered the office in the city of Messrs Acton and Archer, attorneys at law. He was welcomed by the senior partner Mr Tobias Acton, and ushered into a comfortable room at the front of the premises facing out on to the bustle of Lombard Street.

Waving aside the offer of a glass of canary and ignoring Mr Acton's polite enquiries as to the health of Mrs Stamppe and his son Mr Edwin Stamppe, Mathew cleared his throat and got straight to the point. 'What is this urgent matter that requires my presence post-haste? It had better be good.'

Tobias Acton assessed the man sitting opposite him with a lawyer's shrewd gaze. His client was a tall man with a spare frame. Eyes of washed-out blue peered at him testily above the aristocratic Stamppe nose, but overall his features were weak, giving him rather the look of a hunted hare. Mathew favoured the plain dress of the country squire he had been for the best part of the last twenty years, living on his brother's estates in Hampshire. Under his careful stewardship the lands of the Earl of Vespian were in excellent heart. Mathew had looked after them as prudently as he would have done had they been his own. In fact, Tobias Acton thought, he had looked after them for so long that he probably thought of them as exactly that—his own.

And now they were. The lawyer composed his features into those of a man about to deliver ill tidings. 'I'm afraid, Mr Stamppe, we have received the saddest of news. Your brother Philip is, I must regretfully inform you, deceased. He died some months ago from injuries sustained when he was robbed, I believe in Paris. Please accept my deepest condolences, sir. Or, I should say, Lord Vespian.'

At last! Mathew struggled to contain the smile that tugged at the corners of his thin mouth. Careful not to show his satisfaction, he shook his head sadly. 'My dear brother's passing cannot be said to be a shock, given the way he chose to live, but it is a blow none the less. I shall arrange for the appropriate notices and such, but the main thing is to confirm the legal transfer of the estate to my name. I take it he left his will with you?'

Tobias Acton shuffled uncomfortably in his seat. 'Well, my lord, as to that, I'm sorry to tell you that things are not quite so straightforward. Lord Vespian—your brother, that is—left us none of his personal papers. As trustees we can obviously act with regards to that part of the estate which is entailed, but as to the unentailed property which, as you know, is not insignificant, we have only this.'

He solemnly handed Mathew a sealed packet. 'Our instructions were to give this into your hands in the unfortunate event of his lordship's death.'

Mathew took the packet, his rigid countenance giving no sign of the anger rising in his breast at this caprice of Philip's. Tearing open the seal, he read the contents with impotent fury. Finally, he crumpled the letter into his pocket. 'It seems, Mr Acton, that I have inherited a niece rather than a fortune. My dear brother has posthumously informed me that he was not only married, but that the union produced a daughter who is his rightful heir. The will and testament supporting this was lodged by Philip with a man named Nick Lytton who, to the best of my knowledge, died ten years since. I can only presume my niece—' he broke off to consult the letter '—the Lady Serena, will stake her claim as soon as she has recovered them from his son.'

Tobias Acton's brows rose a notch. 'A most unexpected development, Lord Vespian. May one enquire as to how you intend to handle this somewhat, ahem, delicate situation?'

'That, Acton, is a question I find myself quite unable to answer at this present moment.'

The next morning, Hughes relieved Serena of her hat and pelisse and informed her that Master Nicholas awaited her in the library, which was situated at the far end of the building. Serena opened the door and stepped into a surprisingly modern room with long windows looking out over a paved terrace. The book cases were mahogany, not the oak prevalent in the rest of the house, as was the large desk behind which Nicholas sat. Above the book cases the walls and ceiling were tempered a soft cream. The hangings were dull gold.

'This is quite lovely,' Serena said, 'and so unexpected.'

Nicholas rose from behind the desk to clasp her hand between his in his customary greeting. 'A description I could easily apply to you.'

She felt his intense gaze probe her thoughts, felt the now familiar fluttering that accompanied the touch of his flesh on hers, however slight. They stood thus for what seemed an eternity, the memory of that remarkable, passionate, all-encompassing kiss hanging almost palpably between them.

A polite cough announced the arrival of Hughes bearing a tray of coffee, which he placed on a small table. Serena poured two cups and handed one to Nicholas before sitting down to sip contentedly on her own. 'I've never learned to make good coffee—this is delicious.'

Nicholas raised an eyebrow. 'Not exactly an accomplishment you can have had much call for, surely?'

'On the contrary. There have been times when we were quite down on our luck, Papa and I, unable to afford luxuries such as servants.'

'Not recently, though. No matter how simple

the gowns you wear, I'm not deceived—the simpler the design, the costlier the price, is my experience. You're tricked out in the absolute finest of everything—gowns, shawls, hats, even those little boots of yours are kid, if I'm not mistaken.'

'And what, pray, *monsieur*, would you know about the cost of a lady's apparel?'

'As much as you, probably. I've certainly paid for enough fripperies over the years, to say nothing of having to cough up for dressmakers and milliners when the lady concerned is a—let us say intimate—acquaintance.'

'You are referring to your mistresses, I take it.' She was determined not to be shocked, equally determined to ignore the foolish twinge of jealousy. 'However, my clothes are from Paris, *naturellement*, which makes them a little above your touch.'

He remembered her earlier jibe about a protector. What if she had not been joking after all? The idea was distinctly uncomfortable. '*Au contraire, mademoiselle*,' Nicholas said maliciously, 'I am well enough heeled to be able to insist that any lady under my protection wears only the very best. And well enough versed in the latest modes to see that your hard times are behind you, if your wardrobe is aught to go by.'

She gave him a direct look, alerted by the harsh note in his voice. 'You think a man paid for them?'

'Am I right?'

He spoke nonchalantly, but Serena was not fooled. 'Yes.' She waited, but he said nothing, only looked at her in that way of his that made her feel he was privy to her innermost thoughts. 'Oh, for heaven's sake, Nicholas, stop looking so serious. I meant my father.'

He was unaccountably relieved, but managed not to show it. 'Well, he must have made you a generous allowance.' Serena did not deign to reply. 'Do you still miss him?' Nicholas asked her after a few moments, his voice gentler now.

'Of course. We were very close. Don't you miss your parents?'

'The cases are rather different,' he replied wryly. 'I saw more of the servants than my parents when I was growing up. Outside school, there were various tutors, but being without siblings I was largely left to go my own way— exactly as my father did in his youth. I had money enough to indulge in all my whims, and when I grew older to support my gaming and fund my *amours*. My father introduced me to his club and a few of his influential friends when I came of age, and that's about the sum of it.'

'So you are an only child too. Did you wish for a brother or sister? I know I longed for siblings.'

'I *was* an only child,' Nicholas corrected. 'I've got a half-sister now.'

'Yes, but so much younger than you—it's not the same.'

'She's about the age Melissa was when my father married her. There's no fool like an old fool—he was completely infatuated.'

'But Melissa made him happy?'

'He died before he could be disillusioned,' Nicholas said sardonically, 'but not, unfortunately for me, before he became obsessed with a desire to reform me.'

'Poor Nicholas.'

There was just a tinge of mockery in Serena's voice, but Nicholas could forgive her anything when she smiled at him that way, making him feel she understood him very well. He was becoming accustomed to it.

'I would have thought reforming you a well-nigh impossible undertaking,' Serena continued teasingly. 'How on earth did he intend to achieve it?'

'Oh, he had his ways, believe me. He took every opportunity to lecture me about the benefits of marrying a good woman and the wonders of love. All the usual nonsense that a reformed rake is prone to as he grows old and finds mortality staring him in the face.'

'That seems a rather jaundiced way of looking at it. Perhaps he really was in love?'

'Spare me the romantic twaddle, Serena. He was in lust, not in love. And he was a hypocrite, which is something I cannot be accused of. I indulge my passions for gaming, horses and women, but I never play when I can't pay. I never put a horse at a fence it can't take. I never trifle with women who don't know the score. Which is more,' Nicholas concluded bitterly, 'from what I've heard about my father in his younger days, than can be said for him.'

'Perhaps that's part of it—his wanting to prevent you making his mistakes. My father wrapped me in cotton wool for the same sort of

reasons, and in some ways—I am only beginning to realise it now—it was suffocating. You,
on the other hand, were positively neglected, but
that did not prevent your father from wishing to
dictate your life.'

'The difference between us is that I will not
allow him to. You, on the other hand, are still
dancing to Papa's tune.'

Serena bit her lip, for he had hit a nerve. 'For
the moment. So,' she continued brightly, 'despite
your father's attempts, you have not been con-
verted to the conquering power of love as
espoused by Lord Byron.'

'That deluded romantic! The man has almost
single-handedly brought love and languishing
back into fashion.'

'It seems to me that Lord Byron is more interested in indulging his own rather eclectic tastes
and encouraging everyone, poor Lady Lamb
included, to worship at the altar of his ego,'
Serena said scornfully. 'In any case, real love
doesn't come in or go out of fashion, as I have
no doubt Lord Byron will. You can't stop it or
avoid it. You can't be cured of it and you can't
dictate how it happens either. Some people never

fall in love because they never meet the right person. My parents were fortunate. It may be that your father was too, with his Melissa. It is possible that his wanting you to change your ways was not hypocritical, but a desire for you to be as happy as he was.' She stopped abruptly, taken aback by the passion of her own response.

'I'm afraid we'll just have to differ on that,' Nicholas said dismissively. 'It's a pretty point of view, and you are a charming advocate, but I remain unconvinced. You know less of the world and its travails than you think if you really mean what you say.'

With difficulty Serena managed to repress the hot retort that rose to her lips. 'I won't quarrel with you, there's no point. *I* won't persuade you, only experience will do that.'

'Indulge me, though, by explaining one thing to me before we drop the subject.'

She raised her brows enquiringly.

'Yesterday by the trout stream you seemed more than happy to encourage me to—for us to—for things between us to take their course. Today you rhapsodise about true love. I'm concerned that we are at cross-purposes.'

'In what way?'

'I can never offer you love, Serena, I won't be such a hypocrite as my father. I can promise you fun, perhaps, pleasure definitely, but it would be a brief idyll, nothing more. I won't pretend to any finer feelings to ease your conscience. If you choose to pick up where we left off from our kiss, you must do so with your eyes wide open.'

Serena paused for a moment before replying. She was not in love, but tossing and turning in her bed last night, she had been forced to acknowledge the depth of her attraction to him. The pang of physical awareness she had felt when first she encountered him, stripped to the waist in the boxing ring, had grown during the hours they spent together. Hidden away from the rest of the world as they were, time slipped by more and more quickly. Whenever she saw him, the urge to give in to temptation became harder to resist, fuelled by the knowledge that once she had her papers their paths were unlikely to cross again. The sensible voice in her head warned her that to give in to her desires was to risk being burned, but this feeling of rightness when she was with him continued to grow regardless.

Nicholas would take whatever she offered, provided she stuck to his terms. His feelings for her were of a fleeting nature. It had been unintentional, but his reaction to her eulogy on true love was a timely warning. 'My eyes are very wide open,' she told him with certainty. 'We are not at cross-purposes, I assure you.'

Did that mean she would grant him more than a kiss? It was on his mind to ask her, but he thought better of it. 'I have some business to attend to for the rest of the morning,' he said instead. 'I'll join you after lunch.'

Mathew Stamppe, lately become Lord Vespian, had had a busy morning, which included a long-overdue visit to the dentist, a fitting with his tailor and various commissions for his good lady wife. The existence of a niece, a chit of a girl heir to the fortune that was rightfully his, vexed him beyond words and continually dogged his thoughts. Tobias Acton had advised him to sit tight and wait on her contacting him, but this,

Mathew had decided, was not a course of action to which he could inure himself.

His next piece of business took him to a flash tavern just off the Fleet where he was to meet up with an ex-Runner recommended by his club doorman. Mathew sat uncomfortably in a booth, warily eyeing the unsavoury clientele of the dimly lit room, relieved that he had taken the precaution of leaving all his valuables, save the required purse of money, safe in his lodgings.

A short, compact man in a greasy brown coat approached him. 'You Stamppe?' he enquired loudly.

'For pity's sake, man, keep your voice down,' Mathew hissed.

The man smiled. 'No need to worry on that score, squire. Folk in here have learned the hard way to mind their own business, if you get my meaning. Now, let's see the readies.'

He bit delicately into one of the coins from the bag which Mathew handed him. Satisfied with the quality, he called for a glass of fire water and awaited instruction.

Mathew's orders were vague. When pressed to be more specific, he flapped. 'Just do whatever you see fit, I want no details.'

The ex-Runner smiled knowingly. He had come across the type many times before. Happy enough to pay someone else to do their dirty work, but too squeamish to think about what they had paid for actually entailed. It suited him well enough. He signified his agreement by raising his glass in a toast before tossing it back with a satisfied smack of the lips. Then he was gone.

After a lunch alone, Nicholas still being engaged upon business, Serena flicked through some volumes of Shakespeare in a half-hearted way, searching for the source of the last rose of summer quotation. By the time he joined her she was heartily bored.

'Forget about that for today, let's play cards instead,' he said, lounging in the doorway.

'Cards,' Serena exclaimed in surprise.

'Yes, why not? Can you not play?'

'Very well, actually. Whatever you want.'

'Piquet?'

'If you wish. But just for penny points.'

Nicholas laughed. 'I'm considered to be a very good player.'

'Oh, I'm not worried,' Serena said airily, 'I've played a lot of cards in my time.'

'Another of the skills learned at dear Papa's knee, no doubt,' he quipped.

She chuckled. 'If only you knew.'

'Since you're so confident, we should make the stakes more interesting. A forfeit.'

'It depends what you have in mind.'

'You're expecting me to say a kiss, but I won't be so predictable.'

His smile was irresistible. 'What, then?' Serena asked.

'A lock of your hair. Something with which to remember our time here.' He surprised himself at the fancifulness of his request, was still more surprised when she agreed.

'Deal,' she said, handing him the cards with a glint in her eye that should have worried him.

As the rubbers progressed it became clear that Serena's claim to skill had been no idle boast. Nicholas was losing steadily.

'Well, I make that—let's see…' Serena added up the score and showed him the total.

'Confound it, I never lose by such a margin. Are you sure?'

'Quite sure,' Serena said smugly. 'Now you must pay the forfeit.' She opened her reticule, producing a pair of embroidery scissors, brandishing them before him triumphantly. He ran his fingers through his carefully cropped hair, much alarmed. 'Give me those, I'll do it.'

Serena shook her head. 'To the victor the spoils, Nicholas. What was it you said, *"I never play when I can't pay"*?'

'You're enjoying this.'

She nodded primly, her eyes brimming with laughter.

He made a dive for the scissors, but she quickly put them behind her back. 'Kneel before me, Mr Lytton,' she commanded, 'I would not wish to ruin your coiffure.'

He held her gaze as he knelt, a wicked smile curling the corners of his mouth, his eyes reflecting the laughter in hers. 'You will regret this, *mademoiselle.*'

'I don't think so. Stay still.' She bent over his head. Her dress brushed against his face, which was disconcertingly close to her thighs. Heat rushed through her body.

'I told you you'd regret it,' Nicholas said

wickedly, his voice muffled by the material of her skirt. 'I, on the other hand, am finding this position rather delightful.'

Serena froze. *Was that his breath she could feel through her petticoats?* A quick snip and a lock of silky black hair fell into her hand. 'There, you can stand up now,' she managed breathlessly.

He gazed up at her with such a smile that her knees almost buckled. 'Why don't you come down here and join me? It's very—good God!'

'What is it?'

'The last rose of summer left blooming alone. I've just remembered, it's a song. And there it is. Come here.'

'Very funny. Get up.'

'No, I mean it,' Nicholas said. 'Look.'

She carefully placed his curl in her reticule with her scissors and dropped to her knees beside him. He took her by the shoulders and pointed her at the fireplace. Two panels decorated with delicate plasterwork filled the gap on each side between the mantel and the book cases. On one the figure of a man held a flower stalk in his hand. On the opposite panel was a tomb, around and on top of which the petals of the flower were scattered.

'*Oh!*' Serena clapped her hands together in excitement.

'*The last rose of summer*. Melissa used to sing it—damned melancholy thing, but it tickled my father. He knew the poet who wrote it, years before it was set to music. I can't think why I didn't remember until now. Go on then, they're your papers, see if you can find the latch.'

The panels were not large, starting from the wainscoting and ending at head height. Carefully, Serena felt her way around the edges of the one on the right, with shaking fingers seeking a gap or a mechanism, but there was nothing. She tried again. Nothing. Disappointed, she sat back on her heels.

'Maybe it's on the other one. Let me try.' Nicholas joined her, kneeling on the floor beside the panel depicting the young man and the flower stalk. As Serena had, he felt his way around the panel. Then he looked more closely at the stalk, which seemed to be detached from the plaster beneath it. Carefully, he twisted it. It turned. The tombstone with its rose petals slid back to reveal a cavity in the wall. Inside lay a small packet sealed with red wax, a name written in faded ink on the front.

Serena reached in. *Philip Stamppe, his last will and testament.* Her father's name leapt out from the paper in flowing script. She felt herself go faint, and staggered to her feet.

Nicholas poured her a small measure of brandy. 'Sit, drink this.'

Serena drank, spluttering as the cognac seared the back of her throat. Then drank some more, savouring the calming effect of the liquor. 'I'm sorry, it's the shock, seeing his name, that's all. I'm better now.'

He was almost as shocked himself, to find that the papers actually existed. As the implications began to make their way into his brain, Nicholas cursed inwardly, for now his precipitate action had ensured that Serena had no further reason to stay and he was not ready for her to go. Not yet.

She turned over the little packet of documents on her lap, but made no attempt to break the seals.

'Am I permitted to know what they are?'

She was sorely tempted to tell him everything, but

to do so would be to call a halt to whatever this thing was between them, and she was not willing to do that. Not yet. 'My father's will,' she conceded, 'and some papers confirming my identity.'

'You don't seem particularly overjoyed to see them.'

She looked up. 'I expect you are, though. It means I won't need to trespass on your time any longer.'

'Must you go straight away?'

'I ought to.'

'That's not what I asked.'

'I know.'

Nicholas stared frowningly out of the window. 'Leave it another couple of days and I'll be able to escort you myself. I should have news of my duelling opponent by then, and in the meantime I can show you a bit of the countryside. Do you ride?'

'Yes, but—'

'Good. We'll go riding tomorrow,' he said decisively.

'I should go to London tomorrow.'

'Stay. Let us have a day's grace, without worrying about papers or panelling or—or anything.'

Serena folded the documents into her reticule along with the lock of Nicholas's hair as she thought through his suggestion. He had not pressed her as to their content. Did that mean he didn't care, or he didn't want to know? And if she stayed another day, what was implied? More than just a gallop across the countryside, or was she reading too much into it? *He would not take what was not freely given.* She believed him, but she did not trust herself. Already, part of her had rushed ahead like a stampeding horse, looking forward to the morrow. She tried to rein it in. 'A day's grace,' she said. 'Yes, I'd like that', though even as she spoke, doubt seized her.

Nicholas took her hand and pulled her to her feet. His smile was warm, drawing from her a response that banished everything save a tingle of anticipation, a rush of pleasure. 'Come on, then,' he said to her, 'I'll walk you back to your lodgings.'

'*Tiens*, I thought you were never coming back, *mademoiselle*, I was about to send someone out in search of you.' Madame LeClerc, arms crossed impatiently, greeted Serena from the doorway. Dressed in her habitual black, her pale eyes peering short-sightedly at her charge, she had the look of a well-fed mole startled from its burrow.

'I'm sorry to have kept you waiting,' Serena said soothingly. 'Let's go in. You'll be wanting your dinner.'

'Pah,' Madame LeClerc said contemptuously, though whether she referred to Nicholas's retreating figure or dinner was not clear. Once inside, she commenced her habitual lament. 'I am tired of waiting, Mademoiselle Serena, when will we be on our way?'

'Not so very long now,' Serena said patiently, 'my business is almost concluded.'

'Business! Is that what you call it. The whole village is talking of you,' Madame LeClerc said spitefully.

Serena turned from the mirror where she had been tidying her hair. 'You shouldn't listen to idle gossip, Madame LeClerc, I'm sure there must be more productive ways for you to pass your time.'

'What am I to do here, exactly' Madame responded angrily. 'The women dress in sacks and aprons. When I try to advise the cook on how to make a nice French *ragoût*, she orders me from the kitchen. And now there is a strange man pestering me with silly questions.'

'What strange man?'

'A round man with a greasy coat. He knocked on the door and talked at me. I don't know what he said, but I thought he was a person most suspect.'

'He was probably just lost; I shouldn't worry about it.'

'That is all very well for you to say, *mademoiselle*, but you leave me alone all day when you go off to the big house. What if he had ravished me, what then?'

Serena spluttered with the effort of turning her giggle into an unconvincing cough. 'I am relieved he did not.'

'Much you would care if he did!'

Realising that she was genuinely upset, Serena spoke more soothingly. 'I promise you we won't be here for much longer. Now let's forget about strange men, and eat whatever nice English food our landlady has prepared for us before it gets cold.'

They sat down to dinner at the table in the parlour, but Madame was not content to drop the subject of village gossip. 'They say you spend all day in the company of this Monsieur Lytton. They say that you are his mistress,' she informed Serena through a mouthful of rabbit pie. 'They say you must be, given his reputation with the ladies.'

'I'm not interested in gossip,' Serena replied sternly.

'Yes, but, Serena—Mademoiselle Cachet—you should be more discreet; your papa would not be pleased.'

'*C'est mon affaire, madame*, none of your business. Since Mr Lytton's father was one of Papa's oldest friends, I'll thank you to hold your tongue. Eat your dinner; I want to hear no more of this.'

It was only village gossip, but it worried her none the less. She did not doubt that much of the speculation had originated from Madame LeClerc herself, but that was no consolation.

Retiring early to the privacy of her chamber, Serena finally broke the seal on her father's will with shaking fingers. By the time she had worked her way through the lengthy and highly technical content, her candle was guttering, throwing strange shapes onto the walls. The sums of money mentioned staggered her. Until now, she had not quite believed it was true, so outlandish had been Papa's tale, but the facts were there in parchment and ink. She was indeed an heiress, a considerable one.

Getting out of bed, she folded the documents carefully into a drawer of her jewel case before taking out the necklace Papa had given her for her last birthday. It was a simple but beautiful piece of jewellery, a gold locket with a sapphire in the centre, surrounded by a pattern of tiny diamonds. She opened it and carefully placed the lock of Nicholas's hair inside, unable to resist pressing upon it a little kiss. Then she snuffed the candle and climbed wearily into bed.

Lady Serena Stamppe. It sounded so strange to her ears. Not at all like herself, but like someone in a book or in a painting. Someone far more dignified, older, more refined than she. Lady Serena. The Honourable Lady Serena. Nicholas would be amused. No, Nicholas would not be at all amused. She would not think about that. Not yet. Not until after tomorrow.

Next door, Madame's snoring stopped. Taking this as a good omen, Serena fell into a deep sleep.

Chapter Four

Serena woke to a fresh sunny morning. It augured well for the promised outing, which she was looking forward to enormously. She checked her appearance in the mirror one last time before going downstairs. Her riding habit was of deep blue velvet, and the small hat trimmed with feathers of a matching colour sat jauntily atop her golden curls. It was not one of Madame LeClerc's creations, having been fashioned for her by an English tailor in Paris, the mannish cut of the short jacket serving to emphasise the very feminine curves concealed beneath it.

Madame LeClerc was wont to sleep late and had not yet risen, and for this Serena was grateful. She could imagine the fevered speculation that would be aroused by the sight of herself setting off to ride out alone with Nicholas. Madame's expressive Gallic eyebrows would shoot up to new heights, possibly to disappear entirely under the frill of her cap. With a chuckle, Serena gathered the long trail of skirt over her arm and closed the door of her lodgings quietly behind her. She stepped gaily out into the bright April sunshine and set off for the Hall with a sense of anticipation and well being.

The way was damp underfoot. The scent of fresh earth and wet grass carried on the gentle breeze stimulated her senses. Though she missed Paris and greatly looked forward to seeing London, with all the famous sites she'd heard so much of, at this precise moment she was in no rush to get there. In a way, she was starting to think of this lush green land as home. How she envied Nicholas the beauty of Knightswood Hall. How she envied him the casual acceptance and ease of manner with which he took it all for granted. Papa had imbued his daughter with his own excellent address and confidence, but there were nevertheless times when Serena felt overwhelmed by the elegance of Knightswood Hall and its dashing owner. She was not at all convinced of her ability to play the role of a lady for the London Season in which her father had insisted she should take part, once her true position was known. She was even less convinced than ever of her desire to do so.

Overseeing the saddling of the two horses as Serena made the now-familiar short walk from the village, Nicholas was also musing on the subject of his family's ancestral home. During past visits to the Hall the solitude, lack of entertainment and the early country hours had been a trial. In Serena's company he looked on it all with a fresh eye. Seeing the house from her perspective, he could admire its beauty anew, could appreciate its quirks and inconveniences as the product of its evolution, tangible evidence of its history and provenance. For perhaps the first time ever he felt a genuine sense of pride at being the owner and custodian of the Lytton estate.

The fresh green loveliness of the English spring bursting forth in all its glory before him was something else he had missed, since it coincided with the height of the Season and the hustle, bustle and grime of London. He was making up for lost time now. At some point its appeal would begin to pall, he had no doubt. As would Serena's. But not yet.

He knew enough of her to be certain that she would not change her mind about leaving. At best he had only today and tomorrow. He would wait no longer to sample more of her charms. The thought ignited his senses, an unaccustomed sense of anticipation making him jerk on the bridle in his hand. Titus whinnied and flared his nostrils. The dappled grey mare standing next to him pranced skittishly.

'I'll take them round the front myself,' Nicholas said, casually dismissing the groom. Grabbing both sets of reins, he set off on foot through the archway, out of the stable block and towards the house. Rounding the path which led to the front, he met Serena coming from the opposite direction.

Seeing Nicholas stride towards her, leading a horse in each hand, a dazzling smile illuminating his handsome features, she felt her breath catch in her throat. His cravat was snowy white against the strong line of his jaw. A plain dark-brown riding coat buttoned tight across his chest emphasised the width of his shoulders. Looking down, past the cutaway of the coat, the waistcoat of biscuit hue adorned with a single fob, she drank in long muscular legs clad in his favourite buckskins and impeccably polished short boots with long tops. She swallowed. The soft leather of his breeches seemed moulded to his shape so tightly she would swear she could see his muscles ripple underneath as he walked, the square-cut tails of his coat flying out behind him. His hands were clothed in gloves of the same close-fitting soft leather. In one of them he carried a riding whip. He was, Serena thought, not beautiful, that was quite the wrong word, but astonishingly, compellingly attractive.

Trying not to stare like a besotted schoolgirl, she turned her attention to the horses he was leading. The large imperious stallion could only be his. The other horse was smaller, a lovely dappled grey with expressive, intelligent eyes. 'Oh, is this my mare?' She ran the last few steps, going straight to the horse's head, producing some lumps of sugar from a pocket in her habit. 'She's lovely.'

'Yes, she is,' Nicholas said, his eyes on Serena.

He took her hand, pressing a kiss to her knuckles, smiling into her eyes in a way that left her in no doubt of his thoughts. Serena felt a responsive shiver. Beside her the horse pawed nervously at the ground.

'Her name is Belle,' Nicholas told her, handing over the reins. 'She can be quite lively—do you think you'll be able to handle her?'

'I'm sure we'll get along splendidly. I expect she just needs a gallop. I'm looking forward to it almost as much as she is.'

'Well, just take it easy until we're out in the fields. Come here and I'll help you up.'

She mounted with ease, draping her long skirts gracefully over the pommel. Belle pranced and pawed, held firmly in a light grip. They set off at a brisk trot side by side down the lane and out into the fields. Serena rode well, straight-backed and light handed, the feathers in her hat flying out in the breeze as she urged the mare into a gallop. Beside her, Nicholas and Titus kept pace. The countryside rushed by in a swirl of green and brown accompanied by the thud of the horses' hooves, the whistle of the wind in her ears, an occasional rustle in the undergrowth as some small animal fled from their path. Gradually they slowed to a canter and then to a trot, lazily following the meanderings of a burbling stream.

Flushed from the exercise, her eyes bright with curiosity, Serena asked Nicholas to tell her more about their surroundings, surprised to find that almost all the land belonged to him. Her questions forced him to dig deep into the recesses of his brain for answers. It was gratifying, how quickly it all came flooding back to him.

'I hadn't realised you were such an expert on farming,' she teased.

'I'm not really. My bailiff manages it all; I can't claim any credit for the good heart the land is in.'

'But you clearly understand how the estate works.'

'I spent a lot of time here in my youth, even though I don't come down so often now.'

'It's so beautiful here, I love it. You're very lucky.'

'I suppose I am. Do you plan to stay on in England?' he asked curiously.

'Yes, I think so.'

'In London?'

'I don't know.' In truth she had no idea. 'Maybe I'll find my own place in the country.'

'So your father's will left you well provided for?'

'Yes. But we said…'

'I know, that we wouldn't talk about it today.' He reined in his horse. 'We should go back. If we follow the stream for another mile or so, we can loop round through the West Farm and approach the Hall from the north.'

Serena nodded her agreement. They had passed the main buildings of the farm and were approaching the edge of the grounds of the Hall when she dropped back a little, distracted by a sound from the hedgerow to her left. As she leaned over in the saddle to try to see what creature was making the strange noise, the unmistakable sound of a shot pierced the air. The bullet whizzed over her head, missing her by inches.

Hearing the crack, Nicholas pulled Titus up sharply, turning round in the saddle just in time to see Serena's horse rear up into the air before bolting, with Serena still clinging on. Quickly wheeling Titus round, pressing his heels into the horse's flanks to urge him on, Nicholas galloped after Serena as she hung grimly on to her horse's neck and careered across the field. Coming alongside, Nicholas leaned over precariously to grab the horse's bit. 'Whoah, Belle, whoah, girl,' he said gently. The mare slowly came to a halt.

'Are you all right?' he asked anxiously.

'Yes, I'm fine, I'm fine.' Serena sat up in the saddle. She was as white as a sheet, but had herself firmly in hand. Taking her reins back from Nicholas, she focused her attention on soothing Belle, whispering calming platitudes in her ear. Gradually, the mare ceased her fidgeting. Serena looked up to find Nicholas frowning heavily, staring over her shoulder at the direction from which the shot had been fired. 'What is it?' she asked him.

'Did you see anything?'

'Nothing at all. I felt something whizzing over my head, but I didn't see where it came from.'

'It came from over there.' He pointed to a clump of trees leading into a wood at the boundary of the property. 'I'm going to have a look. There's a barn at the other side of the field, you and Belle can wait there. You've had quite a shock. Are you feeling well enough to ride?'

'I'm fine. But—can't I come with you?'

'No, go and wait for me there. I won't be long. I expect it was a stray shot fired by a poacher, in which case he'll likely be long gone. What he was shooting at this time of year in broad daylight I have no idea though—rabbits, maybe.'

'They would need to be flying rabbits,' Serena said with a weak attempt at humour. 'That bullet would have gone into my head if I hadn't bent down.'

'That thought had not escaped me,' Nicholas replied grimly. 'Go and rest, Serena. I'll join you shortly.'

Giving her no time to protest, Nicholas galloped off in the direction of the wood. Serena headed for the barn, where she dismounted and tied the mare up beside a convenient water trough. The sky was lowering, the morning's brightness giving way to a squally April breeze. Rain threatened.

By the time Nicholas returned half an hour later it had started to pour, and Serena was beginning to fret.

'I thought something had happened to you.'

He grinned at the charming picture she made, framed by the doorway in her blue velvet suit with her bright gold hair dishevelled. 'Don't be silly, did you think the poacher would shoot me? More likely the other way round, as punishment for his recklessness. Go inside, I'll just put Titus beside Belle. We might as well wait out the rain here, it will pass over soon enough'

He had found no trace of a poacher, not that he had really expected to do so. He had checked with Farmer Jeffries, whom he had spotted working the fields nearby, but he had seen nothing either, although he had heard the shot. The poacher had aimed high, possibly startled into loosing the gun. It was the only explanation that made sense, Nicholas told himself, for the alternative was that someone had shot deliberately at Serena, and that made absolutely no sense at all. He decided not to worry her unnecessarily with this absurd notion. 'It was an unfortunate accident, nothing more, but a most unsettling experience none the less. Are you sure you're all right, Serena?'

She gave him a weak smile by way of reply. She

seemed determined to appear little shaken despite the closeness of the bullet. She had real pluck, Nicholas thought with admiration. Every other woman of his acquaintance would have swooned.

'I'm fine,' she reassured him again. 'I got a fright and let my horse bolt, for which I am ashamed. Thank you, Mr Lytton, for being my knight errant. I'm sorry to have put you to the trouble.' She dropped a curtsy.

'It was an honour, *mademoiselle*,' Nicholas replied with a bow.

He closed over the door to block out the rain, which was now falling heavily. 'It's not exactly salubrious, but at least it will keep us dry,' he said, surveying the space. The barn was small, enclosed on all sides. Apart from some bales of hay stacked in one corner and a pitchfork leaning on the wall beside them, it was empty.

Rain pattered on the roof. A gusty wind whistled through the rough wooden walls. Serena shivered, making for the bales of hay, which formed a break against the draughts. 'We can sit over here, it's at least a little more comfortable.'

Nicholas followed her. Serena perched on one of the bales, reaching up to remove her hat. The action stretched the tight-fitting jacket of her habit against the contours of her body, the soft velvet outlining the fullness of her breasts. The long line of her throat showed creamy white above the lace of her collar. Turning, she found Nicholas gazing down at her, desire writ plain across his face.

Her heart picked up a beat. They were alone in an isolated barn. A ramshackle building with only bales of straw for comfort, hardly the setting she would have picked for her first experience in seduction. But the raw need on Nicholas's face was unmistakable. She had only to acquiesce.

Nervously, Serena pushed a stray curl from her eyes. *Did she want this?* Her whole body screamed yes, but still she tried to be certain in her mind. It was an irrevocable step to take. An idyll, that's how Nicholas saw it. She was not so sure she would be able to think of it in quite the same way afterwards.

Afterwards. *Had she then already made up her mind?* The atmosphere between them crackled with tension. Nicholas stood looking down at her, one brow raised. She knew what he was asking. Knew too that he would accept her no, though he wanted her yes. *She* wanted to say yes. Right here, right now, she wanted to say yes more than anything. But would she feel the same way tomorrow, and the next day, and the next? To surrender herself to him could be to cast the dice irrevocably. Was that really what she wanted? But to draw back from the game now would be to regret having done so for ever, wouldn't it?

'Serena?'

Why must he ask? Why must he look at her like that, so she could not think straight? She stood up, reaching to brush a lock of hair from his brow. It was damp from the rain. Black as coal. Soft as silk. She pushed it back, running her fingers along the contour of his skull, trailing them down his neck, fluttering against his skin. *What was he thinking?*

He smelled of rain and horse and man. His skin was cool and damp. She ran her fingers up through the short hair on the back of his neck. *What was she doing?*

Their eyes locked, blue on grey, deepening into dark pools of desire. With a harsh intake of breath, Nicholas pulled her roughly to him, holding her close, gripping her waist, cupping her head through her curls. Angling his mouth on to hers, he kissed her hard, engulfing her in sudden heat and passion and fire. Soft curves melted into hard planes.

He deepened the kiss. She reached her arms around him, under the material of his coat, against the soft linen of his shirt, the silk of his waistcoat, feeling the heat of his skin through the delicate material. Her hands roamed across his back, kneading the rippling muscles, tracing the knotted line of his spine. He was all bone and muscle and sinew. Power and strength coiled tight. Heady. Strange. Frighteningly, dizzyingly exciting.

Nicholas groaned, thrusting his tongue into her mouth, his kisses demanding, hardening, deepening. Long passionate kisses. Tiny licking kisses. Nibbling on the corners of her mouth, sucking on her bottom lip, his tongue tangling with her own, sweeping across the tender skin on the inside of her mouth. Licking and sucking and thrusting.

He pulled her closer, pressing his arousal

against her through the soft leather of his buck-skins. Shockingly hard. Unimaginable. *Now, now was the time to stop.* To stop before she *did* imagine. What it would feel like. What it would feel like…

She was hot. Her body thrummed, pulsed, pounded, throbbed. She was a hard core of heat, yet she was melting.

Nicholas licked, and she followed. He bit her lip gently, and she nicked his bottom lip between her own teeth. Tentatively touched her tongue to his when he thrust. She wanted to touch him, but did not know how. She knew she should stop, but did not know how. 'Nicholas,' she heard herself say, though surely that was not her voice?

He was still kissing her. Drugging, swollen, swooning kisses, as if he would suck the life-blood from her. She gave and gave and gave and still he kissed her more. He undid the large buttons of his riding coat and waistcoat, shrugging out of both together. The tiny buttons on her own jacket surrendered to his hands, though she could not have said how. They stood chest to chest. She was breathing as if she had been running. Nicholas, too, his chest heaving, like in the fight. She had no will, no will of her own any more, save to do as he bid.

He tugged the folds of his shirt free from his breeches and took her hands, placing her palms flat on his heated skin. She ran them wonderingly along his ribcage, down the line of his torso to the indent at his waist, relishing the shivering response her touch elicited as she used her hands to draw the map of his body. Her fingers encountered the barrier of his breeches. She pulled her hand back as if she had been burned. She *was* burning.

Nicholas looked down at her anxiously. Her eyelids were heavy over the deep blue of her eyes, the long dark lashes fanned out over her cheeks. Her hair was undone from its pins, rippling down her back in long ringlets, one tress curling provocatively over her flushed cheek. Her lips were swollen from his kisses. She looked every bit as wanton, even more arousing than in all his fevered late-night imaginings.

'Serena?'

She stared up at him. He took her hand again, placed it back on his chest, relishing the feel of her skin on his, while desperately trying to read her thoughts. *Was she frightened?* For a moment he thought so. *Because this was the first time?* For a moment he hoped so. *Because it was not?* No, don't think of that.

Beneath the soft silk of her blouse he could see her breasts rise and fall. He could see the hard peaks of her nipples. Carefully he tugged the lace at her neck, finding the fastenings, slowly undoing them, until her blouse was open to the waist. Her breathing quickened. Her hand curled into the muscle of his chest, but she did not stop him. He pulled the blouse free from the waist-band of her skirt. He tugged at her undergarments, expertly freeing her breasts from the wisps of lace and fine lawn cotton that constrained them. At the first touch of his thumbs on her nipples Serena moaned, slumping back against the bales of hay.

She wanted him. Nicholas arranged her gently, supporting her against the straw. She was a picture to rob any man of control, with her golden hair spread out like a fan, her countenance flushed, her eyes heavy with desire. The creamy mounds of her breasts with their rosy-tipped peaks rose and fell alluringly against the white of her undergarments. Just exactly as he'd pictured. The blue velvet of her skirt trailed out beneath her. Nicholas drank his fill of the vision, his breathing heavy, his heart thumping erratically as desire surged painfully through him.

'Nicholas.'

Serena breathed his name in that special way of hers, watching him through eyes slumberous with desire. She was no vision. She was flesh and blood and heat and luscious, perfect curves. And his, all his. Pushing her legs apart under the voluminous skirt of her riding habit, Nicholas knelt down in front of her. Cupping her full breasts in his hands, he licked the soft undersides, teasing her nipples into hard, swollen fullness between his fingers, pinching them just enough to make her moan with the overwhelming pleasure of it. He leaned in closer, circling her nipples with his tongue, flicking over the hard peaks, sucking gently, then hard, gently, then hard.

She was mindless. She was lost. She was frightened by what was happening to her, but in a way that made her want more. Heat spread out from her belly, a dull glow turning into a burning ember, sparks flying out through her veins, igniting her blood, making her burn. *Was this normal?* Serena writhed restlessly. She didn't want him ever to stop. His mouth on her. His hands on her. He was making her do things. Things she didn't know she knew.

She should stop. She couldn't stop. She arched against him, pushing her body into him, finding the restraining cloth of her skirt, his breeches, an unbearable barrier. 'Nicholas.' She breathed his name again, slanting open her eyes to look at him, hot hands, hot mouth, hot eyes on her. She wanted this, and now she wanted something else too.

Nicholas lifted the hem of her blue velvet skirt, pushing it up around her waist to reveal the long graceful line of her legs. Little boots laced tight around delicate ankles. Silk stockings clinging to the outline of her calves, their ribbons tied under the lace-trimmed edges of her underwear. *God, so beautiful.*

Serena blushed because he was looking. Blushed because she could see he liked looking. Blushed because she liked him looking. She shifted under his gaze.

The movement caused the gap between her

pantaloons to open, giving Nicholas a brief, tantalising view of blonde curls. He inhaled sharply, drinking in her body hungrily, feasting on the full length of her legs, the outline of her thighs under the delicate lawn of her underclothes, breathing in the smell of hay, her flowery perfume, the elusive musky scent of vanilla which seemed to emanate from her skin. With his eyes closed, he ran one hand teasingly from the top of her boot up over her stocking and along the velvet-soft skin on the inside of her thigh, feeling her rippling response. Running his hand over her other leg, he breathed in deeply, relishing the smell of her, the feel of her, the lines and textures of her. A multitude of sensations bubbled through his blood, making him swell with desire, wild with the anticipation of possession.

He reached for the gap in her pantaloons, unerringly finding the source of her heat. Gently, he touched, stroked, pressed. She responded, pushing against his hand. He pushed her legs apart, revealing all the glory of her soft curls, her creamy white thighs, her wet centre.

Serena felt the heat of his mouth, a gentle

breath on her thighs. She tightened, her body a bow stretched taut to breaking point. He was licking. The slow sweep of his tongue made her gasp. He licked again, teasing her, circling around the rough edges of desire, homing in, then out again, stroking her with his fingers, pushing her back when she arched against his mouth, his determined control of her frustrating and stimulating at the same time.

Lost, lost, lost. Serena moaned and pushed and twisted against him, wet with need, overcome with wanting. Still the licking teased, brought her to the edge, withdrew, driving her into a frenzy, making her feel as if she teetered on the brink of some huge chasm, wanting Nicholas to push her, wanting to jump, unable to do so without him. She was terrified he would not make her.

Make me, Nicholas, she wanted to say, though she didn't, she couldn't, she wouldn't. *Please.* He heard her. *Did he hear her?* Heat erupted suddenly, ripped through her, and she shattered, her whole body pulsing outwards from the centre of her climax, mindless, falling, whirling, lost. Her hands clenched on the straw at her sides, her heels dug into the bales supporting her, and she moaned over and over in a rhythm of her own, shaking, hot, trembling, wet.

Nicholas raised himself up, bending to kiss her. Serena reached up to pull him close, her mouth hot on his, kissing him back passionately, wild with the need to taste him, to make him feel what she was feeling, to take him to the place where she was.

He breathed hard against her, struggling with the fastenings of his breeches, desperate now to finish what they had begun. The final button on his buckskins gave way, and at last he was free from constraint. He took her hand, placing it on his erection, closing his eyes in pleasure at the feel of her butterfly touch fluttering over him. He was so highly sensitised he could almost feel the ridges and swirls of her fingertips.

Serena looked in awe at the thick jutting length of him. So strange. She could feel the pulse of his blood. She could feel the tension in him etched into every muscle. Here, here was where the centre of all that power was. He took her hand and wrapped it around his hardness. She watched his response with a mounting sense of excitement as she touched him carefully, stroking him, cupping him, watching him, learning from the way he moved, throbbed, moaned under her caresses. Something fierce clutched at her insides. Something powerful and horribly addictive. She ran her thumb over his silky smooth tip. She thought she'd done something wrong. Then she saw from his face that she hadn't.

With a low husky growl Nicholas pushed her back against the hay. As he stood over her, made ready to plunge into her wet, honeyed centre, he became dimly aware of an insistent noise. The door to the barn was being rattled fiercely. He stilled, unable to believe his ears. *Not now. Please God, not now.*

'Who's in there? Is that you, Master Nicholas?'

Nicholas swore furiously. Tearing his eyes from the vision in front of him, he quickly fastened his breeches, carelessly thrusting the ends of his shirt into them. 'Stay here,' he whispered to Serena, making swiftly for the door, slipping outside before Farmer Jeffries could glimpse the scene inside.

'I thought I recognised Titus,' the farmer said. 'Is there anything wrong, Master Nicholas? Only, after the shot, I came out to check things over for myself, and found your horses tied up.'

'The rain,' Nicholas said, running a hand through his dishevelled locks. 'We were sheltering from the rain.'

The farmer looked as if he were about to say something, but to Nicholas's relief he contented himself with a nod. 'Just as you say, Master Nicholas. I'll keep an eye out for that poacher. Good day to you.'

'Good day, Jeffries.'

Nicholas returned to the barn. Serena was huddled on the hay, struggling with the buttons of her jacket. Her skin was flushed, her lips raw and swollen. 'You look quite delectable. Here, let me help you.' He pulled a piece of straw from her hair.

She blushed fiery red, getting to her feet, studiously avoiding his eyes as she brushed out her skirts. 'I should go.'

Nicholas studied her as she adjusted the lace at her neck and pinned the little hat, its feather still drooping with rain, rather lopsidedly back in place. A few moments ago she had been like molten heat in his arms. Now she was simply embarrassed. The horrible suspicion that he had completely mistaken her could not be ignored. He looked around him at the draughty barn, the forlorn bales of hay, and abandoned any idea of continuing where they had left off. *What had he been thinking!*

He picked up his hat and riding crop. 'You're quite right, you should go home. We'll finish this tomorrow, when we can be sure of no interruptions.'

'Tomorrow.' Serena gave a rather forlorn smile. 'Yes, we'll finish this tomorrow.'

He was perturbed by her tone. 'I'll see you home. We'll ride to your lodgings, I can lead Belle back.'

'There's no need.'

'Come on, before the rain starts again.' He threw her efficiently into the saddle and they cantered back to the village in silence. As she handed him Belle's reins, the rain began again in earnest.

Serena opened the door of her rooms on her return to find an empty grate and a note from

Madame LeClerc informing her that the *modiste* had accepted a ride to London with their landlady's son. Crumpling the letter and hurling it into the grate, Serena cursed shockingly fluently in Madame's native language. Her own journey to London would now have to be undertaken alone. Unless Nicholas escorted her. Serena sighed. She doubted very much he'd be inclined to do so after tomorrow.

She lay awake for most of that night, deeply troubled by the day's events. The feelings that Nicholas's love-making had aroused in her were frightening in their intensity. Despite her lack of experience, she knew it was more than mere physical attraction—at least on her part. She was out of her depth, in danger of drowning in the heady potion of desire, attraction and affinity that made up their relationship. In her heart of hearts she knew what she felt for Nicholas was not the fleeting fancy of a spring idyll. If the farmer had not interrupted them, she would have lost more than her innocence. She would have lost her heart.

As a grey dawn crept through the folds of the

heavy curtains, Serena forced herself to acknowledge the inevitable. The time had come for her to fold her cards. Any notion she had of returning to Knightswood Hall and finishing what they had started yesterday was foolish beyond belief. Casting all chances of future happiness with someone else to the winds for the sake of a few hours' idle pleasure would be madness. No matter how much she might yearn for it. No matter how right it felt. Madness.

She tried very hard to picture that someone else of her future, but he stubbornly refused to resemble anyone other than Nicholas. Her country house always turned into Knightswood Hall. Her children all had dark hair and slate-grey eyes. It was useless.

Perhaps she would have more success when this was over. Perhaps, after all, immersing herself in the balls and parties of the London Season would be a wise next step. Not towards matrimony, but away from danger. At least it would give her something to occupy her mind other than what might have been. What now would never be, she thought morosely. For Nicholas would not, in any case, be interested in her once she told him the truth. She had come close today to making him break his own rules, though he did not yet know it. Nicholas Lytton was not a man who would take kindly to that sort of betrayal. A lonely tear tracked down her cheek. Whichever way she looked at it, she dreaded the coming interview. However she tried to imagine it, right now, at this moment, her future seemed bleak.

Nicholas did not sleep much either. Tossing and turning in his tangled sheets, he cursed his over-vigilant tenant. The image of Serena spread out on the hay occupied his mind with tortuous clarity. He had never felt so desirous of a union of the flesh in his life. He had never felt so frustrated in his life. He groaned, turning over again in a vain attempt to find a cool spot in the rumpled bed. Tomorrow. If he did not have her tomorrow, he would go insane.

He was rudely awoken in the morning by a brisk rap on his bedroom door, which most certainly did not emanate from his considerate valet.

'Nick, you dog, get up.' Standing in the

doorway was Charles, Lord Avesbury, a notable Corinthian and Nicholas's best friend. Closing the door behind him, he strode over to pull back the window hangings before sitting himself on a chair by the dressing table.

Nicholas sat up in bed. 'Lord, you must have made an early start. What the devil brings you here? Not, you understand, that I'm not delighted to see you, but your timing is appalling.'

'I was staying with the Cheadles,' Charles replied. 'It's not more than fifteen miles away. There was talk of a picnic or some such nonsense today, so I thought I'd make my escape for a few hours.'

'I see. Lady Cheadle still hopeful, is she?'

'It's my mother's fault. She and Lady Cheadle are bosom buddies. She will have it that it's the dearest wish of her heart to see me leg-shackled to her friend's eldest daughter.'

'And you, Charles? Is it the dearest wish of your heart, to wed Penelope Cheadle?'

'Steady on, Nick, I wouldn't put it that strongly. I'm getting on though, about time I was setting up my nursery. I'm turned thirty.'

Nicholas stretched up to tug the bell for his

valet. 'I hope you know what you're doing, Charles. Rather you than me. I'm going to get dressed. Go down to the breakfast parlour, Hughes will bring you some coffee. I'll join you shortly, then you can tell me all the news.'

'Not much to tell. Truth is Nick, you're mostly the news at the moment.'

'Don't tell me my duelling opponent has inconveniently died?'

'No need to worry on that score, he's making an excellent recovery. You may come back to London whenever you're ready. No, it's not the duel. Get dressed, we can talk over breakfast. I'll be dammed if I'll sit here with you when you're not even wearing a nightshirt.' Refusing to be drawn any further, Charles retired downstairs.

Chapter Five

Nicholas did not tarry over his *toilette*, joining his friend in the breakfast parlour some twenty minutes later. Charles was gazing out of the window where a long line of men were scything the lawn. He was a good-looking man, famed for the perfect cut of his coats, which he had always from Weston, and the intricacy of his cravats, which he always tied himself. He was neither as tall nor as well built as Nicholas, but he had a leg shapely enough to look well in the tight panta-loons and tasselled Hessians he wore—from Holby, naturally—and his amiable countenance showed surprisingly few signs of wear despite his solid membership of the hard-drinking, hard-playing Corinthian set.

As Nicholas entered the room, Charles raised

his quizzing glass. 'I'm not sure I like the way you've tied your cravat. These country ways are making you lax. Time you were back in town.'

Nicholas laughed, sitting at the table to carve some ham. 'I was never so fastidious as you, Charles. Tell me, for I'm on tenterhooks, what on earth can have made me the talk of the *ton*.'

'Hear you gave Diana Masterton her *congé*.'

'Yes, she was becoming tedious in her demands, I told Frances Eldon to pay her off. Don't tell me that's it?'

'No, of course not. At least…' Charles took a sip of coffee. 'Bumped into your cousin Jasper at White's the other day. Asked me if I knew aught about the Cyprian who's keeping you company here. Wondered if she was the reason you'd rid yourself of the fair Diana. Needless to say I couldn't tell him anything, except that I doubted the truth of the rumour, since you're always so careful to keep your fancy pieces at a safe distance.'

Nicholas paused in the act of cutting into the slice of ham on his plate, frowning at his friend. 'She's not a fancy piece.'

'*What!*' Charles exclaimed, startled into

spilling his coffee. 'You mean to tell me it's true, there's a woman here? Come on, Nick, that's not your style. What are you thinking of?'

'She lodges in the village, not here. And I'd like to know how Jasper found out about her.'

'I never thought to ask. Wouldn't surprise me if he bribes your servants though, sort of thing he would do. Seemed mighty put out about it in any case, on account of your birthday being so close.'

Nicholas gave a sharp crack of laughter. 'So that's what he's worried about. He's well off the mark—I have no intentions of marrying Mademoiselle Stamppe.'

'Oh, so she's French,' Charles said dismissively, as if that explained everything.

'No, English actually, although she's lived on the Continent all her life.'

'What's she doing here with you, then, if she's not your mistress?'

'It's a long story, Charles.'

'You can't fob me off so easily, Nick.' Lord Avesbury took an enamelled box from his waistcoat pocket and flicked it open expertly with the tip of his thumb. 'Tell me the whole tale.' Taking a delicate pinch of snuff, he sat back in his chair with a grin. 'Anything's preferable to Lady Cheadle's picnic party. Go on, I've got all day.'

Cautiously skirting over the more personal aspects of their relationship, Nicholas recounted the events of the past few days.

Charles listened, running the full gamut of emotions from incredulous to sceptical. 'So what's in those papers of hers, then?'

'Her father's will and proof of her identity.'

'Why would she need proof of her identity? Sounds a bit shady to me. And now I come to think about it, her name sounds familiar too. Can't put my finger on it just at the moment, but it'll come to me. What's in the will?'

'I don't know. She promised she'd tell me, but events yesterday got in the way somewhat.'

'Events?' Charles laughed. 'I see. That's what you meant by my bad timing. Take it she's a looker, then, your *mademoiselle*?'

A bell clanged in the distance. Nicholas stood up, looking towards the door. 'You'll see for yourself in a few moments. I fancy that's her now.'

Serena entered the parlour a few minutes later.

'Oh, I beg your pardon, Hughes didn't mention that you had company.' She had been so busy rehearsing over and over in her mind the speech she intended to deliver to Nicholas that it quite overset her composure to find he was not alone.

Nicholas came over to take her hand in his familiar clasp. 'Serena, this is Charles, Lord Avesbury, my dearest and oldest friend. Charles, may I present Mademoiselle Serena Stamppe.'

Charles produced his quizzing glass to inspect the goddess who had appeared before him, his brows rising as he took in the perfection of Serena's beauty. She was dressed in a printed cotton dress of Turkey red, the small puffed sleeves intricately pleated and tapering tightly down almost to her knuckles. The neckline was trimmed with freshly laundered white ruffles, matching the frilled hem of her petticoat, beneath which her feet were clad in her favourite half-boots of kid. She had discarded her pelisse and hat when she arrived, and the full glory of her golden curls, piled high on her head, competed with the morning sunshine gleaming through the window panes.

Tucking the eyeglass into the pocket of his

waistcoat, Charles trod over to take Serena's hand, bowing with great elegance. 'Your servant, ma'am. Forgive me, Nicholas did not warn me I was about to encounter such a vision of loveliness. Your presence alone has made my journey worthwhile.'

Serena smiled politely, rather nonplussed to find herself in such obviously elevated company. 'How do you do,' she said, remembering her manners just in time, and dropping an elegant curtsy. She turned to Nicholas. 'Forgive me, if I had known you had a guest I wouldn't have intruded.'

He smiled reassuringly. 'Charles is a very good friend, there's no need to worry. Stay for coffee at least.'

She agreed because it would seem rude not to, sitting down in her usual chair by the fire. In the presence of Nicholas's friend all the impropriety of their situation hit home with a vengeance. She was embarrassed and disconcerted. Frustrated, too, for she had hoped to get the difficult conversation she had resolved to have with Nicholas out of the way as soon as possible.

Charles chatted amicably about the house party he had temporarily abandoned, the latest *on dits*, and a wager made on a race between a frog and a chicken. By the time Nicholas recounted the story of his first meeting with Serena, she had relaxed enough to be able to laugh about it.

'I thought he was a groom. It never occurred to me that I was watching the master of the house stripped to the waist and fighting the local blacksmith.' She looked up teasingly at Nicholas, who was standing with his back to the fireplace. He returned the look with a smile of such warmth that she raised a hand towards him, remembered that they were not alone, and dropped it. Remembered, too, her resolve to put an end to things between them.

Charles observed the by-play with interest. Now he had met her, it didn't surprise him that Nick had kept such a beauty hidden away. She was almost flawless, the mysterious Mademoiselle Stamppe, it would take a strong man indeed to resist her charms. It wasn't like Nick to be so reticent about his lady loves. He had carefully refrained from discussing Serena, though it was obvious they were intimate. Their bodies gave them away, constantly moving towards one another. The way they looked at each other, too. And that smile—they might as well have kissed. Nick was in deep with his adventuress. Charles wondered if he realised just how deep.

'I hope you won, Nick. The fight, I mean.'

'Of course I did. Samuel landed a couple of good punches, but he's slow.'

'You're getting too old for that sort of thing.'

'I know, I know.' Nicholas looked down at his hands, the faint scars the only reminder of the recent mill. 'I tell myself that I won't do it any more, but you know how it is. I can't resist a challenge.'

'Yes, but the next time you might lose. Give it up, Nick, you're almost thirty. Time you settled down.'

'I'll be the judge of that,' Nicholas said curtly. He didn't want to think about his father's damned will.

'You've got less than three months left,' Charles continued blithely.

'Not now, Charles.'

Watching him, Serena was confused by the less-than-subtle change of subject. The awkwardness of her situation returned to her. She rose to go. 'I'll leave you two to catch up. It was a pleasure to meet you, Lord Avesbury.' She curtsied, then turned to Nicholas. 'May I speak with you tomorrow? There is a matter I am most anxious to resolve with you.'

'You are not the only one who is anxious for resolution,' Nicholas whispered in her ear.

Serena blushed furiously, then looked stricken. 'I will see myself out.' She left, resolutely closing the door before he could demand to know what was wrong.

Nicholas and Charles passed a pleasant day tooling Charles's phaeton round the countryside, before partaking of a rustic meal at an inn some miles from High Knightswood.

'I bumped into your sister and your stepmama at Almack's the other day,' Charles said, touching his whip to his horses. 'Georgie was queening it over a pack of young pups.'

'Brat. Did you speak to them?'

'Of course I did, for I had already determined to come and see you. Georgie wanted to know when you were coming back to town, and said to be sure and tell you that she's a blazing success. Melissa was—well, you know what Melissa's like.'

Charles concentrated on overtaking a lumbering cart. 'Dashed attractive woman, that Serena of yours,' he continued when the manoeuvre had been stylishly executed.

'Very,' Nicholas agreed drily. 'What are you implying?'

'Ain't implying anything. I'm happy to tell you straight to your face, Nick, it's obvious how things are between you two. The way you were looking at each other put me to the blush. Don't tell me it's finally happened,' he said with a sudden guffaw of laughter. 'Has the lovely *mademoiselle* given you a *coup de foudre*?'

'You're being ridiculous Charles, I'm not in love with her.'

'Whatever you say. It's just occurred to me, though—maybe Jasper wasn't too far off the mark after all.'

'What's my cousin got to do with this?'

'Fretting himself to death at the thought of you getting hitched.'

'But I've no intention of getting married. Leastways, not until it's absolutely necessary.'

'Lawyers still claiming they're making progress? Depend upon it, they'll be saying that on the day of your birthday, it's what you pay 'em for. Don't believe a word of it. You need to get hitched, no two ways about it, and the perfect candidate's fallen like a ripe peach into your hands. Beautiful, obviously more than willing—in fact, I'd say the chit's besotted with you, although you don't notice, of course—and, what's more, not someone who will give you any trouble.'

'You're serious,' Nicholas said incredulously, staring at his friend as if he had just escaped from Bedlam.

'Of course I am. Think about it for a moment. I don't think you've quite grasped the severity of your plight. If you don't marry, you'll lose everything.'

'Not everything, I'll still have the Hall and estate.'

'Much good they'll do you without funds. You'll have to give up your gaming, your expensive women, your hunters. You'll have to rusticate here for ever, in penury.'

'It won't come to that.'

'It's coming mighty close,' Charles said exasperatedly. 'You can't let Jasper inherit, Nick. What isn't swallowed up by his debts will be tossed away on the hazard table. He's playing very deep these days, he'd be back under the hatches in less than a year.'

'I am aware of that. But it doesn't alter the fact that I have no desire at all to be married.'

'What makes you so much against it?'

'An inherent dislike of being coerced into doing something I have no desire to do, for a start.'

'Bloodymindedness, in other words.'

'If you like.' Nicholas sighed deeply. 'Of course I don't want Jasper to inherit.'

'Then marry your Serena,' Charles said stubbornly. 'Devil take it, Nick, it's not like you to be so dense. She's perfect. My guess is she's the by-blow of some gentleman, you don't get a nose like that from common stock. She's well mannered, well turned out—need I go on?'

'So you're suggesting a marriage of convenience.'

'Convenient enough for both of you, certainly. You keep your fortune. She gets your name. You can pension her off after a respectable time—say a year.'

'You underestimate my dear parent. There is a clause in his will that no one else, not even Jasper, has knowledge of. If my marriage is terminated by anything other than death, Jasper inherits.' Nicholas smiled at the shocked expression on his friend's face. 'My father constructed a matrimonial prison for me, with a life sentence as punishment. I will find a way to break it—I must. Now let us drop the subject, once and for all.'

Charles pulled the phaeton up at the front door of the Hall, refusing the offer of a bed for the night. 'Didn't mean to offend you, Nick.'

'It's all right, Charles. I simply won't be told how to run my life. Not by my father, not by Jasper or even, my dear fellow, by you.'

Charles grinned. 'Truth be told, Nick, I'm pretty set on doing the deed myself. Don't want to offend the future mother-in-law, best be on my way before they send out a search party.'

'Give my regards to Lady Cheadle, and accept my felicitations, if I'm not being premature.'

'Well, it's fairly certain. I'm to have an audience with Lord Cheadle in the morning—settlements, you know. She's a compliant little thing, Penelope, she'll do well enough. Take a leaf from my book, Nick, before it's too late.' Charles pulled his caped driving coat more securely around him and tightened the reins. With a crack of the whip he set his horses trotting briskly down the path, only to pull them up almost immediately. 'Stamppe,' he called back, 'knew it would come to me. It's the family name of the Vespians. Saw the announcement in the *Morning Post* the other day, the fifth earl died in Paris last year. Your Serena must be some distant relative.' With a twirl of his whip, he set off again.

Nicholas headed for the library, demanding the last few days' copies of the *Morning Post*. While Hughes retrieved the newspapers from the butler's pantry and hastily ironed them flat, Nicholas poured himself a glass of Madeira and thought about Serena.

Inevitably his mind returned to the image of her yesterday lying wanton in the hay, her hair fanned out, brighter gold than the supporting bales, her creamy flesh flushed. He couldn't wait to plunge into the hot wet core of her, to feel her tight around him, to… Damnation! He was fantasising like a school boy. If he continued in this vein he was in for another night like the last one, tortured by adolescent fantasies and frustrated with longing.

Looking at the clock on the mantel, he realised that it was almost dinner time. Tomorrow he would make sure their love-making was not interrupted. Tonight he would have to content himself with trying not to think about what that would entail.

Hughes arrived with the stack of newspapers and the day's post. There was a letter from Frances Eldon at last. Nicholas opened it with a smile of anticipation. As he quickly scanned the neatly crossed pages his smile faded. By the time he had finished, his face was a mask of fury.

He was waiting for her on the front steps of the Hall the next morning. The day was dry but cold, making Serena glad of the warm woollen cloak she wore over her dress of pale blue muslin. At the sight of Nicholas's tall figure her heart did a little flip of excitement. It was all very well to tell herself that they must never share so much as another kiss. Faced with the man himself, her will power weakened.

You are not the only one anxious for a resolution. His parting words to her yesterday. Excitement turned to anxiety, which dissolved into dread when she saw his face. No sign of his usual careless smile, his mouth was drawn into a tight line and he was frowning, his eyes a cold slate grey that seemed to glitter like polished granite. 'Is there something wrong, Nicholas?'

She faltered to a halt on the step below him. He looked down, his eyes travelling slowly over her, from her face, sweeping down her neck, the length of her body, with contempt. An icy coldness clutched at her heart. 'Nicholas?'

'Come in. There's coffee waiting,' he said curtly, preceding her into the house, giving her no choice but to follow him, hastily abandoning her bonnet and cloak to Hughes's care.

They sat opposite each other in front of the fire as was their custom. The clock ticked on the mantel. Outside, the sun danced in and out of scudding clouds, slanting shadows of light and dark onto the polished wooden floors. Everything familiar, in its usual place, yet somehow nothing felt the same.

Nicholas's brows met, giving him the look of a brooding devil. The long fingers of his right hand drummed a slow beat on the arm of his chair. He sat with careless grace, his long legs, clad today in tightly fitting pantaloons and polished Hessians, sprawled out in front of him, but there was no mistaking the tension in him. He was coiled. Ready to spring. And Serena felt horribly like his prey.

His mood alarmed her, all the more because he had himself so tightly under control. She carefully replaced her half-full coffee cup on the tray lest her shaking hands betray her. Nicholas had not touched his. The clock ticked.

'Alone at last, Serena,' Nicholas said, looking positively predatory.

She managed an uncertain smile.

'I've given Hughes instructions to deny me to any callers. What with Farmer Jeffries and then Charles, I think we've had too many interruptions lately, don't you?'

Her mouth was dry. She licked her lips. 'Nicholas, I…'

He raised an eyebrow. 'Nervous, Serena? There's no need to be. Surely our experience in the barn was sufficient to prove that the conclusion to our little idyll here will be pleasurable— on your part, at least. We have yet to determine how I will like it.'

Colour flooded her face and drained just as quickly, leaving her ashen. 'Why are you being so beastly?'

'You're tense. We should do something to help you relax. A game of piquet, perhaps? Or what about dice? I'm sure Papa taught you how to load the bones as well as how to fix the cards.'

'I don't cheat.'

'Oh, but you do, Serena. You have been cheating me since the day you turned up on my doorstep.' He stood, the tension in him blatantly obvious now, in the way he clenched his fists by his side, the way he held his shoulders rigid. He reached into his coat pocket and pulled out a letter. 'I had this from Frances Eldon, my man of business, yesterday. Combined with your uncle's announcement in the *Morning Post* and your own revelations, it has helped to make a lot of things much clearer.'

She realised at once that it was too late. If he knew from someone else what she should have told him from the first, he would never forgive her. 'You had your man of business investigate me,' she said flatly.

Nicholas coloured. 'Since you were so sparing with the truth I had no option.'

She stood up shakily. 'Don't say you had no option, it's not true. You could have waited. I came today to tell you, but I see there is no need, your Mr Eldon has saved me the trouble of a confession.'

'You lied to me.'

'You did not trust me,' she flung at him, her temper flaring. 'And I did not lie to you, Nicholas. I may have misled you, but you were perfectly happy for me to do so.'

'What do you mean by that?'

'You claim you were suspicious of me from the start. Suspicious enough to have someone investigate me. But you never asked me. You never said, *Serena, I'm not sure about this story of yours.*'

'Would you have told me?'

'Yes! No! Probably. It doesn't matter, you

didn't ask because you didn't want to know. And then when I found my papers, the same thing. I would have told you straight away, even before I had read them, if you had pressed me. But you did not. Instead you suggested a day's grace.'

'Which you were more than happy to agree to.'

She nodded and took a calming breath. 'Yes. Yes, I was. It was wrong, I knew it was wrong, but I agreed because I wanted…' She blushed, but forced herself to continue. 'Because I wanted what happened in the barn. Now I know it was a terrible mistake.'

Her admission threw him. He reached for her, but she stepped back. 'No, Nicholas. It's too late now. I must go. I should have gone two days ago.'

'Sit down, Serena,' Nicholas said coldly, 'you don't get off so lightly. I want to hear it for myself. All of it.'

She would rather do almost anything, but she owed it to him, and he was mostly in the right, so she sat down, stiff-backed, hands clutched tight together in a bitter parody of their first meeting. Nicholas sat down too, his gaze unwavering. That look of his that made her feel he could read her mind.

'Well, as you have obviously surmised, Papa made his money from gambling. Gaming salons, but I assure you he was neither a cheat nor a sharp.' As she sketched a picture of their life, she watched Nicholas watching her, but his face gave away nothing. 'We followed the wars, for where there are wars there are officers and hangers-on and plenty of money,' she continued. 'Most recently we settled in Paris.'

'And you, did you preside over the tables?'

Despite the circumstances, the very idea forced a smile from her. 'Hardly. I've told you several times, Papa was extremely protective. He forbade me from entering the salons when they were open. I was his hostess at private parties—when he played for pleasure with his particular friends, all older men, respectable men. I played too, sometimes. And of course, I practised with him.'

'A fine education for you!' He was unaccountably angry on her behalf. 'What about the dangers you must have been exposed to, the sights you must have seen, the type of men you must have met?'

'It wasn't like that. You don't understand.'

'No, I don't. What did he intend for you, your

sainted papa? You're—what, twenty-two, twenty-three? Did he not wish to see you settled?'

'I'm almost five and twenty. Of course he wanted to see me settled, that's why I am here. He would have brought me himself if it was not for the war.'

'That is complete nonsense, he could have returned any time if he'd really wanted to. Your father sounds to me like a selfish bastard.'

Serena was silent. Papa had explained, but even then, through the grief of knowing he had only a few hours left to live, his excuses had sounded weak to her ears. It had been more than thirty years, after all. 'You're right, he was a little set in his ways. I suppose the truth was that he had grown used to his life and did not wish to be constrained by his responsibilities in England.'

'His life as the Earl of Vespian.'

'Yes, my father was Lord Vespian.'

'Which makes you the Lady Serena— assuming, of course, that a marriage actually took place between your parents. Was there one?'

She cast him a wounded look. 'Of course there was.'

He was unrepentant. 'I'm only saying what everyone else will ask. Charles did say it was curious, your need to prove your identity.'

'You told Charles all this? You had no right.'

'Charles won't say anything. He liked you.'

'Well, I'm relieved to know that someone does.' Serena reached for her reticule and pulled out a small leather pouch, which she handed to him. 'I thought my father was being excessively cautious, but he insisted I should have this as well as the legal documents.'

Nicholas undid the ties. Inside was a ring, intricately worked in gold, a strange antique setting wrought around a large black pearl. Frowning, he traced a long finger over the pattern. 'An heirloom, I presume,' he said, returning the ring to its pouch and handing it back to Serena.

'Another of his deathbed bequests,' she said with intentional irony. 'I've to give it to my uncle. It seems it is always worn by the heir to the earldom.'

Nicholas strode over to the window. In the brief time they had spent together the narcissi had started to fade, the cherry blossom to fall.

In the distance he could see a horse and plough readying a field for planting. He had been beguiled, even Charles had spotted it. Locked away from the world, he had been careless of everything save the overwhelming attraction between them, the shared laughter, the gravitation of their bodies towards each other. He had been happy. And no matter what she claimed, he had also been duped.

A gust of rage seized him. 'Tell me, Lady Serena,' he said, turning back from the window to the beautiful deceiver sitting in front of the fire, 'just why you felt it so necessary to keep your real identity a secret.'

'You know why.'

'I'd like to hear it from you.'

Her knuckles where white, so tightly was she gripping them. 'Very well, if I must. I did not tell you because I knew that while you would be happy enough to dally with Mademoiselle Cachet of no particular place and no particular family, you would run a mile from Lady Serena Stamppe. I needed to find my father's papers. You only helped because you were bored and you thought I was fair game. You would not have thought Lady Serena fair game, would you, Nicholas? And I would not then have found my father's will. I don't know why you're making me say this—no doubt you wish to humiliate me. No doubt I deserve it—but do not paint yourself as whiter than white in this tawdry episode.'

'I did not think you *fair game*, as you call it. How dare you!'

'You hardly treated me as you would a respectable female.'

'You hardly gave me grounds to do so. The first time I set eyes on you, you kissed me while I was half-naked in front of a crowd of spectators.'

'*You* kissed *me*!' She flung herself to her feet. 'And then you kissed me again, here in this very room.'

'You didn't put up much of a fight.'

'Oh, how dare you. *How dare you!* You turn everything to your own account. I came alone here because I *am* alone. What relatives I have don't even know I exist yet. I thought I was calling on a man my father's age. You made it perfectly clear from the start that you didn't think my papers existed, or if they did that they had long been lost. I've told you, time and again I've told you, that I led a sheltered life, yet you chose not to believe that either. You talked about the rules of the game, and not playing if you couldn't pay, and no commitment, at every opportunity so that I knew—*how could I not*—that you would consign me to the ends of the earth if you found out that I was the type of female who could be *compromised*.'

'That explains why you lied, it does not explain why you let me make love to you. The other day—in the barn—I gave you every opportunity to say no. *Dammit*, Serena, you know I did.'

'Yes, you did,' she whispered. 'And I didn't. I should have, but I didn't. I don't know what came over me. I was not thinking straight. I thought I could play to your rules, that I could indulge in what you call a spring idyll, but I realise that I am not, after all, the type to treat such *affaires* lightly. It meant nothing to you, but I discovered it *should* mean something to me.'

'You left it rather late in the day to discover something so fundamental. There is a name for that type of behaviour, but I will not sully your ears with it.'

Serena recoiled as if he had hit her, but met his gaze resolutely. 'I deserved that. I know how it must look, but it was not my intention to—I mean, it *was* my intention to—what I mean is, at the time I meant it. But afterwards, I realised that I risked throwing away my chances of future happiness with someone else. Throwing it away on someone who did not—would never—offer me what I want.'

'Marriage, of course,' Nicholas said disgustedly. 'I should have known you weren't really that different from the rest of your sex. Well, you'll be able to take your unsullied pick now, Lady Serena.'

'Yes, I will,' she said, finally driven by hurt to goad him. 'I'm not only titled, I'm vastly wealthy too, you know. An heiress and a lady— you're right, I *will* be able to take my pick.'

Charles had been right. The perfect candidate, he'd called Serena, and that was before he knew all. That Frances Eldon had also urged matrimony on his employer in his latest epistle added fuel to the flames. 'I hope you will be more honest with the poor clunch, whoever he turns out to be, than you were with me. Will you tell him that he's taking a lying, scheming, card-sharping temptress to his bed? Will you tell him that he's not the first to touch you? To kiss you? To make you cry out with pleasure? Or will you play the innocent virgin with him? I warn you, you will have to polish up your act a bit if you do. Respond to him as you did to me, and he will not believe you any more than I do.'

Serena flinched. 'You don't mean that, Nicholas. You know I wasn't acting.'

'I know that I am the one left aching with frustration, while you at least were satisfied,' Nicholas responded crudely. 'All I've been thinking about, day and night, is you, you, you. The vision of you lying there with your hair undone haunts me. And now it will always haunt me. I will never be rid of you,' he said heatedly, grabbing Serena by the shoulders. 'Don't you see what you've done? Because I will never have you I will always be imagining what might have been.'

He pulled her towards him and kissed her roughly. His lips were hard on hers, his tongue thrusting into her mouth. She could smell the scent of his soap, feel his breath warm on her skin, sense the barely controlled anger in the tension of his fingers bruising the soft flesh at the top of her arms.

It was a punishing kiss, a possessive kiss, the hungry kiss of desire too long pent up. It was the kiss of a man intent on slaking his thirst. Then suddenly it was a passionate kiss. Unable to stop herself, Serena responded, kissing him back urgently, meeting fire with fire. Nicholas groaned, releasing his grip to slide his arms around her, pulling her close into the hard length of his body. Then abruptly she was free. 'It would have been better for us both if your father had left his papers with a lawyer.'

'You wish we had never met?'

'With a passion.'

'Don't be like this, Nicholas, don't let us part on such terms.'

'For God's sake, what other terms can there be?'

'We are both overwrought. You think I have deceived you, but I have not. I'm the same person I was when first we met. A title does not change who I am. I admit, I did not tell you the whole truth, but I did not lie to you. And as to what has happened between us—you have not broken your rules. Your conscience is clear, you did not take anything I was not willing to give, and thanks to the arrival of your tenant, I did not give you enough to be truly compromised.' She managed a watery smile.

Her willingness to absolve him from the blame he suspected he deserved melted Nicholas's anger, leaving him feeling strangely empty. He saw she was making a valiant attempt not to cry, and felt guilt perch like a brooding raven on his shoulder. 'Go and pack,' he said gruffly, struggling to resist the desire to pull her back into his arms. 'I'll pick you up at noon tomorrow.'

'Don't be foolish, Nicholas. I'll hire a chaise. I won't be more than a night on the road.'

'It is you who are being foolish. It's too dangerous for you to travel alone with only your snoring Madame for company, and Charles told me yesterday that I'm no longer *persona non grata* in London, since my duelling opponent is well on the road to recovery.'

Serena coloured. 'Madame LeClerc is gone ahead of me.'

'Then that settles it. There have been a spate of robberies on the London road. A highwayman, Hughes says. It's not safe.'

'I'll hire some outriders,' Serena said stubbornly.

'Serena, I insist. If you don't agree, I'll simply make sure you can't hire your own chaise in the village. One of the advantages of being the local landowner.'

'That's not fair. Nicholas, it's better if you don't, really…'

He took hold of her hand between his own. 'I could not be happy with you travelling alone. Indulge me in this. We both need time to order our thoughts, and I to cool my temper. You are right, we should not part on such terms. We deserve better.'

Her conscience warred with her desires, and her desires won. She could not resist the temptation of a few more days of his company. 'Very well.' Refusing his escort on the grounds that he too must attend to his packing, Serena departed Knightswood Hall.

It was only when she had gone that he realised she had still offered him no explanation for her willingness to make love to him.

Chapter Six

The air in the public room of the King's Arms, the tavern owned by the legendary heavyweight Thomas Cribb, was stifling. Acrid wood smoke from the roaring fire hung heavy, despite the grimy windows flung open wide to the street. The pungent aroma of unwashed human bodies mingled with the smell of spilt ale and cheap spirits.

Jasper Lytton paused on the threshold, wearing the habitual sneer that marred the handsome lines of his countenance. Of late the place had become overrun with the *hoi polloi*, so much so that even the distinction of being invited to partake of daffy within the sanctity of Cribb's own private parlour was become a dubious pleasure. He raised his quizzing glass to survey the room. From the window embrasure a thin man beckoned with a long white finger. Jasper joined him reluctantly.

'I th-thought you weren't going to turn up, Jasper. I've been here an age.' The man spoke with a slight stammer. He was young and elegantly dressed, but dissipation was already taking a heavy toll, thinning his hair, etching a deep groove on either side of his mouth. The pale eyes were bloodshot. His hand shook as he reached for the decanter to top up his glass, filling Jasper's at the same time.

'God, Langton, you look like hell.' Jasper lolled on the hard wooden seat, watching his friend's hand tremble with malicious pleasure. Though Langton could give him at least five years, and he himself drank harder and gamed deeper, no one would take Jasper for the senior man.

'S-so would you, in my position. Well, do you have it?'

Jasper shifted uncomfortably, unwilling to meet the other man's gaze. 'No, not yet.'

'*You promised!* I need it back immediately. If I d-don't have it—God, you know what these people are like.'

'Only too well, I introduced you to them myself, remember?' Watching his friend gulp down the fiery liquid, Jasper felt a minute twinge of guilt. It wasn't as if the five thousand he owed Langton was such a great sum, but it *was* a debt of honour. Introducing Hugo Langton to his own moneylender of choice had been intended as a stalling tactic, nothing more. Carefully reaching into his jacket pocket, Jasper withdrew a small roll of notes. 'There's two hundred here on account. I'll get the rest soon. I just need a run of luck.'

'Or your cousin to bail you out,' Langton muttered, snatching at the money.

Jasper's smile hardened. 'That's unlikely. Nicholas made it perfectly clear that he wouldn't be towing me out of the River Tick again.' The bitter memory of that last uncomfortable interview with his cousin still rankled. Why couldn't Nicholas see that paying off Jasper's debts for him was simply advancing money that would be rightfully his in the very near future anyway?

'How long is it now until the great day?'

'Less than three months.' He'd be lucky to hold his creditors at bay that long. There were bailiffs at his lodgings. Duns at his club. Damn Nicholas, why was he making him wait?

Across the table Langton emptied the dregs of the decanter into his glass. His hand no longer shook. The rough liquor gave him courage. When he spoke his voice was free from its stammer. 'Three months, and you'll be a rich man—provided your cousin doesn't get leg-shackled in the meantime.'

Jasper's thin lips tightened. Waving an imperious hand at the beleaguered landlord for more brandy, he quelled the panic that threatened to overwhelm him every time he thought of the consequences were his cousin suddenly to announce his nuptials. 'He wouldn't do that,' he said grimly.

The fierce look that he drew forced Langton to cower back in his seat, all thoughts of teasing banished. 'If you s-say so. I merely thought…'

'What have you heard?' Jasper asked sharply.

'Just a rumour. Came from Charles Avesbury, if you must know.'

'Avesbury,' Jasper exclaimed. 'He said Nicholas was to be married?'

'Well, not as such. But he did see the lady in

question. Said the two of them were smelling of April and May.'

Jasper scowled. 'We'll see about that.'

'What d'you mean?'

'Never you mind.' Jasper pushed back his chair. 'I have business to attend to.' Swatting the landlord's arm from his shoulder, Jasper indicated, with a careless nod of the head, that the new decanter was Langton's responsibility. Without a backward glance he strode for the door of the inn, casually kicking a flea-bitten terrier from under his feet.

'Business,' Langton mused, pouring himself another glass of brandy. 'Dirty business, if I'm any judge.'

At mid-morning the next day Nicholas's travelling chaise and four arrived outside Serena's lodgings. After a curt greeting, he stood by the chaise, watching as she supervised the loading of her luggage, admiring the graceful figure she cut in her woollen travelling cloak, the gold of her hair glinting under a poke bonnet.

Yet another sleepless night had taken its toll on Serena's mood. She had expected Nicholas to be angry, but had not anticipated he would feel quite so betrayed. Castigating herself for not having been truthful with him from the start only served to make her feel worse, however, for she could not ignore the fact that only by doing so had she come to know him so intimately.

As her dressing case and jewellery box were stowed inside the chaise, Serena wearily acknowledged the truth of the matter. She had fallen in love with Nicolas Lytton, plain and simple. No wonder his touch set off such extreme sensations. No wonder she felt a fizz of excitement every time she looked upon his handsome figure. No wonder she felt as if the sky was falling down when she thought of a future without him. She loved him. She wished with all her heart it had been possible, just once, to make love with him. Now her only consolation was that he had no idea of how she felt. And that was how it must remain, for if ever he had an inkling of her feelings—knowing Nicholas—he'd probably see it as another form of entrapment.

He helped her into the coach, his expression unreadable. Serena disposed herself beside her boxes as he took the seat opposite. The coachman pushed shut the door and they were away. She leaned back against the squabs and closed her eyes. She was exhausted, but sleep would be impossible with Nicholas sitting so close that his knees brushed hers. He was angry still. She knew better than to try to coax him out of it, could only hope that at some point on the long journey ahead his mood would mellow. Today should be a time for looking forward to whatever her new life would bring. She had an uncle, an aunt, perhaps even cousins. She was rich. She was in the fortunate position of being able to suit herself, neither beholden to an employer nor dependent upon a husband. The future was hers to define. Yet she could not bring herself to think about anything other than the brooding man sitting impassively opposite her. As they left High Knightswood behind, Serena fell into a troubled doze, her head resting awkwardly on her shoulder.

Nicholas watched, torn between frustrated desire and guilt. A surfeit of brandy last night had failed to prevent their last conversation replaying over and over in his mind. Serena was right, she had not really deceived him. He had asked

Frances Eldon to investigate her because he knew her story was not the whole truth. And she was, unfortunately, right about his willingness to be deceived. He wanted her so much that he had deluded himself. Had failed to examine closely the inconsistencies in her story, the apparent contradictions in her character. It was a bitter pill to swallow, that she had also ultimately saved him from breaking his own damned rules. He had not compromised her, but he could not stop imagining what it would have been like if he had.

This morning he had an aching head and an unusually active conscience. Time would cure the former. The latter, having little experience of, he was less sure how to tackle. He owed her an apology at the very least. She had every right to reproach him for the things he had said yesterday, but she had not. He still couldn't understand why, if her claims to innocence were the truth, she had allowed him such liberties. It didn't make sense. He wished to hell she hadn't. He wished to hell she'd allowed him more. He wished—he didn't know what he wished any more. The only thing of which he was certain was that he was not ready for Serena to quit his life.

*   *   *

As the horses slowed to turn into the yard of the posting inn for the first change, Serena was startled into wakefulness. Reaching up to straighten her bonnet, she smiled at Nicholas, an unaffected smile, forgetting for a moment all that had gone between them.

'We should take some refreshment while they put the horses to the traces,' he suggested.

She nodded her agreement. 'Coffee would be most welcome.'

Nicholas helped her down the step, calling imperiously to the landlord to see to her request. It was late afternoon, the day dull and damp, not actually raining, but the smell of rain was in the air. Serena stretched her aching limbs, removing her gloves and reaching up to rub the stiff muscles on the back of her neck. She looked over to find Nicholas watching her, and smiled tentatively.

'I must apologise for my overreaction yesterday,' he said stiffly.

She put a hand on his arm. 'Don't say any more. We both spoke in haste. Let us cry friends and forget about it.'

'Friends with a woman,' Nicholas said with a rueful smile. 'That will be a first, but for you, *mademoiselle*—Lady Serena—I'll try.'

The ostlers made the final adjustments to the tackle holding the four new horses to the chaise, then they were back in the carriage and on their way. The atmosphere was restored—almost—to the easy camaraderie of Knightswood Hall.

Lulled by the motion of the coach, Nicholas slept fitfully. Dusk approached and darkness began to fall. Serena was cold despite the rug she had tucked round her knees and the swansdown muff enveloping her hands. Outside she could hear the pounding of horses' hooves, the occasional snatch of conversation between the two coachmen. Once, she heard the hooting of an owl.

Opposite her, Nicholas stirred restlessly against the squabs, one leg stretched forward, resting against her knees. She longed to sit beside him, to pull his head on to her shoulder, to smooth his silky black hair away from his brow, to feel the warm, reassuring heat of his body against hers.

In an effort to distract herself, she stared out

at the night sky, where a waning moon could just be seen through the scudding light cloud. Surely it could not be much longer before they stopped for the night? She was stiff and sore from the journey. Nicholas mumbled, shifted in his seat, and quieted again. The sharp crack of a shot startled her from her reverie.

The coach jolted forwards as the horses reared at the noise, throwing Serena from her seat. Strong arms clasped her, preventing her from falling. A solid wall of warm muscle supported her. A reassuring voice asked her if she was hurt.

'No, no, I'm fine. Nicholas, I think I heard a shot.'

He pulled her up on to the seat beside him and held her close as the coach slowed to a stop, feeling in his pocket for his pistol. 'I didn't hear anything—are you sure?'

'Yes, it was quite unmistakable. Nicholas, do you think…?'

The words died on her lips as the door was wrenched open. A man stood framed in the doorway, his body muffled from head to toe in a black frieze coat, a large handkerchief wound up over his face so that only his eyes showed.

The muzzle of his pistol pointed directly at Serena's head.

'Don't move, lady, or I'll use this, make no mistake.' The man turned to Nicholas. 'You, cully, do as you're told and no harm'll come to you.'

Realising that the highwayman would search him, finding not only the large purse of money he carried, but the silver-mounted pistol too, Nicholas carefully slipped the gun into Serena's hand, which was hidden in her swansdown muff.

A warning squeeze of her fingers and the faintest shake of his head were enough to make her understand. Serena grasped the pistol carefully, her eyes on the highwayman. Nicholas prayed she knew how to shoot.

'All's safe, Jake.' The guttural voice came from outside, obviously an accomplice.

The highwayman jerked his head, indicating that Nicholas and Serena descend from the chaise. 'Any false moves and the mort gets it,' he warned.

Nicholas nodded coolly. Outside, the coach-man was calming the team of horses, the second highwayman's gun trained on him. The other coachman was neatly trussed up at the side of the road, where two saddled horses were tethered to an old gate post.

'Keep yer ogles on him, Ned.' The highwayman named Jake nodded in the direction of the man holding the horses, then turned his attention once more to Nicholas, although his gun remained pointed at Serena. 'You, empty yer pockets. Let's see the rhino.' His voice was harsh, his small eyes hard, the hand holding his pistol unwavering. With a curse, Nicholas handed his purse over.

'Now the watch,' Jake said, emitting a soft whistle as he felt the weight of the purse.

Serena stood rooted to the spot, the long muzzle of the horse pistol pointing at her stomach. She was not frightened. Knowing that highwaymen did not risk killing unless they had to, her overriding emotion was anger. Desperate as she was to put Nicholas's pistol to use, however, she was not foolish enough to risk her life. She prepared herself for the loss of her jewels, an obvious target in their distinctive box, and was grateful that her precious papers, along with the black pearl ring, were sewn carefully into the lining of her muff. She was wearing her locket under her travelling dress.

The horses whinnied, pawing the ground nervously. The tackle jangled against the poles as they moved a couple of paces forwards in an effort to bolt again. 'Keep them prancers still,' Ned, the more nervous of the two men, growled threateningly at the coachman trying to hold them.

Jake pocketed the valuables he had retrieved from Nicholas. 'Right now, cully, I'm afraid Ned here's going to have to tie you up, just to keep you out of harm's way,' he said, nodding to his accomplice.

Ned left his position by the coachman, threatening the man with instant death if he so much as moved from the horses. Producing a length of rope, he moved towards Nicholas.

'There's no need for that,' Nicholas said angrily. 'You've got what you wanted. If any harm comes to us, you'll hang for this.'

Jake cackled as if heartily amused by Nicholas's wit. 'Lord love you, we'll be dancing the Newgate hornpipe if we're caught on the bridle way whether we kills you or no. You've no need to fret, we don't mean you any harm, sir. And just to prove that to you, I'll leave off this here gag if you promise to keep your mouth shut.'

As Ned started to bind Nicholas by the wrists, juggling pistol and rope, Jake turned his attention back to Serena. 'Move.' His voice changed to a snarl that made her skin crawl. For the first time since the chaise had ground to a halt, she felt fear. Making no attempt to search her for valuables, Jake indicated that she walk to the other side of the coach, out of sight of Ned and Nicholas.

'What are you doing with her?' Nicholas demanded sharply.

'Shut your mouth.' All traces of humour were gone from Jake's voice. 'Might as well say goodbye to the mort, she's as good as dead.'

It all happened so quickly. 'No,' Nicholas shouted, bringing his half-tied wrists up under Ned's chin, sending him flying back.

'Now you've done it,' Jake snarled, turning his gun from Serena to Nicholas.

'Nicholas,' screamed Serena, withdrawing the silver-mounted pistol from her muff and firing in one fluid movement.

The sharp report of the bullet leaving the gun startled the horses again. They plunged forwards. It startled Ned, too, still reeling from the blow Nicholas had given him, watching in comical disbelief as Jake crumpled to the ground, a bright red stain blossoming on the back of his coat.

But it didn't startle Nicholas. Almost before the bullet entered Jake's shoulder, he kicked the pistol from Ned's hand with one booted foot. Ned swore and lunged, wrapping one filthy hand around Nicholas's throat, but he was no match for a man who had sparred with Gentleman Jackson, and severely hampered by his highwayman's cloak into the bargain. Nicholas landed a doubler clean in the middle of Ned's abdomen, winding him so that he dropped his hand from Nicholas's throat. Showing a singular lack of sportsmanship, Nicholas followed up with a swift kick to his adversary's knees. Grabbing the rope which had been destined for his own wrists, he quickly deployed it on Ned, neatly trussing him hand and foot.

Serena stood rooted to the spot with shock, hypnotised by the dark stain of blood spreading slowly over the wounded highwayman's coat. Jake moaned and stirred, his hand creeping towards his horse pistol, lying on the ground where he had dropped it. As his fingers closed on the muzzle, the polished toe of a Hessian boot kicked it from his grasp. Jake swore long and hard. Nicholas picked up the pistol.

Serena blinked, as if waking from a trance, moving like a sleepwalker towards him.

'Nicholas.'

He caught her with his left arm as she tottered, holding her upright, all the while pointing the pistol at Jake, prostrate and groaning on the ground. 'Serena, don't faint on me now. *Serena*,' Nicholas said urgently.

She blinked again, focusing on his face. Though she leaned heavily against him, he could sense her struggling to regain control over herself.

'Go and sit in the coach. I'll join you shortly, I promise. Go on.' He pushed her towards the chaise, watching to see that she climbed inside, before turning his attentions to the highwayman at his feet.

Unbuttoning Jake's frieze coat, Nicholas retrieved his purse and watch. Then he inspected the bullet wound. It was high in the right shoulder, not likely to be fatal. A perfect disabling hit. Grinning, he wondered if Serena had managed such a shot by luck or design. Whatever it was, her courage was impressive. Where other women would have swooned and screamed, Serena kept a cool head. Perhaps the *bon papa*'s upbringing had been to some purpose after all.

A groan reminded him that he had unfinished business. Nicholas hauled Jake into a sitting position, the rough movement causing blood to flow anew from the man's wound. Paying no attention to the stream of expletives that ensued, he pulled the muffler from Jake's face, revealing a weasel-like countenance made distinctive by the long scar running from the his left ear to the corner of his mouth.

'Shut up,' Nicholas said harshly, as the man continued to curse. 'You're lucky not to be dead. I want some answers or you *will* be dead. I'll have no compunction in shooting you, and no doubt either that the law will be on my side.'

Jake groaned. 'Ain't nothing to tell. We meant you no harm.'

'No, but you had other intentions for the lady.'

'Aye,' the highwayman agreed with a leer.

With a snarl, Nicholas positioned the muzzle of the pistol close against the man's temple. His other hand tightened around Jake's throat until he choked.

'Stop! Stop, guvnor, I…'

The grip relaxed enough to allow Jake to take a few breaths. 'The truth then.'

'We was to kill her. That's what we was paid for—and mortal good pay it was. No harm then, I thought, since she was such a fine-looking wench, in having a bit of fun before we put a bullet in her. No harm…'

But Jake's sentence was destined never to be completed. Strong fingers clenched round his throat and Nicholas's face, a grim mask of white teeth and black brows and slate-grey eyes, closed in on him. *Like the very devil himself*, thought Jake as he lost consciousness.

He came to trussed and bound beside his comrade. The coachman had been freed, and was readying the chaise for the road.

'Who paid you?' Nicholas demanded icily.

'I can't tell you that,' Jake replied groggily, clutching at his throat and coughing.

'Can't or won't? I'll find out either way, you

know, but it would be far better for you if you co-operated.'

Jake shook his head. 'It won't make any difference. We're bound to dangle for this night's work.'

'Perhaps. But I am a gentleman of some influence. If you co-operate, I can put in a word for you. You may get away with deportation.'

'Truth is, I couldn't tell you either way, guvnor. He was a flash cull, that's all I know. Found Ned and me at the Queen's Head tavern on the Fleet. We was to come down here and watch you, report back if we saw you with the mort—the lady. Which we did. So he sends word, the flash cull, that we've to bide our time and kill her. Not to harm you, just her. When we heard yesterday you was heading for London, it seemed too good to be true—a hold up on the King's highway being what comes natural to me and Ned, you understand.'

'And this *flash cull* who paid you—if you did not know who he was, how then did you keep in touch with him?'

'We'd to write to a Jimmy Ketch, care of the Queen's Head. But Jimmy Ketch ain't his name, as anyone there'll tell you.'

'How do you know?'

Jake gave a wheezy laugh. 'And here was me thinking you was a wise one. Jimmy Ketch is flash cant for the hangman.'

There was obviously no more to be had from the man. The two coachmen were mounted on the seat and the chaise positioned on the road. Leaning over to check the ropes that bound the captive highwaymen, Nicholas gave a satisfied nod.

'You can't be leaving us here,' Jake shouted. 'If I don't get this bullet out I'll die.'

'Yes, possibly.' Nicholas's saturnine smile made Jake cringe in genuine fear. 'And if you don't die of the wound, I have no doubt you'll face your Maker on the gallows soon enough. However, you won't be alone for long, don't fret. I shall be sending the local magistrate to attend to your needs as soon as we reach the next posting inn.'

Nicholas turned his back on the highwaymen and rejoined Serena in the chaise.

'Nicholas, thank God,' Serena cried with relief, throwing her arms around him. 'Are you all right? Did they hurt you,' she asked anxiously, scanning his face in the pale glow of the moonlight.

He hugged her tight against him. 'I'm fine. And you? You're chilled to the marrow. Come here.' He pulled the door closed and sat down on the seat, taking Serena with him. As the chaise started off, he wrapped his arms protectively around her. 'You'll be better directly. It's not far to the posting house.'

Serena laughed shakily. 'I've never shot anyone before.

'I should think not. I could only hope when I gave you my gun that you knew what to do with it.'

'Papa taught me.'

'The *bon papa*. I guessed as much. I never thought I would say this, but I am grateful to him. You were very brave Serena.'

'Oh, no, I'm so ashamed, I went to pieces after I fired the shot.'

'Don't be silly. The important thing is that you didn't go to pieces beforehand. You kept your head, which is more than any other female—and probably most men—of my acquaintance would have done.' Nicholas reached for her hand, holding it in his own reassuring clasp. Serena nestled against his shoulder. He could smell the flowery scent she wore, feel her hair tickling his chin.

Now he had her safe, cold fear gave way to overwhelming relief. When it dawned on him just exactly what the highwaymen intended, he had been overtaken by a terrifying mixture of rage and horror. It had taken all his will power *not* to kill Jake with his bare hands. He dared not think what would have happened had he not given Serena the gun. His hold on her tightened. She was safe, he reminded himself, which was the most important thing.

Serena sat up, reluctantly disentangling herself from Nicholas's grasp. 'What did that man— Jake—what did he mean to do with me?'

'It's best not to think about it.'

She stared at him, trying to discern his expression in the gloom. 'Was he going to kill me?'

'Yes,' Nicholas admitted curtly.

'But I heard him tell you that you wouldn't be harmed, when he was tying you up,' she said in a puzzled voice. 'That doesn't make sense. And why did he take me out of sight behind the coach? Was he going to—oh!' Serena turned chalk white.

The horses turned into a brightly lit courtyard. The door swung open and the steps were let down. Calling for a parlour and brandy—at once—Nicholas scooped Serena up and carried her into the welcoming warmth of the posting inn, laying her down on a settle beside the fire in the private room to which the landlord directed him.

Brandy arrived. Serena took a sip from the glass Nicholas held to her lips, choking as the alcohol burned its way down her throat. She sipped some more and sat up, reaching with relief to untie the strings of her hat, casting it on to the floor at her feet. Recklessly, she downed the remainder of the drink, feeling a warm glow working its way up from her empty stomach to her face.

'Do you want another?'

'Thank you.' This time she sipped cautiously, placing the glass on a side table to stand and remove her cloak and gloves, sighing with satisfaction as the heat from the fire warmed her numbed fingers. 'Have you ordered dinner?'

'Yes, in half an hour. Your room is ready too, I asked one of the maids to unpack your portmanteau.'

'That was thoughtful. I think I'll go and tidy myself before we eat, I must look a fright.' She got unsteadily to her feet, waving Nicholas away. 'I'm fine, I promise. I won't be long.'

While she was gone, Nicholas occupied himself by writing a note summoning the local magistrate to the scene of the crime. Then he stared anxiously at the door until Serena reappeared, telling himself he was being ridiculous, only just resisting the urge to check on her.

She returned to the parlour with her hair tidied and a fresh fichu round the neck of her gown, just as dinner arrived. She was pale but calm. Her smile lit up the room. Her presence had the usual immediate effect upon his body. Nicholas grimaced inwardly. It seemed it would take more than a couple of highwaymen and a near-death experience to quell his desire for her.

They ate the rustic meal of roasted capons and game pie followed by a ewes'-milk cheese in companionable silence, but, knowing Serena only too well, Nicholas was not surprised to be faced with an enquiring and very determined countenance as soon as the covers were removed and the servants gone from the room.

'Nicholas, you're keeping something from me—what is it?'

He did not answer immediately, pouring himself a glass of port to buy some time, swirling it around in the glass thoughtfully. He was immensely reluctant to tell her, but she should know, especially since he could claim no right to protect her in the future. 'Those two men were hired with specific orders to kill you, Serena. Who would stand to benefit if you did not claim your inheritance?'

Her mouth went dry at this bald statement of fact, though it was no more than she had already surmised herself. 'I'm not sure. I suppose my fortune would go to my Uncle Mathew, who is now Lord Vespian.'

'Is it a lot of money?'

'An immense amount. I can't quite believe how much.'

'So you really are an heiress. And your uncle would inherit it all?'

'Yes, I don't have anyone else. But although he may well have learned of Papa's death by now, he knows nothing of my existence,' Serena replied confidently, blissfully unaware of the letter from her father, recently come into her uncle's possession, which informed him of precisely that.

'Are you sure? If he knows your father is dead, then surely…'

'No. The circumstances are such that Papa did not tell Mathew of either his marriage or my birth, I don't know why. Your father was the only one who knew, and even then, I think just the bare bones of his marriage to my mother and my birth—they did not keep in touch after that. Papa wrote once a year to his lawyer, just to let him know that he was safe. I presume that if he has not had a letter this year he will have made enquiries, which is why my Uncle Mathew may know that he is now Lord Vespian. But as to me—no, he knows nothing about me.'

'Why was your father so secretive?' Nicholas asked exasperatedly.

'I don't know, and I didn't get the chance to ask him. All I do know is that when he was dying he told me most particularly to go to your father and retrieve my papers before seeking out my uncle. Those were his instructions, so that's what I did.'

'Well, it seems to me that your papa has put you in a damned awkward situation.'

'You're thinking that if he had left everything in my uncle's hands we wouldn't be in this mess together. I'm sorry.'

'I didn't mean that at all,' Nicholas said with a twisted smile. 'I tell myself it would be better if we had not met, but I cannot bring myself to regret it.'

'Nor can I,' Serena said softly.

In the silence that followed a dog barked outside in the courtyard. A gust of male laughter came from the tap room. Serena had never felt so alone. Nicholas would leave her in London. If he was right in his surmise, her family, whom she had been relying on to introduce her into society, were trying to kill her! She remembered the shot from the poacher's gun at Knightswood Hall, and wondered if that too had been an attempt on her life. She realised it was what Nicholas thought, but had not said.

Her life really was in danger. Then Nicholas's life was in danger too, as long as he was near her. If things had turned out differently along the post road… She shuddered. They could both have been killed, their existence cruelly snuffed out; denying them for ever the chance to experience what might have passed between them. It was an unbearable thought. 'Nicholas, do you realise that we might have…?'

'Don't think about it,' he said roughly, taking her in his arms. 'We are alive. You are safe now.'

'Alive,' she repeated. She recalled that first day they met, and the sense of recklessness that had infected her ever since. She felt it again now, a gust of desire so strong it was as if she was being squeezed breathless. 'Make love to me Nicholas,' she whispered, reaching up to touch his face, tracing the high planes of his cheek bones, the strong line of his jaw, the sculpted line of his bottom lip. She loved him so much, her heart ached with it.

He removed her hand. 'Don't, Serena. You're upset, you don't mean it.'

She reached for his hand, spreading open his fingers, measuring her own against it palm to palm, marvelling at the contrast in size, her own white skin against his tan, her veined wrists narrow beside his more sinewy, masculine width. She remembered him stripped to the waist in the boxing ring. She recalled the scent of battle, his lust for victory. The thought of his strength, the sheer male power of him, so different from her own fragile femininity, made her shiver. She kissed his wrist, a butterfly touch, tracing the line down to his thumb with her tongue.

'Serena, stop it.'

His voice sounded harsh. He did not pull his hand away. She remembered how he had guided her most intimate touch on him. Remembered how it had felt, touching, watching, feeling. Pleasure and pleasuring. She glanced up at him. Pressed another butterfly kiss on to the tip of his thumb. He exhaled. Daringly, her heart pounding, she pulled his thumb into her mouth, caressing the length of it with her tongue, releasing it to taste the skin between his thumb and his index finger.

'Serena. Oh God, Serena, you don't know what you're doing. It would be a mistake. You'll regret it.'

More butterfly kisses along the next finger, then the length drawn into her mouth a little more confidently. Something—fear, excitement, anticipation—twisted inside her. She reached the next finger, sucked a little harder, held it there a little longer.

She looked up through eyes hooded with burgeoning passion to find Nicholas's face a mask of untrammelled desire. He swept her into his arms and carried her from the room, striding effortlessly up the stairs, along the corridor and into her bedchamber. Closing the door firmly behind him, he gazed searchingly into her eyes, shaking his head before laying her gently down on the bed.

'This is insane,' he said, as if to himself.

Chapter Seven

Serena could feel the soft feather mattress moulding itself to her contours, the solid weight of Nicholas lying next to her. He was staring at her, his eyes glittering, watching her. She could feel his breath, his mouth as he pressed urgent kisses on to her eyelids, her cheeks, her ears, her neck. She could smell him, male heat and the elusive scent that was just Nicholas, distinctively Nicholas, only Nicholas. And she could hear him. 'Serena, Serena, Serena', his voice so weighted with need that she could not be mistaken and she could not resist, not now.

He kissed her. No butterfly kisses this time, no teasing, just unleashed, untamed passion. Lips and tongues and teeth clashing, biting, licking, kissing. Hot kisses, hard kisses, deep kisses.

Kisses which sought to know. And now hands too, seeking, searching, learning.

There were too many clothes between them. Nicholas released Serena's mouth, pulling her upright. 'I need to see you.' He shrugged his own coat off, dropping it carelessly to the ground before turning her round to untie her dress, loosening it, easing it off, kissing her neck, licking into the hollow of her throat, trailing a line of kisses across her shoulders. He pulled the long sleeves down her arms, helping her step out of the dress, leaving it pooled on the floor on top of his coat.

He made short work of the intricate lacings of her corset. A tiny part of her mind noted jealously how expert he was with buttons and ribbons and fastenings, then she forgot all about it. Her long petticoat was next, carefully pulled over her head, his hands running over the curve of her waist, her ribcage, the outline of her breasts as he removed it, touching each indentation, learning her body as if memorising it. Standing before him in her chemise, Serena shivered under his scrutiny, a wild excitement taking hold of her in the heat of his gaze, relishing the feeling that he was devouring her with his eyes. No fear this time. Not even embarrassment. His urgency made her shameless. Her nipples hardened, clearly outlined against the thin cotton.

His eyes on her were like polished slate as she reached up to remove the pins that held her hair in place. Long tresses uncoiled from her coiffure. Nicholas groaned, kissing her, twisting the molten gold in his hands, fanning it out over her shoulders, crushing her hard against his body.

Still too many clothes. Impatiently he tugged off his neckcloth. Equally impatiently tugged his shirt free from his breeches and over his head, sighing as Serena pressed herself against his muscled chest, her hands roaming over his torso, across his back, his shoulders, his ribs, her mouth trailing kisses.

And still too many clothes. Nicholas rapidly divested himself of his top boots, buckskins and undergarments, to stand before her naked. Watching him from the bed, Serena shyly drank in the long legs, the line of his buttocks, the indentation of his waist, the breadth of his chest and shoulders. Beautiful, she thought. 'Beautiful,' she whispered, sitting up on the bed, reaching out to touch as he stood before her, allowing him to part her legs so that he could stand between them. She stroked his chest, flattening her palms over his nipples, feeling him shiver beneath her touch as she stroked downwards, spreading her hands over his muscled buttocks, round to the soft skin on the inside of his thigh, experimentally running her fingertips along the silken length of his erection.

Nicholas closed his eyes, his expression strained, almost grim with pleasure as she stroked and touched, learning this part of him in the same way as she was learning the rest of his body. *He wanted her. He ached for her.* It made her head spin. It made her heart contract. It made her into a wild creature she barely recognised.

Leaning forwards she cradled his heavy length between her breasts, rubbing the hard peaks of her nipples against his stomach, relishing the hot surge of pleasure the movement gave her, reaching round to pull him closer, moaning with the heat and roughness and satin smoothness of him.

Nicholas muttered something incoherent. He disposed of her chemise, her pantaloons. He pushed her back on the bed. She was completely naked save for her silk stockings, their ribbons fluttering at her knees, and her little laced boots. A vision. He drank it in, breathing heavily. Exactly as he remembered, golden hair, alabaster skin, luscious pink mouth, cornflower blue eyes. Downwards his gaze went, to the dark pink of her nipples, the curls between her legs. She was a dream, like the painting of a courtesan kept discreetly locked away in the back room of a certain type of club. Like a wanton. Ripe, lush, and ready.

Mine, Nicholas thought possessively, *mine*, his last coherent thought before he lowered himself on to the bed beside her, skin on skin, muscle, bone, soft curves and hard planes melding into one as they kissed, pushing, arching, rubbing urgently closer.

Serena was on fire, driven by the insistent beating pulse deep within her that made her writhe against him, moaning his name, demanding something, anything, to satisfy this burning quivering knot of pleasure inside her. 'Don't stop, don't stop, don't stop,' she said to herself, or whispered aloud, feverishly reaching, anxiously searching for the place she wanted to be, was almost afraid to find, the place Nicholas knew, where he would take her.

He kissed her again, a deeply possessive kiss, a thirsty kiss. He licked his way down her throat, the valley between her breasts. She heard herself moan. He turned his attention to her nipples, biting gently, sucking hard, each movement sending out a current of feeling which connected up to the pulse further down. She felt his erection press hard against her stomach. She dug her nails into the muscles of his back, bracing her heels in their laced boots into the mattress the better to push against him.

Nicholas rolled away, moved down her body, his fingers stroking the inside of her thighs, touching her curls, parting the folds of the skin underneath, uncovering the source of all her heat. He touched her delicately. Serena tensed. He touched her again, sliding his finger over the heat, down, back, around, rubbing, delicately increasing the pressure until she felt as if she would break with the exquisite tension. He stopped. She clutched at his shoulder, then moaned as she felt his mouth, his tongue on her, even more knowing than his fingers, a long sweeping movement just exactly where it needed to be, and she couldn't stop it, she was lost, flying, soaring, plunging towards pleasure.

Nicholas pushed carefully into her as her climax pulsed around him, breathing hard as he entered her, cupping the rounded flesh of her bottom to tilt her up towards him. Gently he pushed, discovering she had not lied, meeting resistance, overwhelmed with the knowledge, pausing, trying to stop, thinking he should stop—or trying to think he should stop. Then she tightened her muscles around him and arched up and he was there, where there was no going back, engulfed in hot wet desire, and it felt so right. He pushed, withdrew, pushed deeper. Serena urged him on with tiny gasps of encouragement, gripping him tight with new-found muscles until they found a rhythm, and he was lost to everything save the need to drive towards his own climax, pouring himself into her, taking her with him over the edge, released, lost as he never was before, in the terrible beauty of shared passion.

They breathed, entwined together, limbs tangled, bodies joined, hearts thumping, savouring the warm glow of their lovemaking. She could no longer tell which was Nicholas and which was Serena. Floating in the euphoric aftermath of sated desire, Serena wanted to stay this way for ever. This was lovemaking. It felt so right. Surely he felt it too. For a moment she allowed herself to dream.

The dream did not last. Nicholas opened his eyes, staring at her as if seeing a stranger. *What had he done?* He rolled away abruptly, ignoring the empty feeling the movement created.

He had never felt this way before, wild elation and crushing guilt clashing so strongly it was as if he were being ripped in two. He was angry. With himself for succumbing, with Serena for being irresistible. As he looked at her, the little voice in his head whispered *mine, mine, mine*, and he exalted in the knowledge that that part, at least, was true. She *was* his, she had given him what she had given no one else. Which fed his fury *and* his desire. Nicholas wasn't used to feeling remorse. Or possessiveness. Or out of control. He had never been so swamped by emotions when making love. *What had he done?*

'What's wrong?' The bleakness of his expression made Serena's stomach churn.

'What's wrong?' Nicholas sat up, his muscles rippling. His torso glistened with sweat. He stared past her, his brows drawn together in a fierce frown, trying to garner his thoughts. 'We shouldn't have let ourselves get carried away. A not-unnatural release from the emotion of our ordeal perhaps, but unwise all the same,' he said, spouting the first thing that came into his head.

He might as well have slapped her. One thing to be told not to expect anything from him, another to be dismissed so degradingly quickly. Her first time, and he knew it. He should have been holding her, soothing her, telling her how wonderful it was. Except it obviously hadn't been wonderful, for him. Serena felt a flare of temper. *He could at least have pretended!* Her whole body yearned towards him, seeking comfort, reassurance, tenderness, and there he was no doubt already wondering how soon he could be rid of her when they reached London. She deserved better.

She sat up, wrapping the sheet around her body. With her hair streaming down over her naked shoulders and her lips swollen from kissing, she looked both unbearably lovely and unbearably vulnerable. 'Serena.'

She brushed his hand away dismissively. 'How can you talk so, calling it a *release*! And an unwise one, at that.'

'It was unwise. If anyone ever hears of this night's doings, you'll be ruined.'

'So that's what this is about! You're feeling guilty. What is it you're worried about, Nicholas, that I'll tell?'

'Of course not.'

'No, it's not that, is it? It's your precious rules. You've broken them and now you're worried about the consequences. Well, you needn't worry about that either, I have no desire at all to drag you up the altar and spend the rest of my life shackled to someone who doesn't give a damn about me.' She bit her lip. 'You have forgotten that it was I, and not you, who *initiated* this—this episode. You did not take. I gave. Obviously *what* I gave didn't live up to your expectations. I must apologise for my lack of experience, perhaps my next lover will be more appreciative.'

Next lover! 'Don't talk like that, as if you are some lightskirt,' Nicholas growled, gripping Serena by the shoulders. The sheet slipped, revealing a tantalising glimpse of pink nipple before she grabbed it again and pushed him away.

She glared at him, angry flags of colour flying in her cheeks. As suddenly as it came her temper fled, leaving her deflated and fighting back the tears. 'Look, Nicholas, it's been a very traumatic day,' she said shakily. 'Highwaymen, attempted murder, now this.' She blinked, managing a weak smile. 'Let us put it down to shock, write it off as an emotional release, call it what you will. Call it the end of an idyll, even, but let us put it from our minds. Don't let us quarrel any more, Nicholas, because I can't bear it.'

'Serena, I didn't mean…'

'It doesn't matter, it is done, let us forget it. Go to your room and rest, for we have an early start. In the morning we will wipe the slate clean, there will be no need to mention it again.'

'Serena, I…'

'Please, Nicholas, do as I ask,' she said with a catch in her voice.

Her very refusal to reproach him made his

guilt swell to unbearable proportions. What she said made such perfect sense he could almost have said it himself, but it felt wrong to leave her like this. He battled with the urge to take her back into his arms and tell the world and the consequences to go hang, but his instincts told him this would be to heap madness upon folly. 'Very well,' he agreed finally. He took her hand, pressed a warm kiss on her palm. 'It shall be as you wish. But you are completely wrong about one thing. You lived up to and beyond all my expectations.' He kissed her swiftly. Before she could muster a reply, he had pulled on his breeches, picked up the remainder of his clothing, and hurriedly left her room.

Even without the conflicting voices of his conscience, temper and libido, Nicholas would have spent a sleepless night, since his chamber faced the front yard of the busy posting house, which seemed, to his rattled senses, to tend to customers constantly throughout the long hours of darkness. As a grey dawn rose and his exhausted brain was on the brink of succumbing to sleep, the horns of the Bristol Mail jolted him rudely into full wakefulness. The Mail was followed by the stage, and then any number of vehicles and deliveries, for the inn was on the main road to London. By the time he joined Serena in the parlour for breakfast he was pale, exhausted, short-tempered and no nearer to understanding how he really felt than when he had left her in the early hours of the morning.

Though she too had lain awake for most of the night, Serena presented Nicholas with a determinedly collected countenance. Lying alone in the bed rumpled by their frenzied caresses, wrapped in the sheet that bore traces of Nicholas, she had finally given way to tears. The perfection of their lovemaking served only to confirm beyond doubt the perfect nature of her love for Nicholas. She would always love him, but it changed nothing. She must take her own advice and start the day with a clean slate. She would not flatter his ego by wearing the willow for him. He would never know how she felt. She would not waste her life wishing for the impossible.

Clad in her travelling dress and showing, to Nicholas's exhausted eyes, infuriatingly little signs of yesterday's traumas, Serena responded to his abrupt good morning with a polite smile. He sat down at the table, watching gratefully as she carved him some ham and placed it, with a large chunk of fresh bread and a foaming tankard of ale, in front of him. Reluctant to meet her eye while confusion still reigned between the opposing voices in his head, Nicholas took a reviving draught of the excellent ale, and addressed himself to his plate. Serena sat opposite nibbling a slice of bread and sipping on her coffee. Her papa had been right after all, thought Nicholas, when he named her. *Serenity.* She was the easiest company he had ever kept. A calming presence when he wanted quiet. Lively and witty at other times, making him laugh with her teasing, filling him with a zest for life he usually only felt when boxing or fencing. She was brave, unfaltering in a crisis, and a truly passionate lover. He had never before encountered anyone who could so perfectly match their needs with his. Never before met anyone to arouse such needs in him in the first place, he acknowledged ruefully.

Nicholas sighed. It was all true, but it added up to—nothing. He had no idea what today would bring, save their parting. The one thing he didn't want to have to contemplate.

'Would you like another slice of ham?'

'No.' He rose from the table. 'I'll go and pay the shot. Be ready to leave in ten minutes,' he said brusquely. Try as he might, he could not rid himself of the ill temper brought on by this most unsatisfactory state of affairs.

The mood between them did not improve within the confines of the long coach journey. Each of her careful conversational gambits was greeted with a monosyllabic response. Eventually, Serena surrendered herself to sleep.

By the time the mud-spattered chaise, horses steaming, finally pulled up at the Pulteney Hotel, Nicholas had come to no decisions, save the certainty that he could not simply abandon Serena to her fate. He was almost certain her uncle had arranged at least one, if not two attempts on her life. She had been vague about her plans and he had not pressed her, but his conscience demanded he do something. He needed time to think. 'I'll call for you tomorrow,' he said curtly, cutting short Serena's stumbling, awkward attempt at a farewell. 'I'm coming with you to the lawyer's office. The sooner your identity is established, the safer you will be. In any event, you will need me as a witness to authenticate the papers.'

'Nicholas, there is really no need. I am perfectly capable of looking after myself, I have been doing so since Papa died.'

He shook his head, unwilling to attempt to explain what he could not himself wholly understand. 'I'll call for you at eleven tomorrow.' Leaning towards her, he kissed her swiftly on the lips, then pushed her towards the open door of the carriage, giving her no time to object.

Serena stood alone on the street, watching as her bandboxes and portmanteaux were unloaded efficiently and taken through the doors of the hotel. Through the thick glass of the chaise she could see Nicholas rubbing his forehead with his hand. Then he leaned back on the squabs, closing his eyes. He did not wave farewell. With her shoulders back and her head high she entered the hotel and demanded their very best suite of rooms.

When Nicholas stepped through the front door of his town house in Cavendish Square not long after, his butler informed him that both his step-mother and half-sister were at home, taking tea. Resigning himself to an hour of tedium, he discarded his driving cape and hat and adjusted his necktie in the large mirror in the hallway before mounting the stairs to join them.

The drawing room on the first floor was pleasantly proportioned, the plainly plastered walls tempered a pale yellow. The curtains at the long sash windows, which looked out on to the square, were of dull gold damask, matching the coverings of the assorted chairs, sofas and *chaises-longues* set out in conversational groups around the room.

'Nicholas!' Georgie jumped from her seat by the fire, rushing to greet her elder brother. She was a pretty girl, obligingly free of any tendency towards either puppy fat or spots despite her tender years. Aside from her striking grey eyes, Georgie was unlike her handsome brother in almost every way. Her hair was dark brown, her little mouth a perfect rosebud, and her skin as correct a blend of white and pink as any English rose could desire. A crooked front tooth, a schoolgirl giggle and a slight clumsiness of manner, which in some young women might have been a drawback, were deemed in a girl with such an excellent portion to be merely part of her charm.

Decked out in sprig muslin trimmed with ribbons, she presented a pretty enough picture as she reached up to plant an affectionate kiss on her brother's cheek. Nicholas responded with a hug, telling her she looked bang up to the mark.

Georgie grinned and dropped him a curtsy, spoiling the effect somewhat by treading on one of his toes. 'Dearest Nicholas, I'm so pleased to see you, I've got much to tell you. Why did you not send word of your arrival, we had no idea you were coming today? I met Charles at Almack's last night and he was so kind as to compliment me on my *toilette*. Coming from such a notable Corinthian, that is high praise indeed. Did you get my letter? And did you—?'

'Georgiana, hush now. Ring the bell for fresh water, your brother will be wanting some tea. Nicholas, how do you do?'

The voice from the fading beauty on the sofa gave the impression of suffering stoically borne. Like her daughter, Melissa Lytton was petite, her sylph-like frame giving her the appearance of a wraith on the verge of fading for ever into eternity. She was impeccably attired in a grey silk dress with long sleeves, her raven locks dressed in an intricate knot on the back of her head, the tiny little cap she wore the only indication of her widowed status. Not yet forty, in temperament and appearance she was nearer fifty. Melissa did not rise to greet her son-in-law, merely extending a long thin hand from her semi-prone position.

Nicholas grazed the hand with a kiss, and sat down beside her. 'Well, Melissa, I can see you are in your usual health.'

'Alas, I was never strong, Nicholas, and though I am determined to make sure your sister has a good Season, it is already taking its toll.' She raised her vinaigrette to her nose and took a delicate sniff. 'I try my best, and as you know, dear Nicholas, I never complain,' she said with a sad smile.

'Oh, Mama,' Georgie said impatiently, 'the Season's barely started. I hope you're not going to sell me short, we've got engagements every day for weeks and weeks still.'

Melissa sighed. 'Pour your brother some tea, he will be glad of it after his journey, then no doubt he will want his bed. Have you the tic, Nicholas? I know that if *I* had made such a journey, I would be prostrate. I shall have them put a hot brick in your bed. You should rest before dinner.'

'Don't fuss, Melissa, I'm perfectly well.' Nicholas sipped distastefully on the dish of Bohea his sister handed him. He abhorred tea. 'Tell me all about your latest conquests, Georgie. Did you know Charles is betrothed? He's giving a party.'

'Yes, we already have the card, though Mama thinks it may be too much for her.'

Judging by his stepmother's few words and pained demeanour, it wouldn't be long before Melissa took to bed to indulge in one of her regular—and lengthy—recuperations. Poor Georgie, she deserved better than to be left to her own devices while Melissa quacked herself.

His sister was not the only one in need of a companion. Serena and Georgie would be perfect for each other. Of course Serena had not exactly said that she wished to launch herself into society, but what else was she going to do here in London? She could certainly not rely upon her murderous uncle to help her. Life above a gaming salon did not prepare one for *ton* parties. Nicholas knew only too well how cruel and vicious genteel society could be, what sport could be had with the naïve outsider. He doubted Serena was prepared for this. It mattered a great deal to him that she be well received. It would go a long way to ease his guilty conscience if she were established.

Established. The word gave him pause, for he was not prepared to think too specifically about its implications. He decided not to, and instead set about putting his idea in train. 'I brought a new acquaintance into town with me,' he said, interrupting his sister's account of a visit to Vauxhall Gardens. 'The only daughter of an old friend of our father's. She's older than you, Georgie, but she's new to London; it might be a good idea if she accompanied you to a few parties, give your mother some much-needed time to rest and regain her strength.'

'Oh, *no*, Nicholas, not if she's old.' Georgie pouted.

'I said older than you, not old, silly. She's four and twenty. Very beautiful, but luckily she's blonde; she'll be the perfect foil for you. What do you say, Melissa? That way you won't be so knocked up by having to escort Georgie everywhere.'

'Is she a respectable female, Nicholas?' Melissa asked dubiously.

'Very,' he said emphatically. 'She's the daughter of Lord Vespian. The previous, recently deceased Lord Vespian, that is, who was Father's friend many years ago. Her name is Lady Serena Stamppe.'

'You may bring her to meet me,' Melissa consented, 'then we'll see.'

It did not seem to occur to his mother-in-law to ask Nicholas how he became acquainted with Serena. Melissa was a caring enough mother, but vacuous, and consequently rather poor company for a vivacious girl like Georgie. In comparison, Nicholas had no doubt that Serena would be an instant hit with his sister.

Satisfied with his afternoon's work, Nicholas placed his half-full dish of tea back on the tray. 'I'll present Serena to you tomorrow. I'm off to my club now. I'll see you at dinner—if you're not dining out?' Receiving a graceful assent, Nicholas went upstairs to change into clothes more suitable for the stroll down Bond Street to St James's.

He was greeted warmly at White's and with some surprise, his erstwhile duelling opponent having only just been given a clean prognosis. The club was thin of company, but Nicholas found Charles at the window table along with some of his cronies discussing a race that was to be held the next day. Nicholas listened with little interest, waiting until the odds were settled and entered into the book, before requesting a private word with his friend.

'I am to congratulate you, Charles. I take it your discussions with Lord Cheadle went well the morning after you left me?'

Charles smiled thinly. 'Yes. I hadn't appreciated just how tedious settlements could be. Not content with dowries and dowagers, the man actually wanted to talk about his grandchildren. We're not even married yet, and he wants to dictate which school my sons will attend.' Charles shuddered. 'I tell you, Nicholas, it's one thing to bring yourself up to the mark and tie the knot, but it's quite another having to discuss your future offspring with your future father-in-law when you're future wife hasn't even allowed you to kiss her!'

Nicholas laughed at the pained expression on his friend's face. 'Well, you can't say I didn't warn you. I trust you have kissed her now? After all, you *are* officially engaged.'

'Oh, you know how it is,' Charles said with an embarrassed laugh, 'we're never permitted to be alone. On the odd occasion we've been left together, Penelope is the soul of propriety. When I asked her for her hand I was granted a peck on the cheek. I can only pray that her mama has informed her she'll be expected to give rather more of herself on her wedding night, otherwise Lord Cheadle is going to be deprived of those damned grandsons he's counting on.'

'Charles, you can't go to the altar without at least being sure she'll be compliant. What are you thinking of, man?'

'Lord, Nick, there's nothing unusual in the case. She's an amenable little thing and she's not repulsive, I'm sure we'll get on well enough once we're married, provided she can breed. What strange notions you have about marriage. I don't look to a wife for that sort of pleasure, I get that elsewhere, as you do—as most men we know do.'

Nicholas stared at his friend, struck by the casual callousness of his words, though he could not argue with the truth of them. More strongly than ever he felt that marriage on such terms as those would never be for him.

'I'm glad you're back, Nick,' Charles said. 'Never mind my wedding, did you think any more about your own? You didn't by any chance take my advice and ask Serena?'

'I believe I've already told you not to be ridiculous on that subject, Charles,' Nicholas said sharply. 'She's here in town, as a matter of fact.'

Charles raised both eyebrows, for him a sign of extreme surprise. 'Is Jasper aware of this?'

'What's it got to do with him?'

Charles smiled. 'I told you, Jasper knows that you had a female in tow at the Hall. He was worried enough about it to ask me what I knew. He's up to his neck, you know, and from what I hear he's playing deeper than ever. Some hell down in Piccadilly, you know the sort of place. I don't say the dice are loaded, but…'

'Does he know her name?' Nicholas interrupted sharply.

'Well, if he does, it didn't come from me. What does it matter?'

'Because you were right about her aristocratic nose,' Nicholas responded with a wry grin. 'Turns out my Serena, as you call her, is the Lady Serena Stamppe, daughter of the late Lord Vespian, and a considerable heiress.'

'Good Lord.' Charles paused in the act of taking snuff, a comical expression of disbelief on his face. 'And you haven't asked her to marry you? Are you mad? Devil take you, Nick, what's stopping you?'

Nicholas paused. What was stopping him, exactly? Serena could be his, and only his. She would be safe with him. He would with a single act secure her presence in his bed and his father's fortune. He would be set up for the rest of his life. But that was just it of course—*for the rest of his life*. 'You're becoming a bore on the subject, Charles. Just because you're getting leg-shackled doesn't mean you have to wish it on everyone else.'

'Thing is, Nick, don't you think you *ought* to marry her now? If word gets out that she was at the Hall—practically living there—to say nothing of what I presume has been going on between the two of you—well, I don't need to say any more.'

'Fortunately there is no one to tell, save yourself, and I know that I can trust you implicitly. Serena assures me she does not consider herself compromised,' Nicholas said, choosing his words carefully.

'Does not consider? What does that mean?'

'I have nothing more to say on the matter,' Nicholas responded angrily. 'Now oblige me by changing the subject, if you please.'

Charles grimaced. 'God, you're like a stag being baited by the hounds. I know something that will cheer you up. The divine Eleanor is on the market for a new protector. Since you paid off the Masterton, the odds have shortened in your favour. She's a choice piece.'

Nicholas shrugged. A few weeks ago the news would have intrigued him. Eleanor Golding was reputed to be even more talented than Diana Masterton. Now, the only emotion he could summon up was indifference. It was all Serena's fault. He cursed her roundly. He had to get her out of his system.

Watching his friend frown, Charles decided not to waste his own blunt by betting in Nicholas's favour, and diplomatically turned the conversation to less controversial affairs. Soon they were joined by a group of friends intent on a hand or two of whist before dinner.

Nicholas played, but his mind was on other things, and he lost badly. He returned to Cavendish Square for dinner but ate sparingly, listening with detachment to the chatter of his sister and the gentle remonstrations of his stepmother before retiring unusually early to bed.

The next day at eleven o'clock precisely Serena was waiting for him in the foyer of the hotel. She was turned out extremely modishly in a silk walking dress of her favourite blue with a pleated hem. A pelisse in matching blue velvet and a poke bonnet trimmed with three ostrich feathers made her the most elegant and most admired woman in the hotel. Nicholas, who had until now seen her only in simpler clothes more befitting the country, bowed formally over her hand and complimented her on her outfit.

She smiled, trying to ignore the beating of her heart, which seemed to leap into her throat at the sight of his familiar tall, handsome figure. 'Thank you. Coming from such a self-confessed arbiter of ladies' costume, that is a high compliment indeed.'

'Are you comfortable here? Did you sleep well?'

She nodded, hoping that the large rim of her bonnet hid the dark shadows under her eyes. Nicholas climbed into the very high-perched phaeton which he had left in the care of his groom, and leaned over to help Serena up.

At the offices of Messrs Acton and Archer, Mr Acton received the woman claiming to be the Lady Serena, daughter of the late Lord Vespian, with undisguised interest. 'I take it that you have proof of your status,' he asked, his natural cautiousness quickly reasserting itself.

From her reticule, Serna took the packet of documents. 'I think you will find all the proof you need here. My papa lodged everything that you have in front of you with an old friend, a Mr Nicholas Lytton, for safekeeping. The gentleman here with me is his son, Mr Lytton having died some ten years ago. He can vouch for their authenticity.'

Tobias Acton inspected Nicholas carefully. 'Indeed,' he said. 'Perhaps if you will be so good as to give me a moment to peruse these papers?'

They waited as the lawyer read his way painstakingly through the will with frequent reference to the other documents. Finally, he looked up. 'Well, this seems to be in order. I don't like to ask this, but I'm afraid I must. How can I be sure that you came about these papers legitimately, Lady Serena?'

'Papa gave me this.' Serena withdrew the antique ring from its leather pouch and placed it on the blotting pad of the desk in front of Mr Acton.

'Ah! I know this well. The black pearl. Yes, the last time I saw your papa—I was just a clerk—he wore this. I have to say, now that I see you, you do bear a strong resemblance to you dear departed father. Well, this settles things. Welcome, Lady Serena. I am most—indeed ex-

tremely—pleased to make your acquaintance.'
The lawyer made Serena a low bow. 'You are
aware, I take it, that you have an uncle, Mathew,
now Lord Vespian? With your permission I will
send him an express informing him of your
arrival.'

'He is aware of my existence then,' Serena asked.

'Indeed, yes. Your father left him a letter informing him of his marriage and your birth. I
gave it to Lord Vespian myself, here in this very
office a few days ago.'

'Is her uncle aware of the extent of Lady
Serena's inheritance?' Nicholas asked.

'I did not read the letter myself, you understand, but I believe that is the case,' Tobias Acton
said cautiously.

Nicholas looked at Serena. 'How did he
react?' she asked.

Mr Acton pursed his mouth. 'I'm afraid your
uncle was rather shocked at first. "It seems, Mr
Acton, that I have inherited a niece rather than
a fortune." Those were his very words. As I said,
it was a shock. I expect he has now become reconciled to the idea and is looking forward to
welcoming you into the family.'

'I doubt it,' Nicholas said. 'In fact, he—'

Serena placed a restraining hand on his arm, and shook her head. 'Not here.'

The meeting came to an end shortly afterwards, with Serena agreeing to return the next day once the lawyer had time to assimilate the full implications of the will. Nicholas helped her back into his phaeton and took the reins from his groom, who had been walking the horses. 'We'll go for a drive in the park, it should be quiet at this time and there's something I need to discuss with you.'

Chapter Eight

Sitting in the carriage, Serena felt curiously numb. Now that the long-awaited meeting with Mr Acton was over, her future was a blank canvas she had neither the energy nor inclination to paint. Beside her, Nicholas's expression gave her no clue as to his feelings. She admired his skill as she sat beside him, making their way through the crowded streets of the city, and resigned herself to waiting. Hawkers called their wares from every corner, everything from pints of ink to quarts of milk. Clerks carrying thick bundles of papers tied with ribbons wove fearlessly through the traffic. Two men selling rival newspapers competed with each other to see who could ring their bell the loudest. In comparison, the park was an oasis of peace, occupied mostly by children and nannies, the fashionable hour for the *ton* and the *demi-monde* alike not having arrived.

Nicholas allowed his horses to slow to a sedate trot. 'You're very quiet.'

'Are you surprised? I no sooner discover I have a family only to have it confirmed that they wish me dead. Do you really believe my uncle hired those highwaymen to kill me?'

'I'm really sorry, but it does seem likely.'

'Papa's only brother.' She opened her reticule to search for a handkerchief. 'I'm sorry, I'm just so—it's just so incredible.'

'At least he is not likely to make another attempt, now that Acton has met you.'

'The way I'm feeling right now, he's quite welcome to make another attempt.'

'Don't say things like that, Serena. If I didn't know you better, I'd think you were about to indulge in a fit of the vapours.'

She managed a watery chuckle. 'I don't think I know how to.'

'That's better.'

'I have an aunt and a cousin as well as an uncle. Do you think they wish me dead too?'

'No, of course not. No one who's met you could wish you other than well.'

She blushed. 'Compliments now?'

'The truth.'

'Do *you* wish me well?'

'You shouldn't have to ask that. I wish you more than well. I wish you to be happy. Have you thought about what you're going to do next?'

'Not really. Everything seems to be happening so quickly. It's only a few days since I first visited Knightswood Hall, but it seems like weeks. I must see my uncle, I suppose, though what I am to say to him I have no idea.'

'Shall I deal with him?'

'No, I am perfectly capable of looking after myself, you know, and he is hardly likely to pull a gun on me over a glass of sherry. What is it you wished to say to me, Nicholas? If it's about the other night, I don't want to—'

'No, it's not. What you said made perfect sense.'

'Oh.' She did not know what to make of this and could see no possible good in asking him to clarify, so she inspected her gloves and waited.

'I've told you about my sister Georgiana,

haven't I? She's here in town with Melissa, her mother, my father's second wife.'

'Yes, I remember you said,' Serena replied, now completely at a loss.

'Georgie needs someone to take her about— to parties and balls and such. It struck me that you and she could bear each other company. You'll like her.'

'I'm sure I will, but I haven't decided—'

'It's a perfect solution,' Nicholas interrupted ruthlessly. 'She's pretty much up to snuff is Georgie, even though she is young; she'll see that you meet all the right people, do all the right things. Melissa will get you vouchers for Almack's and I'll hire a caper merchant for you, too, so that you'll know all the latest steps.'

'With what purpose in mind, might I ask?' Her voice was decidedly cool.

Nicholas kept his eye on his horses. 'Your father wanted you established, that was surely his purpose in sending you here.'

'Yes. But as you've pointed out, had he been absolutely set on it he would have brought me himself. In any case, I am not so sure it is what I want.'

'Of course it is—what else will you do?'

'You have it all thought out.'

Nicholas glanced over, but her face was set, she looked firmly ahead. 'I'm trying to help you, Serena.'

'Yes, I'm sure you are.'

'So you'll come to tea in Cavendish Square?'

'I'll think about it.'

He was tempted to ask her what was wrong, but was not at all convinced he would like the answer and opted, in what he assured himself was a sensible manner and not at all cowardly, to revert to the earlier subject. 'I was thinking, perhaps your father was more prescient than you realise.'

'How so?'

'I thought it strange before, his insistence that you find your papers and take them with that ring to the lawyer, rather than seek out your uncle. Strange, too, that he did not trust his brother with the knowledge of your birth.'

'You mean he suspected that Uncle Mathew would—surely not?'

'What we've taken for whimsy on his part has probably saved your life. I've been meaning to ask you, why did he leave England in the first place. Was it a duel?'

Serena hesitated.

'I sense another secret.'

'He left under something of a cloud. He was accused of murder.'

The horses, used to the lightest of hands on their sensitive mouths, veered off the path as Nicholas jerked the reins. He swore under his breath and quickly got them back under control. 'I should have known. Mitigating circumstances, no less—now I understand why he didn't come back sooner. Nothing involving your papa is straightforward, is it?'

Serena gave the ghost of a smile. 'He was no more a murderer than you are. He took the blame for a friend.'

Nicholas looked sceptical.

'I know what you're thinking,' Serena said, 'but it's true.'

'Go on then, reveal all.'

She closed her eyes, forcing her mind to drift back to that night. The sickroom, the sense of impending gloom as she watched her father fade in front of her eyes. 'He and some close friends had been playing cards most of the night,' she said, doing her best to recall his exact words. 'Dawn was breaking when one of them took it into his head to visit his *chère-amie* and Papa decided to accompany him.' She smiled ruefully. 'I asked him why he would do such a thing, and he was very embarrassed. He said she had a sister.'

'Charming. His determination to keep you wrapped in cotton wool did not prevent him from sullying your ears with some sordid tales.'

'I'm sure you could come up with something equally sordid if you set your mind to it,' she said acerbically.

'I don't tell tales, sordid or otherwise.'

She was silent.

'I'm sorry. Please carry on.'

'They arrived at the village where the two women lived, but their brother answered the door. He was drunk, and refused them entry to the house. Papa's friend had a temper. They started brawling, he and the brother, right there on the doorstep. The fight was vicious. The brother was a brute. Papa's friend was distracted by his light o' love, standing on the doorstep wailing like a banshee, apparently.'

Nicholas gave a crack of laughter. 'I can imagine.'

'Papa's friend succumbed to a—a sweet uppercut, Papa said. Have I that correct?'

'Quite correct. If you recall my fight with Samuel, I delivered just such a punch myself.'

'And just as successfully too. Papa's friend went down, just as Samuel did. Papa thought it was all over there and then. He went to help his friend up, laughing at his muddied clothes.' Serena stopped to assemble her thoughts, finishing the story in a rush as it came back to her. 'His friend suddenly pulled a dagger from his coat and plunged the blade straight into his opponent's heart. For an instant Papa thought it some cruel jest, but the man crumpled to the ground, lay completely still in the mud, blood pooling around him. Papa's friend begged him to help him. He was engaged to be married at the time, you see, whereas Papa had no ties, so he agreed to take the blame. He always expected to hear word from his friend that he had made things right. He always intended to return, but…'

'But he never did,' Nicholas finished for her. 'And who was he, the real murderer?'

'I don't know. Papa wouldn't tell me. He wanted me to know he was not guilty, but right to the end he insisted on protecting his friend's identity.'

Nicholas shook his head slowly. 'Serena, I swear your life is like a Gothic novel come to life. No wonder you find Byron's poetry insipid! If you tell me your papa left you no clue, I will be horribly disappointed.'

Serena bit her lip guiltily in an attempt to suppress a slightly hysterical laugh. 'No.'

'It bothers you, doesn't it?'

'I don't like to think of Papa branded a murderer if he is innocent.'

Nicholas looked thoughtful. 'It may be possible to trace the woman involved by finding out the name of the murdered man. Through news sheets or court records. I could set Frances on to it.'

'I think you've asked Mr Eldon to do enough investigating of my family.'

'I suppose I deserved that.' They had arrived back at the gates to the park. A few moments later he pulled his carriage up in front of Serena's hotel. 'You'll come to Cavendish Square this afternoon, won't you?'

'I'm not sure.'

'Please. Come to tea, that's all I ask.'

It would be churlish to refuse. She nodded. Without waiting on his help, she leapt nimbly down from the carriage and entered the hotel.

Jasper Lytton awoke to the sound of persistent pounding on the front door of the Albany lodgings where he rented rooms. Clasping a hand to his head in a vain effort to suppress the sensation that his brain was being pierced by a selection of steely knives, he opened one blood-shot eye and felt with the other hand for his watch, lying discarded on the table by his bed. Two o'clock. Cautiously, he peered over at the window. Daylight. Afternoon, then.

The pounding stopped. His man must have answered it. No doubt it would be duns. A scratching at the door of his chamber preceded his valet. 'There is a gentleman demanding to see you.'

'I am not at home,' Jasper said curtly, wincing as he sat up. The knives in his brain were joined by a red hot poker.

'I said a gentleman, not a creditor,' his valet responded impatiently. An employer such as

Jasper, who owed him the last two quarters' wages, did not merit politeness.

'R-r-rather a gentleman *and* a creditor,' Hugo Langton said, pushing past the valet and closing the door in his face.

'What do you want,' Jasper asked wearily.

'I w-want my money,' his one-time friend said angrily. 'I have it on excellent authority that your cousin is about to get hitched, and I want what you owe me before you land in the Fleet prison.'

'Been listening to Charles Avesbury, have you?' Jasper sneered. 'He's talking nonsense.'

'Not Avesbury, my sister,' Langton responded. 'She had it from some new dressmaker who's all the rage. A Frenchie, just come from High Knightswood, if you must know.'

'*What?*' Jasper got out of bed, clutching his head.

'Thought that would make you pay attention,' Langton said, his stammer disappearing as his confidence grew. 'The woman told my sister that she came over from France with a young lady who subsequently spent the duration of their stay closeted with your cousin at Knightswood Hall.'

'One of his bits of muslin,' Jasper said dismissively, though he knew it was a lie.

'No, thought about that,' Langton said vehemently, 'but can't be. Your cousin's not a loose fish, wouldn't keep a mistress in his own house. Must be something more to it than that. Face it, Lytton, you're done for.'

'Don't be so sure,' Jasper said with a nasty smile. 'Now get out, I need to dress.' Ignoring Langton's protests, Jasper pushed him bodily out of the room, calling for his man to bring him his shaving water. Stepping out into the late afternoon an hour later, his rage was cold, his intentions calculated and his step decisive.

Serena presented herself at Nicholas's house in Cavendish Square with mixed emotions. Though she had once looked forward to entering society, she was not at all convinced that she wished to do so now, so alien would it be from the milieu in which she had been raised. She was annoyed with Nicholas for his too-obvious attempt at easing his conscience by fobbing her off on his sister. She was annoyed, too, at the arrogant way he was choosing to assume control over her life, and the mixed signals he continued to give her, first pushing her away, then pulling her back into his orbit. But more than anything, she was angry with herself for granting him the power to do so. Knowing full well she was nurturing foolish hopes, she nevertheless continued to nurture them.

In the end, common sense and a rather shameful curiosity had got the better of her. Foolish she might be in falling in love with him, but in every other sense, Serena was determinedly practical. It would be stupid to dismiss, in a fit of pique, the opportunity that his promised introductions offered. And if she were honest, sharing Nicholas's company for a few more weeks, days, hours, whatever he would give, while immensely difficult, would not be half as painful as not sharing his company at all.

The tea party went well. Melissa was happily uninterested in the circumstances surrounding Serena's arrival in England and her relationship with Nicholas. Pleased to find a sympathetic ear, she passed a pleasant half-hour regaling Serena with the merits of country over town air, debating the possible healthful effect of Lord Byron's reputed diet of vinegar and potatoes, and recommending the services of a Dr Leland whom she had found to be most sympathetic should Serena ever suffer, as Melissa herself did, from sick headaches.

Serena nodded and smiled with good grace, contriving—most of the time—not to catch Nicholas's eye for fear of giggling. Only once, when Melissa offered her an old family receipt for the relief of gout, did she resort to muffling her laughter behind a handkerchief, refusing steadfastly to respond to Nicholas's question into the condition of her own mercifully gout-free joints.

Georgiana's sharp eyes missed nothing. Lady Serena was quite beautiful, even if she was almost past marriageable age. It was so very unlike her brother to take an interest in any female of the *ton* that Georgie had, from the outset, been sure of an intrigue between Nicholas and Serena, and it did not take her long to find evidence of the intimacy between them to confirm her suspicions.

As Serena appeared to listen attentively to a list of Melissa's latest symptoms, Georgie caught a look—a glance, no more—between their visitor and her brother. They were laughing together at some shared joke. When Nicholas turned his attentions to Georgie, his sister had every opportunity to see how Serena's eyes were drawn every few minutes to look at him wistfully. She was convinced that here was a case of star-crossed love for her to help resolve.

Serena did not stay long, but she was enough of a hit with Melissa to be asked to accompany them to a rout party the next day. 'Just a small affair, with some intimate friends. You know the kind of thing, my dear Serena—you will not mind my using your name, since your papa and my husband were such friends?' Melissa dabbed at her eye with a tiny flutter of linen and lace. 'No dancing, you understand. Just cards and pleasant company.' With a sigh, Melissa collapsed back on to the sofa, requesting Nicholas see their visitor out.

He stood to give Serena his arm. 'I would recommend that you stay away from the card tables,' he said, his eyes alight with amusement, 'I don't want to be hearing that you've fleeced all of Melissa's friends.'

'If Melissa's friends are anything like herself they won't have the energy to play cards, so there's no need to worry.'

They spoke softly, but Georgie's ears were sharp. 'Why must Serena not play cards? Does she cheat?'

'Georgie, you let your tongue run away with you overmuch,' Nicholas said sharply. 'What's more, you are being excessively rude to our guest.'

'Oh, I do beg your pardon.' Georgie curtsied, tripping on the edge of a rug. 'But I don't think you're at all offended, are you, Lady Serena? I saw you laughing at Mama with Nicholas when you thought no one was looking.'

'Oh dear, then it is I who should apologise to you, Miss Lytton.'

'Don't be silly. And do call me Georgie, I hope we're going to be friends.'

'Very well then, I will. Thank you for the tea, I look forward to seeing you at the party.'

Leaving the room on Nicholas's arm, Serena turned to him questioningly. 'Can I look forward to seeing you at the party also?'

He shook his head. 'Come in here, I need to talk to you,' he said, pulling her into a small parlour on the ground floor.

'What is it now, Nicholas?' Serena asked, instantly becoming defensive as she wondered what new social solecism he thought she had committed.

'We can't be seen in each other's company.'

'Why not?'

'Whether we like it or not, there is an unmistakable air, an aura between us, which we cannot hide. We may both offer silence on the subject of our lovemaking, but our actions betray us all too eloquently. You saw my sister—she realised straight away that we are not mere acquaintances. Other people would see that too. There would be gossip.'

'And as you have pointed out to me several times, Nicholas, you steer well clear of any friendship with a lady that may be construed as flirtation. I understand,' she said coldly.

'I'm not talking about mere flirtation,' Nicholas said exasperatedly.

'Then what are you talking about?'

'I am talking about your reputation. If people ever found out what has passed between us you would be ostracised. And if they see us together they would know instantly. Georgie noticed. Charles saw it.'

She was angry, the more so because she knew

he spoke the truth. 'You wish to ease your conscience by staying clear of me and having your sister put me in the way of eligible men, in other words.'

'Yes. No, that is not what I meant.' Putting her in the way of other men was the last thing on his mind. 'I just want to see you established.'

'No, that is not what you want, Nicholas,' she contradicted him coldly. 'You wish to wash your hands of me.'

'You are deliberately misunderstanding me, Serena.'

She glared at him. 'Enlighten me, if you please, then. How exactly do you wish me to feel, because frankly I have no idea.'

Nicholas ran a hand through his hair in exasperation. 'What I want is for you to be happy without me. Serena, you must realise that the nature of our acquaintance forced us into an unusual intimacy. What we felt, thought, did during our time at High Knightswood, it was not real. Everything—our seclusion, your circumstances—all served to fuel, to intensify a physical attraction that in any other situation would not have flourished. Had it not been for our near-death experience, I doubt we would have consummated our passion. But we did.'

'Yes, we did. A mistake, we both agreed. But not one for you to feel guilty about. You did not coerce me.'

'It makes no difference,' Nicholas responded hotly. 'Can't you see that?'

'I still don't understand what it is you want of me.'

'What I want of you!' He tugged at his neck-cloth as if it were too tight. 'I want nothing more on earth than to make love to you until we are both totally sated.'

'No,' she said flatly, 'I will not be your mistress. I told you that I would not play the game on such terms. I have no wish for an *affaire* that will end with a few trinkets when you have had enough of me. I have no desire to be the latest in the infamous Nicholas Lytton's long line of conquests.'

She stood facing him, her arms crossed challengingly, a martial glint in her eyes, looking so beautiful, so angry, so infuriatingly, completely desirable, that Nicholas lost his head and shook her.

'You're hurting me.'

He released her immediately, breathing heavily, frightened by his own fury. 'I never, not for one moment, think of you in the same light as any other woman.' The words were clipped, his lips narrow, his eyes almost black, glinting at her beneath a frown so deep that his brows met. 'You asked me what I want of you, I spoke the unvarnished truth. I also know that I cannot have what I crave. But what I can do is ease your entrance into society. I can do that much for you—or at least Georgie and Melissa can. And in this way our relationship will become what it should always have been, that of common acquaintances.'

'In other words, you hope familiarity will breed contempt.' Tiredness washed over her. It had been a very long day. 'Very well, Nicholas. We shall nod and smile at one another from a distance until you become bored. You will sate your passions in your usual way, and perhaps I will sate mine by taking a husband,' she said maliciously, conscious of the need to inflict on him just a little of the hurt she felt.

'With your new-found fortune, I do not

foresee any difficulties on that score,' he agreed sarcastically. 'You can replace me in your bed soon enough.'

But I will find you impossible to replace in my heart, Serena thought wretchedly. Determined not to let him see how much he had hurt her, she curtsied quickly. 'I must thank you for your kind offices. I am not so foolish or so rude as to turn down your sister's offer of friendship. We have both said enough to understand each other perfectly. Goodbye, Nicholas.' Without waiting for a response, she swept from the room.

'Serena!'

She heard him call, but ignored it. Nodding to the butler, who opened the large front door, she left the house in Cavendish Square with straight shoulders and head held high, determinedly ignoring the anguish tearing at her heart.

Serena spent the night telling herself she was well rid of such a heartless beast as Nicholas and torturing herself with imagining in vivid detail just exactly what she would be missing out on in the lonely years to come. As a consequence she was not in the best of humours when she was informed the next morning that two gentlemen wished to see her. Uncle Mathew had travelled post-haste to reach town upon receipt of an express sent by Mr Acton. His son Edwin accompanied him.

She was unprepared. Having assumed that a man who could arrange her murder would not hasten to pay a morning call, she had not yet decided how to handle the situation. Schooling her expression into one of polite surprise, she executed an elegant curtsy and decided that discretion would serve her best for the present.

'My dear niece. I cannot tell you how good it is to meet you at last,' Mathew said effusively. 'As you see, I came up to town as soon as I had word you were here. How do you do?' He bent his sparse frame stiffly over her hand.

'Uncle Mathew.' He had not her father's looks, but the family resemblance was plain. A bluff man, a country squire with little town polish, if his clothes were anything to go by. Serena granted him a cool smile.

'And here is your cousin Edwin come to meet you—my son, you know. Edwin, make your bow lad.'

Like his father, Edwin was tall and spare of frame, with the piercing blue eyes of the Stamppes. Youth lent his hollow features an attraction lacking in his father's countenance. Had he the sense to dress simply, as became his physique, he would have passed as a well-enough looking young man. Sadly, Edwin had no such sense, having ambitions to join the dandy set. In the mistaken belief that he was bang up to the mark, he wore his coats pinched tightly into the waist, the shoulders exaggerated and peaked with the assistance of immense amounts of stiff buckram wadding. As if this was not enough, the enormous brass buttons on the coat served to emphasise the meagreness of his sparrow-like chest, and the tightness of his knitted pantaloons the stick-like quality of his spindly shanks. To this *toilette* he added shirt points starched so high that he could not turn his head, a waistcoat embroidered with pink roses, and so many fobs, rings, quizzing glasses and the like that he positively clanked when he minced down Bond Street each morning.

He had dressed with special care for the meeting with this new cousin. The hat he swept from his pomaded locks was so tall that street urchins competed to knock it off with stones as he passed. His coat required the combined efforts of his valet and the butler to squeeze him into it, so tight was it cut, and his cravat, tied in the intricate *mail coach*, had taken over an hour to perfect. He bowed with a flourish over Serena's hand, bestowing upon it a rather clammy kiss. 'Cousin. *Enchanté.*'

Such a pink of the *ton* would of a certainty have nothing to do with anything so sordid as murder. Serena suppressed the urge to laugh. 'I'm overwhelmed, Cousin Edwin. You'll both take some refreshment, I hope?'

'A glass of Madeira would be most welcome, my child,' Mathew said obsequiously. 'We must sit down and get acquainted, but first it behoves me to offer my commiserations, belated as they are, for the death of your father, my dear brother.' Under her cool gaze, Mathew coloured.

'I believe I should congratulate you on your newly acquired title, Uncle. My loss is your gain.'

'Well, as to that…'

'Though you have been managing the estates

for so long now, you must almost have thought them your own.'

This was rather too close to the bone. 'I have certainly kept the land in excellent heart. I only hope I can continue to do so on the somewhat reduced income I will have once your inheritance has been paid.'

Serena gave him a direct look. Having met him, she could not believe that he posed any further threat to her safety. He was clearly a foolish opportunist, a rather grasping man who acted without thinking. The sort of man who would always bet on the outside odds and blame everyone but himself when, predictably, he lost. Enough had been said—or not said—to make him aware of her suspicions. After all, apart from her ridiculous cousin, he was her only blood relative. There could be no benefit in pursuing the matter.

An awkward silence reigned. Edwin shifted uncomfortably in his seat, aware that his beautiful and rather intimidating cousin was in some way angry with his father, but unable to imagine why, since they had never met.

Finally, Mathew spoke. 'Well, well, there is no

point in dwelling in the past. We should be rejoicing to be reunited as a family,' he said bracingly. 'Now that you are acquainted with your cousin Edwin here, I expect you will see a good deal of one another, what with going to the same balls and—and such.'

Mathew rubbed his hands together as a brilliant idea formed in his head. The marriage of his niece to his son was the perfect solution, well worth the expense of a dispensation, if that proved necessary. He wished it had occurred to him earlier, he could have saved himself the gold he had expended on that incompetent ex-Runner. The man had diddled him, that's what he had done, with his claims that it was too dangerous to try again. Poppycock!

Looking at his son, forced into a rigid sitting position on the small gilt chair by the combination of starched cravat, over-tight lacing at his waist, and pantaloons that threatened to unknit if he moved too suddenly, Mathew experienced a twinge of doubt. Serena was a fine-looking filly, and quite a catch, with all that Vespian gold on her back. She'd be bound to go off well despite the fact that she was near five and twenty.

Nevertheless, he owed it to the estate to make a push on his son's behalf. 'Aye, you can rely on Edwin to take care of you, Serena dear. He's quite a ladies' man,' Mathew said, looking encouragingly at his son.

Serena looked somewhat sceptical. Edwin blushed furiously.

Mathew smiled suggestively. 'I'm thinking it best for now if I leave you two young 'uns to it, and I'll take a look in at my club,' he said with a knowing wink.

His meaning was unmistakable. Serena bit her lip. If only Nicholas were here, how he would have enjoyed it. She couldn't wait to tell him. Then she remembered. She bit her lip again, though she no longer felt like laughing.

'No, no, I'll come with you, Father.' With one eye on Mathew's retreating figure, Edwin looked like a startled fawn yearning for its mother's protection.

'Don't go yet,' Serena called to Mathew. 'I have something for Edwin. Wait here.' She left the room, hastening back bearing a small leather pouch, which she handed to her cousin. 'Papa said it's always worn by the heir to the earldom. I'm not sure it will be to your taste, it's very old-fashioned, but none the less it's yours by right.'

Edwin opened the pouch and took out the ring. Mathew, looking over his shoulder, gave a gasp of surprise. 'The black pearl. Acton said you had it, I knew there was no question of your identity if you had.'

'Papa said it would be thus. It's Edwin's now.'

Edwin regarded the intricate gold that encased the huge pearl with something akin to horror. 'There's not any sort of curse or anything on this? Because if there isn't, there ought to be.' Seeing Serena's face, he remembered that the ring had been her father's. 'What I mean is, thank you for passing it on and everything, but I'm not actually required to wear it, am I?'

'Not wear the black pearl!' Mathew was shocked.

Edwin handed the ring to his father. 'If you're so fond of it, you wear it. Grotesque thing like that, I'd be a laughing stock.'

Mathew was a weak rather than a cruel man. He refrained from pointing out that his son was already such a laughing stock that the addition of an antique pearl ring was unlikely to make much difference, and instead put it on his own finger.

Edwin creaked to his feet. 'Very nice to meet you, Cousin Serena,' he said with a bow. 'Coming, Father?'

Reluctantly, Mathew followed.

Even without the revelation of her true identity and the added benefit of her fortune, Serena's entrance on to the London scene would have caused a stir. The Season was not yet halfway through, but already the *ton* were bored to distraction with meeting the same company, day in and day out, at the various balls, outings, parties and concerts. A new face was always welcome. Such a very pretty face as the Lady Serena's, doubly so. The tale of her lineage and her inheritance ensured that she was besieged with invitations almost as soon as she was introduced.

Nicholas was, as expected, not present at the rout party that first night. Serena, a vision in a half-dress of sea-green gauze with a petticoat of silver muslin, noted his absence with a sinking heart as she nervously entered the coach containing Georgiana and Melissa. She should be thankful, she told herself, but she could not help wondering if he was already pursuing his next conquest.

Becoming an instant success was, however, a pleasant balm to her bruised ego and a boost to her confidence, as were the flood of envelopes, flowers and trinkets which greeted her over the following days. She was little inclined to vanity, and thought the tributes more likely to be a consequence of her fortune than her face, but she could not remain wholly untouched at finding herself so sought after when she had so lately felt utterly alone in the world.

Of Nicholas she saw precious little. As he had promised, they were on nodding terms only. They were not once alone. Only in the dark of night did Serena allow herself to think of him, longing for him with such an ache that her future unravelled before her like a long black tunnel. In the cold light of day she remembered how useless it all was and resolved anew to forget him.

Tobias Acton managed to secure her a pretty little furnished house in Upper Brook Street, into which she moved with astonishing ease. The days passed in a flurry of parties, dances, tea-taking and shopping. Serena did her best to enjoy herself in this new social whirl, but she found it strangely unsatisfying, not to say occasionally tedious. There was no one to share her sense of the ridiculous. No one with whom to laugh. No one in whom to confide. Too often, her quips fell on deaf ears. Too often the phrase *what can you mean*, or, worse, a blank look, were the responses she received to a witty remark. At times she had to stamp down hard on the absurd urge to shock the company with a lurid story from the gaming salons. In the crush of a ball, with her dance card full and her partners fawning, she felt more lonely than she would have thought possible.

She had already decided that this would be her only Season. Her brief stay in Knightswood Hall had made her certain of more than one thing. She had endured enough of city life. Since marriage to anyone other than Nicholas was out of the question, she must turn her mind to a different kind of future. In the summer she would start looking for a property of her own. One with a home farm, and a kitchen garden, where she would churn her own butter and dry her own herbs. She might even start up a village school. Being an only child, she had always planned to have a large family. A nursery full of brats, as Nicholas would say. *Damn!* Resolutely consigning the endearing image to the back of her mind, she turned her attention to her *toilette*.

Chapter Nine

The following Wednesday, Serena accompanied Georgiana and Melissa to Almack's. Dressed in a simple gown of her favourite pale blue satin, with matching dancing slippers and a pair of long kid gloves a deeper shade of blue, which fitted so perfectly that they roused the envy of several other young ladies present, she fastened her evening cloak and tripped lightly downstairs to await the carriage.

Almack's was an old-fashioned club that demanded that all gentleman wear knee breeches and stockings. This fact alone was sufficient to keep Nicholas from ever darkening its portals. Despite being perfectly well aware of this, Serena could not help but look wistfully at the empty place in the town coach, wishing he would make an exception just this once. She had never danced with him. She longed to share the story of her uncle's visit, knowing just how amused he would be at the idea of a match between herself and her ridiculous cousin. She thought of how he would laugh when she mimicked the look on Edwin's face as he saw the black pearl ring. And she would tell him how easy it had been to put what he would call *the frighteners* on Uncle Mathew.

Serena danced, talked and smiled, all the while nursing a growing—and, she was perfectly well aware, irrational—resentment at Nicholas's treatment of her. Without a doubt he was slaking his thirst for her in some other bed. She was well rid of such a fickle, rude, ill-tempered, infuriatingly attractive man. She checked the time on the wall clock. It wanted but fifteen minutes to eleven, the hour at which the doors of the club were closed to newcomers. The evening stretched uninvitingly out in front of her. She longed for the comfort of her bed.

Shutting her fan with a snap, she looked around for Melissa and Georgie. A tall man clad elegantly in knee breeches and a dark, well-fitting coat stood in the doorway, imperiously surveying the room. Her heart lurched. She felt his eyes bore into her. She looked away, opening her fan again, frantically waving it in front of her over-heated face. Her emotions see-sawed annoyingly from resentment to a fizzing sense of anticipation.

'Lady Serena,' the familiar voice said, as he bowed deep in front of her. 'I trust I am not too late to claim a dance with you.'

'Mr Lytton,' Serena responded breathlessly, 'what a surprise.'

'Another first for you to rack up,' Nicholas said drily.

Serena looked up, trying to gauge his mood, raising her brows questioningly.

He indicated his attire. 'I am not in the habit of tricking myself out in this way, but I found I could no longer resist the allure of dancing with you.'

'Wanting to see if the money you invested in the dancing master was well spent, you mean. I am honoured,' Serena said, taking his arm, feeling the familiar *frisson* of awareness, pow-erless as ever to resist him.

The orchestra struck up a waltz. Fortunately she had been granted permission by one of the patronesses to take part in the dance. She stepped into Nicholas's cool clasp, smiling up at him, looking so breathtakingly beautiful that his hands tightened on her waist. 'I've missed you,' he said. The words were out before he could stop them.

Such a simple admission, but it was more than she could have hoped. She had forgotten that feeling, as if her blood was filled with champagne bubbles. It was so lonely, this new world, with no one to share it. Serena responded recklessly, moving closer into his embrace. If he did not care for the gossip-mongers tonight, she would not.

They waltzed effortlessly, gracefully, their steps perfectly in time. Oblivious of the curious glances from the other dancers, they talked, smiled, touched, looked, caught in their own little bubble on the busy dance floor. He laughed wholeheartedly as she knew he would when she recounted her meeting with Mathew and Edwin. When the music stopped, they left the floor still entwined, engrossed in Nicholas's description of his first encounter with his former duelling opponent—taking fencing lessons!

They went down to supper still talking, oblivious of Nicholas's sister staring at them blatantly from a nearby table. Charles Avesbury joined Georgie to watch, his fiancée Penelope, pale and silent, at his side. Nicholas and Serena sat close, their heads bent together, their arms resting on the table, fingers almost touching. Serena said something, smiling with those big blue eyes of hers, the curve of her full mouth tender, making Nicholas laugh. He leaned closer to whisper in her ear, twisting a long strand of her golden hair round his finger. She blushed, picked up her glass, sipped, put it down, never once taking her eyes from his. Charles looked away, embarrassed and envious.

'Nicholas, it's lovely to see you,' said Serena, 'truly it is, but why have you turned up out of the blue like this? I don't understand, I thought we were to remain—'

'I've got a surprise for you,' Nicholas interrupted, smiling at her in a way that made her light-headed. 'Frances Eldon has managed to track down the name of the man your father is supposed to have murdered.'

'What?'

'And his sister. The—er—lady in the case. You look surprised.'

'I'm astonished. I didn't think for a moment that you meant it when you said you would instruct him to look into the matter.'

'Well he has done so, and as usual he has been successful.'

'Is she still alive, the sister?'

'I don't know, I'm afraid. It happened in a village called Mile End, not too far east of here. If she hasn't departed this life, she's probably still there. Aren't you pleased?'

'I hardly know what to think. Do you think you could—no, it's too much to ask, never mind.'

'Ask me. I find it almost impossible to say no to you.'

She looked at him, aware that it was the truth, equally aware that it was only half the story. He would have no difficulty at all in refusing her the dearest wish of her heart. But she would not think such thoughts tonight. 'Would you escort me there?'

'If you're sure.'

'I'm not at all sure. I had quite decided to let

sleeping dogs lie, but now that you've found her…'

'If she's still alive.'

'I can't not go now.'

He laughed at that. 'I think I understand.'

'I'm glad you came tonight. I was angry with you, and hurt when you so patently avoided my company. But the truth is,' she said with a nervous smile, 'that I've missed you too.'

Nicholas thought back over the last two weeks and all his efforts to resume his old way of life. He had watched Charles race his precious greys against an old enemy and win by a gratifyingly large margin. The evening that followed was spent in a dubious tavern in the Haymarket favoured by the opera company. Some of the dancers joined them. Vast quantities of daffy, gin and water were consumed. The alcohol made Nicholas feel curiously detached from the proceedings. Charles disappeared upstairs with one of the dancers. Nicholas brushed one away. He drank more. The result was a deep melancholy and a blinding headache the next day, which did nothing to improve his humour.

Georgie had obligingly kept him informed of

Serena's successes, ensuring that Nicholas was aware of every time Serena danced more than once in an evening with a favoured beau. Nicholas granted his disappointed sister no sign of the insane jealousy her revelations should have given rise to. Of course Serena was a hit, he had predicted it himself, had he not, he told Georgie curtly, setting off to spar viciously at Jackson's. It did not help. He had donned his knee breeches tonight with a mixture of resentment and expectation.

'I think you have cast a spell on me,' he admitted with a self-conscious laugh. 'I can't get you out of my head.'

Serena swallowed. The air between them crackled with tension. She could feel the heat of Nicholas's hand beside her own. A shiver of awareness twisted low in her stomach. Her mouth was dry. She stared at his hand. Beneath the white ruffle of his shirt sleeve she saw that his knuckles had healed. No trace now of that fight with Samuel. No trace in the immaculate ballroom costume of the wild, reckless boxer she had first encountered. But it was there all the same, lurking in his eyes. She felt the response deep in herself, a wakening urge to throw in her lot with him and flee, no matter what the consequences.

'Nicholas,' she whispered, telling herself that it would be madness, knowing already that she had made up her mind.

'Serena,' he said huskily, tracing the plane of her cheek-bone with a long finger.

He didn't love her, he would never love her, she knew that. But he missed her. He had sought her out. Another first, he said. Surely it could do no harm.

It could, and she knew it. Deeper and deeper she would fall. But right now, at this moment, she was ready to hurtle herself into whatever depths Nicholas chose for her, regardless of the consequences. She reached up to touch his hair.

'*Really!*' The exclamation came from a dowager at the next table, her scandalised countenance reminding them both of their surroundings for the first time since Nicholas had entered the club.

'Serena,' Nicholas said urgently, 'let's get out of here.'

'Are you sure?'

He smiled wryly. 'I should be asking you that,

but I don't think I could bear it if you said no. I've never been more sure of anything in my life. Tell me you feel the same.'

'Take me home, Nicholas.'

He needed no further invitation. Across the supper room, Hugo Langton, alerted by the dowager's exclamation, stared at the scandalous couple. With surprise, he noted that one of them was Jasper Lytton's cousin. 'W-what was the name of the female your dressmaker mentioned?' he asked his sister. 'The F-frenchie.'

Lettice Langton wrinkled her brow. 'Serena, I think it was. I remember thinking it was a pretty name. Why?'

Langton nodded over at Nicholas and Serena, now preparing to leave. 'Know who that is?'

'The latest heiress,' Miss Langton replied. 'She's very beautiful, but quite old.'

'And her name is Lady Serena,' her brother told her with a grin and no trace of a stammer.

Lettice Langton's little mouth dropped. 'Well,' she tittered gleefully, 'I wonder what Mama will make of that little bit of news.'

'Never mind Mama,' Langton said, 'I know someone who will be even more interested.'

* * *

The short drive to Upper Brook Street seemed to take an age. Serena was acutely conscious of Nicholas's leg brushing against hers through the thin satin of her gown. Each time the carriage jolted on the cobblestones they touched. Nicholas gripped her long-gloved hand in his own, so tight she thought her fingers would break. She could hear his breathing. She could feel the heavy thump, thump, thump of her heart. She felt weak with anticipation.

He was out of the carriage and pulling her down after him almost before it stopped at her front door. Dragging her up the shallow flight of steps, he summarily dismissed her footman with a curt nod, telling the astonished servant that he would let himself out. Thrusting Serena through the first door he came to—which fortunately was a comfortable parlour—he turned the key in the lock. 'I don't want a repeat of last time.'

'Most considerate of you,' she responded with a shy smile.

'Come here, Serena,' Nicholas said softly.

She walked into his arms. It was like coming home. Loneliness, anger, hurt evaporated with his touch. She rubbed her cheek against his chest, relishing the scent and feel of him, caught up in the magic that was Nicholas, lost in the wonder of the love she felt welling up inside her.

He held her tight, his face in her hair, remembering the scent and feel of her, the combination of skin and curves and light and laughter that was Serena. *His* Serena. The tension of the last few days dispersed into nothing, replaced with tension of a different sort. The pervading sensation that something was terribly wrong took flight, giving way to a heady certainty that everything was right.

Serena stirred against him. She looked up at him, her eyes clouded with desire. 'Nicholas.' She said his name in that way no one else said it, and he was lost in the grip of a crushing, crashing, overwhelming passion.

His hands roamed along her shoulders, pushing aside her heavy evening cloak. Down the line of her back, feeling her curves through the sheer satin of her dress, he remembered every inch of her. 'Serena. Oh God, Serena, I want you so much.' The words were torn from him painfully. He rained kisses on to her neck, tangled long fingers through the spun gold of her hair, kissed her eyelids, the tip of her nose, returning always to her lips to drink deep, thrusting his tongue urgently into her mouth, desperate to cover every inch of her with kisses.

Serena matched passion with passion, kissing, licking, tugging, scratching. The clasp that held her cloak gave way. It fell to the ground, spilling around her feet. The tiny puffed sleeves of her gown were pushed down her arms to free the neckline of her dress and release her breasts. Cupping them in his hands, Nicholas dropped his face to scatter kisses over the yielding flesh, into the valley between, on to her nipples, lighting little paths of fire everywhere he touched, stoking the flames of the furnace burning lower down.

Serena moaned, fierce with desire, urging him onwards with hands and tongue and lips and body. Nicholas scooped her up to lay her down on a sofa, kneeling down beside her. He ran his hand up the inside of her leg under her gown. She felt her skin tingling beneath the material of her underwear. Her pulses thrummed. The focus of her world narrowed. She was aflame with pinpoints of desire.

Writhing on the sofa, she parted her legs, wanton in her need for him to touch her, reaching to caress his erection through the silk of his knee breeches. Nicholas moaned, his fingers curled into the heat between her thighs. He struggled to undo his buttons. 'Touch me, I need you to touch me.'

Serena ran a gloved hand over the throbbing length of him, closing her fingers around his girth, caressing him with aching familiarity, knowing just exactly where to touch, to stroke, to rub, relishing the feeling of power it gave her to make him shiver and close his eyes with the pleasure of it.

His fingers plunged deep inside her, sliding slickly out, up, rubbing harder on her wetness, plunging in deeper again. Serena gasped, tightened her hand around him. That heady, dizzy, terrifying exhilarating need to jump possessed her. She breathed hard in anticipation. Nicholas kissed her roughly on the mouth. Pulled his hand away. Removed hers.

Serena opened her eyes. He pulled them both

to their feet before she could protest, and in one fluid movement bent her over the sofa, hoisted her skirts around her waist and plunged into her from behind.

'Oh!' She clutched at the back of the sofa for support, momentarily overcome by the hardness and suddenness of his possession. Cautiously, she wriggled her bottom against him, drawing a satisfying groan from him in response. He withdrew almost to the tip of his hard length, then plunged again, at the same time reaching under her dress at the front to touch her with his fingers, rubbing and circling as he thrust hard into her, harder, and harder, filling her, until she climaxed around him, and he lost control, pounding into her, clutching at her, pulling her close as he exploded inside her, saying her name over and over.

When he finally withdrew, Serena closed her eyes, bracing herself for the inevitable rejection, but it did not come. He pulled her close, cradling her in his arms, collapsing on to the sofa with her on his lap, stroking her hair, pressing kisses onto her face, hugging her as if trying to mould her to his shape. A sense of euphoria swept over him, so unlike the usual depression that he was afraid to move lest he lose it.

Serena would gladly have climbed inside Nicholas's skin and stayed there if she could have. She felt spent, sated, and blindingly happy. 'We've still got our clothes on.' Her satin evening gown was creased beyond recovery. Nicholas's neckcloth was half-undone, his shirt ripped open, his coat hanging off his shoulders.

Self-consciously, he shifted to adjust his breeches. 'I had not this in mind when I put these dammed things on to go to Almack's tonight.'

'And was it worth the effort?' she teased, made confident as much by the contented look on his face as his earlier admission of his need.

'I don't know. We haven't finished yet,' Nicholas said with an endearing grin.

'Mr Lytton, so soon,' Serena exclaimed in mock astonishment, astounded to feel a stirring of excitement between her own thighs.

'Lady Serena, I do believe so,' he answered. 'Perhaps you would like to investigate for yourself.'

Serena rolled from his embrace to kneel before

him. 'I think perhaps I should,' she murmured wickedly, taking him delicately into her mouth.

Later, they made more leisurely love on the floor in front of the unlit grate, falling asleep, finally naked, in one another's arms.

Nicholas left Upper Brook Street just before dawn, kissing Serena tenderly. At peace for the first time in days, he failed to notice the man lurking in the shadow of an opposing doorway, keeping an eye on Serena's house. He made his contented way north to Cavendish Square under the light of the new-fangled gas lamps. At home, he slept dreamlessly, well into the late morning.

He awoke to a new-found resolution. Charles Avesbury was right. He would never find a better match than Serena. What he felt for her would probably fade in time, it was the way of things, but she was like her name, serene, and would remain an amenable companion for life. She would be his for always, exactly as she should be, for as long as he wanted her. Reconciled as Nicholas was to the fading of his own passion, he could not bear the idea of Serena giving herself to anyone else. The news, broken tentatively by Frances Eldon after breakfast, that his lawyers had failed in the final attempt to break his father's will, only confirmed him in his resolution. The gods had spoken. Nicholas could find no fault with his decision to make Serena his wife.

It was as if a weight had rolled from his shoulders.

He was in excellent spirits as he strolled down Bond Street towards St James's. Until he encountered Mathew, Lord Vespian, coming the other way.

'Ah, glad to have bumped into you, Mr Lytton,' Mathew said. 'I believe I have you to thank for taking care of my niece's papers.'

'It was a pleasure.' Nicholas eyed Mathew appraisingly. 'I wonder, Lord Vespian, if you would care to join me for a drink in my club. It's just here, and I have something of a private nature to impart to you.'

Mathew looked surprised and not particularly keen, seeing the saturnine look in Nicholas's eye. 'Well, I have an engagement, you know.'

'It will take but a few moments.' Nicholas placed a firm grip on the older man's elbow.

Mathew had no choice but to follow him the short distance along the street, through the entrance vestibule of White's, and into a back room, which, at this time of day, was empty of other members. Smoothing the sleeve of his coat, he sat down huffily, demanding that Nicholas be brief. 'I can't think what can be so important, but there was no need at all to compel me, you know. Your father was another such one, impetuous, always in trouble, just like my brother Philip. You are very alike, in character as well as features, if your behaviour towards me is anything to go by.'

'Yes, yes, let us agree that my behaviour in coercing you was abominable,' Nicholas said dismissively. Despite the early hour, he called for brandy. If Serena's uncle did not want it now, he was like to be in need of it once Nicholas had spoken.

'I will be blunt and to the point, Lord Vespian. Lady Serena is a rich woman, and I believe that the price for her wealth comes at a cost to your estates. Am I correct?'

'Not that it's any of your business, but, yes, it's true enough.'

'And may I ask if I'm correct in assuming that the money reverts to you if anything happens to your niece?'

'Yes, naturally. What has that to do with anything?'

'There have been two attempts on Lady Serena's life. In order to deduce who made them, it is necessary to understand who would benefit from her death.'

'*Two* attempts?' Mathew exclaimed in astonishment.

Nicholas frowned. Perhaps the first bullet had been fired by a poacher after all. 'A near-miss not long after she arrived in England. Then a rather more serious attempt by two highwaymen who held up the carriage she was travelling in. Both times, luck was on her side. I would not like her to rely on chance a third time.'

'*Highwaymen!*' Mathew poured himself a brandy with a shaking hand. 'Are you sure my niece was not just unfortunate? To assume that a hold up was an attempted murder is surely rather over-imaginative.'

'Not at all. It was quite obvious that the whole point was to murder Serena.'

'How can you be so certain, Mr Lytton?'

'Because I escorted her to London from Knightswood Hall, which is where my father kept her papers. Her French companion had unfortunately left her quite alone.'

'You spent two days on the road in my niece's company without an escort?' Mathew exclaimed, outrage written large on his face.

'I can assure you, sir, that all the proprieties were observed,' Nicholas said angrily. 'Let us put things in perspective here, my lord. *I* only had Serena's—Lady Serena's—best interests at heart. *I* was trying to protect her. Whereas you, Lord Vespian, have now tried twice to kill her.'

Mathew's face crumpled and his shoulders sagged dispiritedly. 'No, no, not twice. Not twice, I assure you. And the first time was only—oh, I have been so foolish.' He rested his head dejectedly in his hands. It was one thing to hand over a sum of money to arrange for some vague harm to come to a complete stranger. Quite another to have the deed named cold-blooded murder, especially now that he had met his niece, found her quite charming and intended her for his daughter-in-law.

Nicholas waited impatiently for Serena's uncle to regain his self-control.

Mathew wiped his face with a large handkerchief and took a swallow of brandy. 'What must you think of me? It was a foolish thing, done in the heat of the moment. You must understand, my brother's death, the will, the existence of my niece—I found this all out in the contents of one letter. It was a shock, and I admit I behaved very badly. I paid a man to arrange for my niece to meet with a—an unspecified accident. He bungled it, and refused to try again for fear of discovery, for which I am profoundly thankful.'

'Had he not, rest assured you would be having this conversation with a magistrate, not with myself,' Nicholas said acerbically. 'What was he like, this bungler you paid?'

'I can barely remember. He was an ex-Runner. Small, fat, he wore a greasy coat. I don't know any more.'

'And you had nothing to do with the highwaymen?'

'No! No, on my oath. Nothing. I swear, I

thought the better of it, and now that I have met Serena, I could not wish her any harm. You must believe me, Mr Lytton. I'm an honest man. You cannot make me feel any worse than I already do.'

'I'm not concerned with your repentance, only with your promise to take no further action. If any harm should come to Lady Serena, I will know where to look.'

'She will take no hurt from me, you have my word.' Mathew took another reviving tot of brandy, relaxing as the spirit took effect on his empty stomach. He mopped his face once more, and smiled knowingly at Nicholas. 'My niece is a very attractive young woman, I am not surprised that you take such an interest in her. But she has her family to look after her now, Mr Lytton. And—I'm sure you will forgive my blunt speaking—a man of your reputation would be rather a liability to a young woman seeking to make a respectable match. You understand me, I'm sure.'

Mathew made to rise, but a strong hand on his shoulder and a snarling face breathing hard into his own forced him back on to the seat. He sprawled there gasping like a fish out of water, his terrified gaze staring into the face of the very devil.

'Your definition of *looking after* your niece entailed doing away with her, let me remind you, Lord Vespian. I shall not forget that. What's more, Lady Serena is of age, and if she chooses to spend time in my company, that is for her to say—as it is for her—and only her—to choose not to! Your concern for your niece's reputation will, I am certain, ensure that you keep your base suspicions about my own behaviour to yourself. I bid you good day, sir. I can see no need for our paths to cross again unless I find that Serena is in danger. I trust that there will never be such an occasion. If there is, then I can promise you will regret it.'

Nicholas brushed Mathew aside and stormed out of the club, ignoring the offer, from a friend just arrived, of a game of whist.

Mathew lay gasping in his chair, sweat, which had broken out on his forehead, dripping into his eyes. After a few moments he recovered his breath, and with the aid of yet another snifter of brandy, his composure also. Nicholas Lytton had given him much food for thought. Why, if it ever got out that he and Serena were—close?—she would be ruined. There would be no offers for her hand, for who would take Lytton's leavings? No one. Except perhaps Edwin.

Despite the stress of the interview, things might yet work out to his advantage. With something approaching nonchalance, he left White's and sauntered off to meet with his tailor, so content with the morning's findings that he ordered not one, but two new coats.

Though he was deeply perturbed by the possibility that a second person might have designs on Serena's life, Nicholas put it to the back of his mind as he made his way back to visit her in Upper Brook Street for the second time that day. As her legal protector, he would be able to make sure she came to no further harm.

The door was opened by the same footman he had so summarily dismissed the night before. The man boggled at him, and Nicholas grinned good-humouredly. 'Is your mistress at home?'

He was shown up to a sunny drawing room on the first floor with three long windows overlooking the street. He did not have long to wait.

Serena came in, a vision in sprig muslin and green ribbons.

He clasped her hands between his, smiling down at her. Serena returned the smile shyly. 'I didn't expect to see you again until tomorrow,' she said, the day they had fixed upon for the journey to the village of Mile End.

'There is something I wish to discuss with you. Come and sit down.'

She took a seat by the fireplace, looking at him expectantly.

Nicholas sat opposite her, stood, looked out of the window, then sat down again. 'I think we should get married,' he said abruptly.

Silence. Serena stared, trying to muster her thoughts, her heart fluttering in her chest like a songbird in a cage. 'Do you?' was all she could manage, desperately waiting for the words, those three precious words, which must surely follow such a proposal.

'It makes sense,' Nicholas said, staring at his boots.

Not those three words. Hope withered in her breast. 'Why?' she asked neutrally.

Nicholas looked up. Discomfited, he realised

he had assumed Serena would say yes and throw herself into his arms. He should have known better. His smile was twisted. 'There are many reasons, but there is one that I have not disclosed to you.'

Serena's expression brightened, a tiny flicker of hope rekindled. 'What is it?'

'I think I mentioned when we first met that your father was not the only one with a quirky sense of humour.' Bluntly, he explained the terms of his father's will and his lawyer's failed attempts to break it.

As she listened, Serena felt her blood turn to ice. 'I thought there were to be no more secrets between us.' Her voice faded as she valiantly swallowed a sob. *She would not cry!* 'So you think we should marry in order for you to protect your inheritance,' she managed after a few seconds.

'No, that's just a part of it. Last night—'

'I wondered when we would get to that.'

He stared at her, trying to suppress the panic that threatened to engulf him. The possibility of his first-ever proposal of marriage being turned down had not occurred to him. 'Last night confirmed, if confirmation were needed, that we are extremely compatible. I have said it before, Serena, what we have is special.'

'Since I have no previous experience, I will have to take your word for that.'

'Serena, what I'm trying to say is that I think we could make a good marriage,' Nicholas said exasperatedly. 'We enjoy one another's company. We give each other immense pleasure. Even when passion has been spent, I do not think we will make one another unhappy. We understand each other in that way too. I will always be discreet. You will be comfortably established. And on top of all that, our marriage will prevent my cousin from throwing away my inheritance on cards and horses.'

'And when passion, as you say, is spent, what must I do?'

'What do you mean?'

'Am I to live the life of a nun when you are done with me? Perhaps I will occupy myself with the nursery full of brats you want nothing to do with? Or do you simply wish me to be as discreet as you plan to be?'

'Don't be ridiculous, Serena, you will be my wife. I would not tolerate your infidelity.' He spoke without thinking, reacting only to the idea of her in anyone else's arms but his own. It was a mistake—he knew it as soon as the words were out.

'You are a hypocrite, Nicholas, I thought better of you,' Serena said angrily. 'How dare you propose marriage to me on such terms!'

'I didn't mean it that way. You once told me that for you marriage meant fidelity. I was assuming you had not changed your mind.'

'I have not. But fidelity applies to both partners in my book, not just one. And I was actually referring to love, if you remember. Which in your case,' she added pointedly, 'is not an issue.'

'You're being preposterous! I offer you marriage, something I have never in my life offered before. But I am not the hypocrite you accuse me of being. I know passion will fade, it always does. I won't make you false promises.'

'You don't love me, in other words,' Serena said flatly.

'What has that to do with anything?' Nicholas demanded. He stood, paced over to the window, returned to face her from behind a sofa, leaning his hands on the back of it, reminding her of the use they had put a similar sofa to only a few hours earlier.

The urge to take what he was offering was strong. It was not everything, but it was so much more than she had. But she knew in her heart she could not. 'I can't marry you, Nicholas,' Serena said firmly.

Abruptly, he changed tack. 'If you don't, you will be compromised. Last night, our behaviour in Almack's, leaving together in the way we did, can have left no one present in any doubt of our relationship.'

Serena shrugged. 'I don't care. I've decided to leave London.'

'I thought you planned to settle here.'

'I've changed my mind.' Better a clean break than a long agonising death. She saw that clearly now. 'No,' she said with resolution. 'I can't stay here.'

'Can't?'

'Won't. I have no reason to stay. My only relative wants me dead or married to his son. I have no other ties. Perhaps I will return to Paris and open a gaming salon,' she said defiantly.

'Since my reputation is in tatters anyway, it cannot do me further harm.'

Nicholas sat down beside her and took her hand in his familiar grasp. 'Won't you reconsider?'

She knew a marriage based on one-sided love could never succeed, no matter how unshakeable that love might be. He would discover the truth, and he would resent her for it. The more he resented her, the more she would feel guilty. It was impossible. She shook her head sadly. 'No, Nicholas, it wouldn't work. You would not be happy with me. I could not bear that. I'm afraid you will have to resign your inheritance to Jasper.'

'Damn Jasper and my inheritance,' Nicholas said vehemently, 'I simply don't want to lose you. Not yet.'

Not yet. Serena disentangled her hand. 'It's for the best. Last night was perfect. Let us leave it at that and say no more.'

He hurled himself to his feet. 'I will not demean either of us by begging. I will see you tomorrow.' Thwarted, deflated and frustrated beyond measure, Nicholas stormed out.

Alone in the drawing room, Serena tore her handkerchief to shreds in an effort to hold back her tears. It served no purpose. Every flicker of hope had been extinguished from her heart, leaving it as cold and hard as a block of ice. A block of ice that was fissured and cracking, breaking into myriad splintered pieces. Hot tears dripped and burned like acid on to the tattered lace she clenched between her trembling fingers.

Chapter Ten

The next day dawned bright and sunny in stark contrast to Serena's mood. She gazed out of the window on to the street. She knew Nicholas would turn up, for he had promised, but she dreaded his arrival. Her resolution to leave as soon as possible had hardened overnight. She had been fooling herself for too long now. To continue to be in Nicholas's company would be senseless torture. The time had come for her to face the truth. But she was not at all convinced of her ability to cope with seeing him again so soon.

Nicholas pulled up in his high-perch phaeton drawn by a pair of showy chestnuts. Knowing how much he hated to keep his horses standing, Serena hurried down to meet him. She wore an emerald-green walking dress and warm pelisse, and a fetching straw poke bonnet trimmed with ribbons of the same colour.

Nicholas helped her up, tucking a rug around her knees, carefully moving along the narrow seat to avoid touching her. With a sinking heart, Serena met his saturnine smile.

'You look as charming as ever,' he said, flicking his leader's ear with the whip. 'We have quite a way to go and my horses are fresh— you'll forgive me if I refrain from making polite conversation.'

The journey was completed in silence. They travelled out through the city and headed east-wards. Cobbled streets gave way to country lanes as they followed the direction of the River Thames towards the village of Mile End, reaching it around midday.

As they drew nearer to their destination, Serena forgot about the tension between them and thought only of Papa. His deathbed description of the scene that morning almost thirty years ago came back to her with the clarity of a painting. For thirty years he had borne the blame for a crime he did not commit. For thirty years, his unknown friend had avoided justice. Now she was on the verge of discovering his identity. Nervously, Serena smoothed an imaginary wrinkle from her York tan gloves. Anxiously, she gazed at the little village ahead of them.

Nicholas pulled up at the only inn, shouting for someone to stable the horses. Startled to be called upon to deal with such a fine equipage, a toothless ostler tugged at his cap and led the phaeton into the yard.

'Wait here,' Nicholas barked, disappearing into the dark interior of the inn.

Serena sat in the sunshine on a convenient bench, watching the antics of a small kitten playing with a lazy spaniel. The ostler reappeared from the stable yard accompanied by a scrawny boy. They stared. Serena fidgeted with her reticule.

Five minutes later Nicholas returned. He looked down at her drawn face. 'Are you all right?'

'Fine. A bit nervous.'

'I enquired inside. Eliza Cooper is alive and well and still living in the village, amazingly. She's Eliza Baker now, a widow.'

'Oh.' Serena swallowed. 'I'm terribly sorry, but I feel a little faint.'

'Come on, Serena, this is not like you.'

She smiled wanly. 'It's been a—an eventful few days.'

He laughed derisively. 'Eventful is certainly one word for it.'

'Nicholas, I know it's foolish, but I have a horrible premonition about this Eliza woman. I'm not sure I want to know what she's got to say.'

He looked at her in surprise. 'It's not like you to be faint-hearted. We can leave now if you would rather, but I think you would regret it later.'

'The thing is, what if it was Papa after all,' she said agitatedly.

Surprised to see her so distraught, Nicholas chose his words with care. 'Do you think that is a possibility?'

'I don't honestly know.' She stared down at her reticule, whose strings were now hopelessly knotted. 'Papa believed he was not guilty. The problem is, I have come to realise that he could be less than honest with himself.'

'That may be so, but you are a very different creature. I think you would rather know the truth, no matter how painful.'

His perception drew a smile from her. 'You are

quite right, Nicholas. I would always be wondering.' She rose from the bench wearily.

'Serena.'

Blue eyes under fair brows looked up at him. A day resolutely trying not to think of her and a night pacing the floor of his bedchamber had left him no clearer. She could not be his mistress. She would not be his wife. Yet he simply could not let her go. He sighed in exasperation as he looked at her troubled countenance. Now was not the time for whatever discussion his quandary required. Perhaps if he could help her clear her father's name, she would feel differently about—about everything.

'What is it, Nicholas?'

He shook his head. 'Nothing. Let us find the infamous Mrs Baker. I wonder if we will be able to discern any traces at all of her charms?'

Serena giggled. 'I think that's highly unlikely.'

She was proved correct. The woman who answered the door to which the innkeeper had directed Nicholas was enormously fat and rankly odorous.

'Mrs Baker,' Serena asked doubtfully. 'Eliza Cooper that was?'

The woman smiled, revealing several unsightly black stumps that had once been teeth, adding the smell of stale food to the general stench that surrounded her. 'Been a long time since I heard that name,' she said, eyeing Serena curiously. 'Who wants to know?'

'My name is Stamppe. You may have been acquainted with my papa, Philip Stamppe.'

Eliza Baker looked startled. 'Acquainted with him? He killed my brother.'

'That's not true,' Serena asserted, 'and you know it. The man who killed your brother was your protector, and I want to know who he was.'

Eliza narrowed her eyes. 'Why?'

'My papa is dead. I want to clear his name.'

'And who might you be?' Eliza said, turning her attention towards Nicholas for the first time. 'Not a magistrate, I 'ope. I've done nothing wrong.' She gave a gasp, raising a hand to her face. 'Gawd help us. I thought it were him for a minute.'

Nicholas surveyed her disdainfully.

Eliza staggered back against the doorway of her cottage. 'I never told. I kept my promise, I never told,' she gabbled. 'Never, never, never.'

Nicholas looked at her in astonishment.

'I never said a word. Tell your father, I kept my promise,' Eliza continued, backing into the cottage.

'What has *my* father got to do with this?' Nicholas demanded.

Eliza stared at him. 'It was him 'as done it. Your father killed my poor brother.'

'No, no,' Serena said, appalled. 'That can't possibly be right.'

'Are you calling me a liar?' Eliza snapped, recovering quickly from the shock of seeing a ghost from her past. 'I know who was keeping me warm at night and paying for the privilege.'

Nicholas shuddered with distaste at the ghastly image the vile crone's words had conjured up.

'And I know who killed my brother, God rest him. Saw it with me own eyes. I know who paid me to keep my trap shut too. Nick Lytton, that's who. And you,' she said, pointing a filthy finger at Nicholas, 'are his living spit.'

'Nicholas, surely there must be a mistake,' Serena said, looking with anguish at his darkening countenance.

He pushed Eliza's grimy hand away. 'When did you last see him?' he demanded.

Eliza shrugged. 'Not long after it happened. He gave me a handsome sum, helped me turn respectable, become a lady of leisure, so to speak.' Her laugh dissolved into a violent coughing fit, which she relieved with a hawking spit. 'Haven't seen hide nor hair of him since.'

'Nor will you again. He's dead these past ten years.'

'What business have you coming round here stirring up trouble for, then? You'd do well to leave it alone, missy,' Eliza said, looking accusingly at Serena. 'What's done is done.'

'How can we be sure you are telling the truth, that this is not just some kind of sick joke?' Nicholas interjected.

'Want proof, do you?' Eliza cackled. 'Well, proof you shall have. Wait here.' She disappeared into the gloomy recess of her cottage, emerging a few moments later clutching something wrapped in a filthy rag, which she handed to Nicholas.

As he looked at the object within, Serena saw his expression shift from disbelief to horror. 'Nicholas, what is it?'

'A miniature. A likeness of my father. I fear there is no doubting the truth now.'

'Gave it to me as a token of 'is affection, he said,' Eliza informed them. 'Not valuable enough to sell, so I held on to it as a keepsake.'

'As an insurance policy, more like,' Nicholas said disdainfully. He flicked a coin to the ground in front of Eliza. 'For your trouble. You'll get nothing more from me, you've already been paid in full.'

Serena shrank back against him, white and shaking. 'I didn't know. I wouldn't have—oh, what have I done?'

'Let's get out of this abominable place,' Nicholas said bitterly, 'our very presence here offends me.' He took Serena's arm and led her away.

Eliza shrugged, pocketed the coin and slammed shut the door of her cottage.

Serena trembled so much she could barely walk the short distance to the inn. 'I'm so sorry, Nicholas, you must believe I had no idea, not the slightest inkling,' she said desperately, unable to bear the bleak look on his face. 'His best friend! No wonder Papa would not tell me. I should have left well alone. Oh God, I could almost wish it had been Papa who was guilty after all. I am *sorry*.'

'Now you are being ridiculous. You have nothing to apologise for. It is I who am sorry, deeply sorry, and ashamed. That it should have been my father who kept you in exile on the Continent. My father who exposed you to the life you led. My father who deprived you of your rightful inheritance until now. It only adds to the irony that it was I who insisted on uncovering it all.' He laughed bitterly. 'You could say I have been the architect of my own downfall.'

'*Nicholas!* You mustn't think like that. Those were Papa's choices. None of this is your fault.'

He looked at her bleakly. 'What are you going to do now?'

'Do?' She looked confused.

'Surely you wish to clear your father's name?'

She turned even paler. 'I'm not going to do anything, Nicholas,' she said. 'It was thirty years ago. As if anyone even cares any more. If a scandal is more than a week old, it is forgotten about.'

'You don't have to say that just to make me feel better.'

Serena stamped her foot angrily. 'I make my

own choices, and bear the consequences of them myself. Stop trying to appropriate all the blame, it's insulting.'

'As ever, Serena, your unusual take on life astonishes me. You are an extraordinary woman.'

'I wish I could believe that. I don't feel at all extraordinary right now. I feel tired and confused. Will you take me home now?'

'Yes, I think that would be best. We will talk of this tomorrow, when we have both had a good night's sleep and a chance to assimilate the implications.'

'There's nothing to talk about. Now we know the truth it need go no further. Papa would not have wanted it to. Like me, he made his own choices. Papa did not seek justice. He would not have wanted you to make reparation on your father's behalf either, especially not knowing that we are—are friends.'

Nicholas took her hand, pressing a warm kiss on to the palm. 'Friends. At least you grant me that. Thank you.'

Serena was due to attend a farce with Edwin that evening. Her cousin had been as dutiful an escort as her Uncle Mathew could wish, though for very different reasons than the dreams his father nurtured. Georgiana, whose youthful exuberance was much more to Edwin's taste than his intimidatingly beautiful cousin, was the real reason for Edwin's faithful attendance. They had arranged to meet Georgie and Melissa at the theatre. Edwin found Serena alone in front of the unlit grate of the small downstairs parlour. To his horror, she was crying.

'Cousin Serena, I did not mean to intrude. I beg your pardon,' Edwin said, retreating back towards the doorway.

Serena jumped up, brushing away her tears with the back of her hand. 'It's all right, I won't weep all over you. I had forgotten our engagement. I'm afraid you must go without me, I'm in no fit state for company.'

'What on earth has happened to upset you? Is it to do with Georgiana's brother?'

She was taken aback. 'No, why should it be?'

Edwin blushed. 'Nothing. Georgie said—only I'm sure she was mistaken.'

'Georgie said what?' Serena asked in a voice that made Edwin quake.

'Only that she thought it was a case between you,' he stuttered.

'Well, you can tell Georgie she's very much mistaken,' Serena said tartly. 'I'm upset about my papa, if you must know.'

'The murderer,' Edwin said sagely.

'He was not a murderer!'

'Apologies. Only going by what my father says.'

'That is a fine thing, coming from him,' Serena said feelingly, thinking of the bullet her uncle had arranged for her.

Edwin looked puzzled. 'Has my father been plaguing you about it? Thought it was ancient history by now, don't understand what you're so upset about.'

'I know Papa was innocent, but I am not in a position to prove it, that is all.' Serena sat up and mopped her eyes with a handkerchief. 'You are quite right, it is ancient history. Do go on to the theatre and make my apologies. Don't tell them I was upset, I beg of you.'

She retired early to bed, hoping that a night's rest would restore her equilibrium. Instead, the cloak of night brought darker thoughts to the front of her mind. She lay awake for long hours, thinking of the pain today's revelations had caused Nicholas. If only she had not sought that awful woman out. Nicholas, poor Nicholas—she could not bear to see him unhappy. Only two nights ago they had lain together in the room downstairs. Foolishly, she allowed herself the indulgence of reliving their lovemaking. The memories heated her blood, filling her with longing. The thrum of frustrated desire made her toss and turn between the tangled sheets.

She lay, hot and miserable, listening to the muffled sounds of the London night through the heavy window hangings. The watch called the hour. A party of merrymakers passed with a gust of laughter. Eventually the street fell silent, but still sleep eluded her. With an exasperated sigh, Serena pushed away the bed covers and got up, pulling back one of the curtains to open the window, breathing in the cool night air as she looked out on to the quiet street. The lamps cast shadows on to the cobblestones. There was silence save for her own breathing, and a sharp tinkling in the background.

A tinkling? Serena stepped back from the window to listen. It was the sound of breaking glass, and it seemed to be coming from downstairs. Carefully, she opened the door to her bedroom and listened. Nothing. Perhaps she was mistaken? Some sixth sense kept her standing there until the creak of a board informed her that someone was climbing the stairs.

A housebreaker. But why did they not first look in the dining room, the kitchen, even, where the silverware was kept? Perhaps they were after her jewellery. Pulling the bell to summon aid was a waste of time, since it rang in the basement, and the live-in servants slept in the attics. If she was to act, she would have to act alone.

Serena looked round the room in search of a weapon; her eyes alighted on the tall pewter candlesticks that sat beside the mirror on her dressing table. She picked one up, holding it tightly in her hand, and crept stealthily to stand behind the bedroom door, hoping that the small element of surprise this gave her would provide sufficient advantage to overcome the intruder. She prayed there was only one of them.

Her heart pounded like a hammer striking the anvil, so fast and loud she was sure that the man outside must hear it. Her bedchamber faced the top of the stairs at the centre of the house, next to the drawing room. The footfalls paused. The man must have removed his boots, he made so little sound. She could hear his shallow breathing through the wooden door. She heard the door of the drawing room open. A pause, then it closed again. He had not gone in, for she heard the tiny creak of the floorboard as he resumed his inexorable journey towards her.

Everything happened as if in slow motion. The door opened stealthily. The figure paused on the threshold to look in, saw that the room was unoccupied, made to turn away. Noticed that the bed was unmade and stopped. Came into the room. Looked around. Checked behind the thick curtains at the window, leaning out of the open sash to look down into the street. In the dim light she could see that he was a small man, wiry, no more than twenty or so, with a wizened face much older than his years. He turned from the window, paused again. Made to head for the large cupboard standing in the corner. Checked. And then he saw her standing behind the door.

They moved towards each other. Serena

screamed at the top of her voice and pushed the door away, holding the heavy candlestick high over her head. She barely had time to notice the lethal flash of his dagger, hardly registered the cold kiss of steel deflected from her heart to her arm as she brought her own weapon down on the man's head with all her might. He crumpled, an astonished look on his face, his body toppling to the floor as if all the bones had been removed from it. Serena dropped the candlestick from trembling fingers. With surprise, she noticed that the drip, drip, drip she could hear was the blood from her arm falling on to the boards. At the sound of footsteps outside in the hallway, she felt a dizzy, whirling rush through her brain, and dropped in a dead faint beside the prostrate housebreaker.

It was Georgiana who broke the news to Nicholas. She had called on Serena the next morning with the intention of suggesting a trip to the Royal Exchange, and was astonished to find her still abed looking pale and wan, an intriguing sling supporting her arm. Serena's bravery, and the casual way she dismissed the entire incident, raised her to heroic status in Georgie's eyes, casting all thoughts of silk stockings and ribbons with which to trim a new bonnet from her mind.

Georgiana excitedly told her driver to return her to Cavendish Square. Her brother must be told immediately that his Serena—for in her mind, Georgie always thought of her friend in this way—had only narrowly escaped death.

Nicholas was in the library. *The Times* lay on a table by his side, but, judging from the freshly ironed lines, had not yet been opened. As Georgiana stormed into the room, he was engaged in the frustratingly addictive task of trying to decide which made him feel worse— his father's perfidy or Serena's refusal to entertain his proposal of marriage.

'Nicholas, the most awful thing has happened. Serena has been attacked in her own house.'

Her brother turned a most satisfactory shade of grey in front of her very eyes. 'What! Georgiana, don't fun with me. Is this true?'

'Oh, indeed, yes, I have just this minute come from Upper Brook Street. Poor Serena has been wounded.'

'Is she badly hurt?' Nicholas asked, a catch in his voice.

'The doctor came last night to attend her, and will return today to cup her—though she said she would not let him. She looks dreadful.'

Georgiana stood in front of the mirror that hung over the mantel to remove her bonnet, noting her brother's anxious reflection carefully. 'The attacker found her in her bedroom. She was undressed. Alone. In her bedchamber.' She checked Nicholas's expression in the mirror again, and shivered at the fierceness of his frown. 'She says he was a housebreaker, but I could not help wondering if the man was intent on *ravishment*.'

She said the word with such obvious relish that Nicholas laughed in spite of himself. 'I hardly think so. It's much more likely he was intent on her jewellery case.'

'Oh, that is just what Serena said.' Georgie cast her bonnet aside and turned to face her brother, placing her hands on her hips in a challenging attitude. 'Serena has been attacked in her home and is injured. Aren't you in the least bit concerned?'

'Of course I am concerned—don't be so

stupid, Georgie. Do I look as if I am unconcerned?'

Looking at him carefully, she thought he looked more tired than anything else, and said so.

'A few late nights, that's all.'

'With Serena?'

'Don't push your luck, Georgie, and don't interfere. You're far too young to know anything about it. Both Serena and I are perfectly capable of managing our own affairs.' He only wished that were true.

Georgie looked sceptical, managing a fair imitation of her brother's expression. 'You don't seem to be doing very well as far as I can see. Edwin says she was crying last night when he went to collect her. She did not come to the theatre with us after all.'

'I expect she was tired,' Nicholas said curtly. He did not like to think of Serena upset. More importantly, he did not like to think of her in danger. 'Tell me—without any more of your deliberate exaggerations—exactly what happened.'

Cowed, Georgiana recounted what Serena had

told her of the housebreaker, who had been handed into the care of the Watch by Serena's footman. The wound he had received from the candlestick had been sufficient to knock him cold, but caused no more permanent injury than a nasty cut and a large bruise. Serena's own injury had bled copiously because it had been to the fleshy part of her arm, but already it was healing, and the sling, she had informed Georgiana, was more to appease the doctor than to ease her pain. The housebreaker was well known to the Watch—Georgie pronounced the name 'Fingers' Harry with relish—and was acting alone. No, he had not taken anything. It was fortunate that Serena had disturbed him. In fact, Georgie reminded her brother, Serena had been a *heroine*, for she hid behind a door in order to trap 'Fingers' into thinking the room was empty.

'Do you not think that she was very clever?'

'Very.' His response was disappointingly matter of fact. 'She is a very resourceful young woman.'

Georgie sniffed and pouted. 'And she's perfect for you, if only you could see it,' she said defiantly, leaving the room with a flounce, knocking *The Times* to the floor as she passed.

Nicholas was left with much to think about. Housebreakers rarely worked alone and to his knowledge did not normally carry knives. With a houseful of unoccupied rooms, to choose the master bedroom as his starting place was an unlikely tale. It was too much of a coincidence. Yet if not Mathew, who could be at the bottom of it? He had to find out, and at present there was only one person who could tell him. He pulled the bell rope and sent for his man of business.

Frances Eldon was the eldest son of the local schoolmaster at High Knightswood. A plainly dressed young man with a reserved air and a studious countenance, he had received many strange requests from his employer over the years. He listened impassively as Nicholas issued him with very precise instructions. He was to go to Bow Street where a certain 'Fingers' Harry was being held. With the use of a bribe—here Nicholas handed over a purse—he was to induce 'Fingers' to divulge who had paid him to break into a particular house in Upper Brook Street.

Satisfied that he would soon have an answer, for Frances had never yet let him down, Nicholas set off in haste to call upon Serena.

He found her, looking pale and tired, dressed neatly in lemon yellow muslin, with no signs of a sling. She had known he would come. Despite herself, she was delighted to see his reassuring, handsome face. She had so few hours left to engrave him in her memory. She could almost hear the sand dripping through the hourglass, marking them off.

'Georgie told me what happened. How are you?' He took her hand, leading her over to a sofa, where he joined her, sitting so close his thigh pressed against hers.

She shifted, struggling as usual to contain the shiver of awareness his touch set off. 'I'm fine. I think I frightened the poor man—he wasn't more than a boy, really—more than he did I.'

'As usual, you are too modest. No doubt you will tell me that you dealt with worse in those gaming houses on the Continent.'

It was meant as a joke, but served to remind them both of the revelation precipitated by their visit to Mile End. There was an uncomfortable silence.

'Serena, I am so sorry. You cannot imagine how bad I feel to have discovered—'

'Nicholas, please,' she interrupted, 'let us not discuss it. Your father and mine were friends. Papa never sought retribution, and let us not forget that it was his choice to remain on the Continent for all those years. I doubt very much if he would ever have come to England again, whatever the circumstances. He would have seen the responsibilities that the earldom entailed as chains—I realise that now. No, it is another closed chapter in my life. I must move on,' she added bleakly.

'And what of us, are we still a closed chapter?' he could not resist asking.

'Nicholas, we are a closed book. Nothing has changed. You do not love me. I cannot marry you.' She strove for a smile, but could only summon a thin grimace. 'I will attend the Cheadles' ball tonight, I promised Georgie I would go with her. Then tomorrow I will make arrangements to leave London.'

He felt a sinking feeling in the pit of his stomach. 'I can't let you leave.'

'You can't stop me, I'm afraid. It is for the best.'

'Goddammit, Serena, why must you be so obstinate!'

'Not obstinate, clear sighted. The point about idylls is that they are just that, a perfect moment in time cut short. I have no desire to witness the destruction of ours. I most certainly don't want to be around on the day you wake up and find you are bored with me.'

'I think you are being muddle-headed Serena, not clear sighted.'

Everything that had happened in the past weeks—the discovery of Serena's identity, the highwaymen, the disgust and shame at his father's cowardice, this new attack on her, the utter turmoil his mind and life had been thrown into since he met her—all suddenly over-whelmed him. Nicholas flung himself from the seat to pace around the room like a caged tiger. 'You walk into my life, you turn it upside down, and now you are planning on walking casually out of it again without so much as one regret, leaving me weighted down with guilt and no means of easing it. Well, I should be glad to see you go. I should be happy to be able to return to my old ways. I was content enough without you.'

Content, but not happy, he knew that now. 'I have not known whether I have been on my head or my heels since the minute you walked through my door. You have lit a fire inside me that only you can put out and yet you deny me even that satisfaction.' Nicholas raked a hand through his hair, staring down at the beautiful cause of all his ire. 'Leave, then, if you must.'

'I must.'

He pulled her to her feet, wrapped her in his arms so close it hurt, his hands moulding the curve of her spine, as if he would make one person out of two. He kissed her hard on the mouth. Then he flung her from him and was gone.

Serena stayed where she was, listening to Nicholas's footsteps receding down the stairs. The front door slammed with an air of finality. Resolved to shed no more tears, with a dejected sigh and a heart that felt too heavy for her breast, she mounted the stairs to select her outfit for the ball. If this was to be her last appearance in London society, she thought determinedly, then she was going to make sure she made a spectacular exit.

For the first time in his life, with absolutely no idea what he should do next, Nicholas stood on the front steps for some minutes, trying fruitlessly to find a way out of this ridiculous situation, fighting the impulse to turn around and force Serena into submission. No, kiss her into submission, he thought savagely, that made far more sense. Hunching his shoulders, he headed off in the direction of the Haymarket in search of someone to spar with at Jackson's.

Two hours later, emerging tired but if anything even more despondent, he met Charles as he turned into Bond Street.

'Nick. Been meaning to have a word with you before tonight.'

Nicholas groaned. He had forgotten all about the Cheadles' ball.

'You ain't thinking of ratting on me, are you?' Charles asked anxiously. 'You remember that you are engaged to dine with us beforehand? Could do with a friendly face.'

'No, I won't rat, though I could see it far enough.'

'Not as far as I could,' Charles said feelingly. 'Come with me to Brooks's. I've got something I need to tell you.'

They traversed the short distance to the club in silence, settling in a quiet back room.

'Hope you don't mind my saying so, but you look like hell, Nick.'

'Thank you. That is exactly how I feel.'

Charles shifted uncomfortably in his chair. 'Sorry to have to bring this up, bit of a delicate matter.'

'Go on.'

'It's about that Serena of yours. Gossip all over the *ton* is that she's your mistress.'

'I see.'

'People are saying she was living with you down at the Hall.'

'And how would people have found out that particular piece of information?' Nicholas asked threateningly.

'Don't vent your spleen on me, Nick, nothing to do with me.'

'I should have known better. I beg your pardon, Charles.'

'No need.' Charles took snuff. 'Bothered me, too, that question, so I've taken the liberty of asking about a bit. Appears your Serena's French chaperone is behind it. She's set up shop in Bond Street, you know, been dropping hints to everyone she sells a dress to, it seems.'

'Madame LeClerc.'

'Eh?'

'That's her name. The dressmaker.'

'Don't matter a jot what her name is, Nick. What matters is that your Serena is on the verge of being ostracised. Lady Cheadle took quite a bit of persuading not to withdraw the invite tonight. Not surprising, after the way the two of you behaved at Almack's the other day. I saw you myself. Might as well have undressed one another in public.'

'Oh, yes, how could I forget,' Nicholas said bitterly. 'One can behave as one likes in private—' this with a meaningful look at Charles '—but one must stick to the rules in public.'

'You've never had any problem playing to the rules before.'

'I have never met anyone like Serena before.'

'Don't understand you at all, Nick. If you'd set out to ruin the girl, you couldn't have made a better fist of it. Question is, what are you going to do now?'

'I don't know. You don't know the half of it, Charles.' Briefly he recounted the visit to Mile End.

'Good God!' Charles eyed his friend sadly.

'You've made a complete mull of it, Nick, no mistake. Very attractive young woman, Lady Serena. Dare say there's any number of men will still take her on with a fortune like that.'

Nicholas had been thinking he could not feel worse, but he was wrong. Charles was managing to rub salt into his wounds without even trying. 'I've already asked her to marry me. She won't have me.'

Charles seemed unsurprised. 'Expect you put it badly.' He sighed. Discussing such delicate matters seemed to him frightfully bad form, but someone had to set Nick right. 'Did you tell her you love her?'

Nicholas stared at him. 'No, of course I didn't.'

'Why not?'

'She's never actually said she loves me.'

'Have you ever asked her?' Charles waited for an answer. 'No, thought not. It's obvious she's in love with you, anyone with eyes can see that.' Charles shook his head again. 'Not thinking straight, that's your problem.'

He was right. A host of other things flitted through Nicholas's mind. The seeming contradiction of Serena's admission that she could no longer play the game on his terms, followed by her surrender to him. Her views on love. Even her refusal to marry him—*because you do not love me*, she'd said. *Serena was in love with him!* He had been blind not to see it. Had he been similarly blind to his own feelings?

'What about you?' Charles said, echoing his thoughts.

'What?'

'Do you love her, you dolt?'

'How can I tell, Charles?'

Charles looked embarrassed. 'Afraid I can't help you there, never having experienced that sort of thing myself. But I suspect it's something you feel rather than know, if that makes any sense.'

It was as if a light had come on. He couldn't know how things would work out. But he felt, *knew* at some fundamental level beyond thinking, that his life no longer worked without Serena. Really, it was suddenly painfully simple. Nicholas sat up in his chair and smiled ruefully at his friend, the smile reaching his eyes for the first time in days. 'You know, Charles, for someone who goes to such lengths to affect indifference, you can be a most a perceptive fellow.'

Charles looked pained. 'Don't go broadcasting that about, I beg you. It would ruin my carefully assembled reputation.'

With this comforting *non sequitur* Charles called for a bottle of brandy to fortify him prior to the evening's celebrations.

Returning home in much improved spirits to change his clothes, Nicholas found his man of business waiting for him. Frances Eldon had not let him down. Nicholas had not thought he could feel more guilty in terms of the misfortune he and his family had visited on Serena. Now he discovered he had been mistaken.

Chapter Eleven

Serena was due to dine at the Lytton household in Cavendish Square prior to the ball. She made her *toilette* in a defiant mood. A final check in the looking glass satisfied her. Her gown was of gold satin, the low neckline exposing more of her creamy flesh than she had hitherto dared. The tiny puffed sleeves were trimmed with seed pearls and conveniently hid the discreet bandage that covered her wound, but otherwise the dress was completely plain, relying upon the figure of the wearer to show it off. This Serena did to perfection, enhancing the effect with a long scarf of sarsenet around her shoulders. She had piled her hair on top of her head with just a few stray, artfully positioned curls left trailing across her cheeks.

The knocker announcing the arrival of the Lytton carriage sounded downstairs as she turned from the glass, allowing her maid to fasten the buttons on her tight evening gloves and drape the long cloak around her shoulders. She was ready. The world would see whether the Lady Serena Stamppe gave a fig for their gossip. Nicholas Lytton would see just what exactly he was going to miss for the rest of his life. At least, until he found someone to replace her.

'Serena, you look stunning. Doesn't she, Mama?' Georgie's sharp eyes looked at her searchingly. 'Nicholas dines with Charles, so we are a gentleman short.'

'Oh, he did not mention it when I saw him earlier.' He was no doubt avoiding her. Serena told herself it was for the best, but the disappointment threatened to overset her.

'So he did call. I knew he would,' Georgie said with a gratified smile. 'I told him about your housebreaker. He was most concerned.'

'Well, as you can see there was no need to be. I am perfectly recovered,' Serena said with a bright smile. 'Now tell me, who are you going to favour with the first dance? Will it be my cousin?'

* * *

By the time the carriage arrived to take them to the ball, Serena's face was aching from forced smiling, and her head buzzed from rather too much wine and far too little food.

She saw Nicholas immediately, standing just behind Charles at the top of the stairs, looking so absolutely perfect, as she knew he would, that for a moment she forgot to breathe. He saw her and smiled. Without thinking she smiled back. Then she remembered the terms on which they had parted, and her smile hardened.

Nicholas drank in the vision before him. She was breathtaking, a goddess in gold, the bright satin gown emphasising the perfection of her natural colouring, the white of her skin, the deep blue of her eyes, the spun-sunshine colour of her hair, which put the dress to shame. His eyes followed the delicate line of her throat down to the alluring valley revealed by the low décolleté. He could see her breasts rising and falling as she breathed. He remembered the softness, the fullness of them in his hands. He remembered the scent of her, that elusive mixture of floral perfume and vanilla that seemed to rise from her skin, the heat of her as she wrapped herself around him. He remembered…

'Nicholas.' Georgiana waved at her brother. 'Nicholas. You are staring at Serena.'

He started. Georgie, her glance flicking from her brother's flushed face to that of her friend, became all at once perfectly aware of the train of his thoughts, and blushed.

'You must learn, child,' Serena whispered, 'that there are times when it is politic for young ladies to pretend they have not noticed they are being stared at. Men, even your brother, have thoughts it is best to know nothing of.'

Georgie giggled nervously. Nicholas looked as if he would say something, then thought the better of it. Serena curtsied, just enough to allow him a tantalising glimpse of her cleavage, and the three of them joined the line waiting to greet their hosts.

Charles stood in the place of honour beside his intended. His appearance was as immaculate as ever, but his expression was harried, and he gripped Nicholas's hand with all the appearance of a man reaching out to a piece of driftwood to save himself from drowning.

'Penelope, here is Nicholas's sister, Georgiana, and Lady Serena too.'

The future Lady Avesbury was, as her intended described her, a compliant little thing, neither plain nor ugly, neither blonde nor brunette. She smiled nervously, but did not speak.

Nicholas observed Serena's reception carefully. Penelope looked embarrassed. Lady Cheadle barely acknowledged her. Proceeding through to the ballroom, Georgiana was immediately surrounded by swains, but it appeared to him that the claims for Serena's hand were less in number than usual. Charles was right, the rumour mill was turning.

Upon leaving Charles this afternoon, he had been filled with an optimism that he had come, as the evening progressed, to believe was entirely misplaced. Events were conspiring against him. His father's heinous crime, and now Frances Eldon's revelations added significantly to his burden of guilt. Then, too, there had been time—too much time—to reflect on his hasty words to Serena this afternoon. He had been cruel, there was no getting away from it.

He could see she had not forgiven him. She

was brittle tonight, all sharp edges and glittering surface. Whatever she might have felt before, he could see no trace of it now. The certainty that a declaration would put all right had faded as the hours ticked by. The knowledge that he was in love had taken firm root. What Serena felt now, he was almost afraid of finding out. It seemed, to his exhausted brain that there were simply too many things for her to forgive. She had a generous nature, she might forgive him. Then again, she might simply pity him, and he could not bear to be pitied.

To cap it all there was this damned ball. They could not be alone here. He had a whole evening to endure with the sword of Damocles suspended over him hanging by a thread, a thread that Serena could cut or reel in with one word. And with her own reputation in tatters—his doing again—he couldn't in all conscience even dance with her. The sense of gloom that had been threatening him all evening descended like a black cloud. Would that he were anywhere but here.

Serena, smiling tensely and marking up her dances, watched Nicholas turn towards the card room without so much as asking her for a dance.

It was her last ball. She would not let him off so lightly. 'Mr Lytton,' she called after him.

Nicholas turned, frowning. She seemed hellbent on her course to ruin.

'Nicholas—Mr Lytton. I have but one dance left. I saved it for you.'

Devil take it, all eyes were upon them. Serena, perfectly aware of this, looked at him challengingly. If he let her down, she would be crushed. Though all his instincts warned him against accepting, he could not betray her so publicly. They would dance together and devil take the consequences. If she did not care, why should he? He was growing very tired of the hypocrisy that surrounded him. 'Make it the final dance and I will be honoured, Lady Serena.' He bowed low over her hand for effect before turning away. He would wait it out in the card room. He would not torture himself by watching her with anyone else.

The evening passed in a whirl. Georgiana granted her first dance to Edwin. Serena, working her way up the same set, watched in amusement the progression of this flirtation, which would have her uncle tearing his eyes out.

Supper time came. As Serena entered the room, a group of ladies stopped talking to stare at her, one of them quite deliberately turning her back. She shrugged indifferently, but her temper simmered. Unable to face any of the delicate pasties and jellies her swain selected for her, she partook rather more than usual of the iced champagne cup. It made her light-headed enough to flirt vivaciously, showing just how little the Lady Serena Stamppe cared for the opinion of the world.

She surveyed the room under cover of her fan, but Nicholas was not present to be impressed by her popularity with the other gentlemen. Their conversation this afternoon had obviously put an end to all between them. Knowing him so well, she knew he would already be regretting having been so persistent. Another champagne cup did nothing to ease the pain of this thought.

Finally the orchestra struck up for the last waltz of the evening. Seeing Serena standing un-partnered, a small group of men gathered around her, calling for her to take pity on one of them and grant them the honour. Despairing of the stubborn man named on her dance card, she was about to place her arm on the nearest supplicant when it was taken rather forcibly by a tall devil in an elegant black coat.

'Mine, I think.' Nicholas pulled her towards the crowded floor, glaring fiercely at anyone foolish enough to stand in his path.

Serena barely had time to catch up her reticule before he turned towards her, and then she was clasped in his arms and swept gracefully out on to the floor in a firm hold, much closer than propriety dictated, but not close enough for either of the participants.

They danced one turn around the room in silence. Nicholas guided her effortlessly clear of the other dancers, steering her with the lightest of touches. For a few moments Serena noticed nothing save the hand on her waist, the warm clasp of his other hand in hers, the beating of her heart against his chest, the feeling of his breath on her cheek. Gradually, she became aware that every pair of eyes on the floor—and off—were focused on them.

'We seem to be providing all of the other guests with a spectacle,' she said with a bitter smile.

'And you do not care a jot,' Nicholas said,

looking down at her with an unreadable expression. 'In fact, it was your intention to provoke just such a reaction.'

Filled with a wild rashness from too much champagne, too many emotions, too much Nicholas, too much everything, Serena decided she didn't care any more. 'Whatever these people are thinking about us, it's more or less the truth. I've been in your bed. Well, in point of fact we haven't actually made it to bed yet, have we? Let us put it more crudely. We have experienced carnal pleasures together. I am no longer a virgin. Unfit for marriage. No better than a courtesan, in fact, were it not for my fortune. Being an heiress, I can always be sure of finding some man whose need of cash makes the idea of soiled goods palatable.'

'Serena, for God's sake, shut up.' He gave her a little shake. 'You don't know what you're saying. I fear you have had a little too much wine.' The words were growled in her ear lest any of the other dancers, already straining with interest towards them, should overhear.

Serena glared at a couple passing so close that Nicholas had to whisk her round in a turn that would have made his dancing master clap his hand with glee. Following him effortlessly, Serena was unimpressed at his prowess. 'On the contrary, I have not had nearly enough. I am perfectly well aware of what I'm saying,' she said coldly.

'I should never have agreed to dance with you tonight.'

Her cheeks were flushed. By now most of the dancers and many of the onlookers were watching their progression round the floor with open interest, but Serena cared for nothing save the urgent need to provoke a reaction from her infuriatingly heart-stopping and stupidly stubborn partner. 'Yet you were keen enough to dance when I was Mademoiselle Cachet,' she said, deliberately misunderstanding him.

'As I recall, you were every bit as desirous of taking part in that particular dance as I was.'

'That is true, I was. But now I am the Honourable Lady Serena I must pay the consequences by providing these good people with something to talk about over their morning chocolate,' she said, bestowing a dazzling smile on a passing couple.

His grip on her waist was so tight she was sure

there would be fingermarks on her skin. The expression on his face was so devilish that most people would have quailed beneath it.

Not Serena, though. 'My only regret is that you did not enjoy yourself more. Foolishly I thought my somewhat unsophisticated steps would be a pleasant change for you. Since you have repeatedly assured me that the charms of my presence in your bed will inevitably wane, I can only assume I was wrong. I was merely a convenient stopgap until you found someone more accustomed to pleasing such a demanding gentleman as yourself.'

To her astonishment, this sally was greeted with a burst of laughter. 'You know perfectly well that is not true. I have made my feelings on the subject of your presence in my bed, as you call it, perfectly plain.'

She was silent.

'We can put an end to this scandal quite easily you know,' Nicholas said, speaking close to her ear, 'by legitimising it.'

She came back down to earth with a jolt. 'Not here, Nicholas, please don't ask me again.'

'What better place,' Nicholas countered,

suddenly unwilling to wait any longer. 'It is an engagement party after all.'

Serena blinked away a tear. 'Another loveless marriage in the making. No, thank you, Nicholas.'

'You think I want to marry you to redeem your reputation.'

'That, and your inheritance. And because you feel guilty on account of your father. Oh, yes, and because of our *compatibility*.'

'You know, Charles pointed something out to me today that changes everything.'

'It seems to me that you pay far too much attention to what Charles has to say, and very little attention to anyone else,' Serena said sarcastically. 'What was it this time?'

'He said you are in love with me. He said I should ask you if it's true.'

Serena stumbled. Nicholas pulled her closer, leaning into her ear. 'Well?'

'Well, what?' she whispered shakily.

'Is it true? Are you in love with me?' he asked, his breath warm on her ear.

He was mocking her. Serena shivered, cold with mortification. 'What difference would it make, Nicholas? Do you not feel guilty enough, is that it? Do you wish to add unrequited love to the burden you insist on assuming? Well, I won't let you.' As she tore herself from his hold, the music stopped.

'Serena,' Nicholas called after her, cursing his own ineptitude. 'Serena,' he called more urgently, pushing his way through the staring crowds.

A hand on his arm stayed him. 'Congratulations, cousin, for this very public display of dissent, thanks to which I will now have no problems in staving off my creditors.'

Jasper's sneer was not long lived. With a low frightening growl, Nicholas grabbed his cousin by the throat and trapped him against a pillar. *'You!'*

'Remember where you are, for God's sake,' Jasper croaked.

'It is surely rather too late for you to worry about the conventions,' Nicholas hissed.

'Let him go, Nick, now is neither the time nor the place.'

Nicholas looked up. Charles stood by his side with Lord Cheadle. A circle of people watched with eyes agog. In the minstrel's gallery he could see the orchestra leaning over the better to obtain a view. Reluctantly he released his grip. 'My apologies—you are right, of course. Let us repair to somewhere more appropriate, Jasper.' There was no mistaking the glint in his eye.

'No, no, Nicholas, you can't call your cousin out,' Charles protested.

'Can't I? Not even when he insulted my future wife?'

'Your future wife,' Jasper croaked nastily, 'that piece of soiled goods. Even if you still wanted her, it's perfectly obvious that she don't want you.'

Nicholas lunged at his cousin again. Jasper cringed away. Charles and Lord Cheadle grabbed one of Nicholas's arms each. 'Through here,' Lord Cheadle said, puffing with the effort of restraining his guest. 'For God's sake, man, away from the ladies.'

All four repaired to the card room. Lord Cheadle ushered the bemused whist players out and shut the door. Jasper tugged nervously at his neck-cloth.

'You shall answer for this,' Nicholas said through gritted teeth, his hands clenched by his sides. 'Name your friends.'

Jasper paled. 'You can't call me out.'

'Think he can, given the circumstances,' Charles said diffidently. 'Perfectly good reason, as he said. You insulted his future wife.' He turned to Nicholas, the proprieties having been observed. 'Take it you'll want me to act for you?'

Nicholas nodded.

'If you require my services, too, I will be only to happy,' Lord Cheadle offered, to the astonishment of his future son-in-law. 'Pretty little thing, that Lady Serena,' he explained with a roguish smile. 'Happy to defend her honour, provided you do intend to make an honest woman of her, young man,' he said, turning to Nicholas.

'As soon as she'll have me, my lord,' Nicholas replied.

'Name your friends, then, Lytton,' Charles said coldly to Jasper.

Truth be told, he struggled to think of any. 'I will have them call on you,' he replied haughtily.

'Immediately,' Nicholas interjected.

'Eh?'

He smiled grimly at the three startled countenances. 'We fight tomorrow morning. That way it's less likely that someone will inform on us. I don't want to be arrested before I've had a chance to run my cousin through.'

'Come now, Nick, you know it's actually for your cousin to name the time and place,' Charles intervened conscientiously.

'No, if we must fight, then why not let it be immediately?' Jasper agreed. 'Either I will kill my cousin, in which case I will inherit the funds I am in rather urgent need of, or he will kill me. Whichever is the case, my creditors will be satisfied, and my somewhat precarious financial situation resolved. Really, I cannot think why the solution did not occur to me before. Let it be swords at dawn tomorrow in the Tothill Fields.'

'Nick?' Charles looked enquiringly at his friend. Receiving his nod, he announced himself satisfied and handed his card to Jasper. 'I will hear from your friends in due course, I presume.'

With a curt nod, Jasper took himself off.

'I must go too. I have unfinished business.' Nicholas turned towards the door.

'Don't, Nick, not a good idea. Leave her to calm down. Besides,' Charles said practically, 'much better to get your fight out of the way first. If someone does inform on you, you could be deported. If you kill Jasper, you'll have to flee the country, and if he kills you—well, you see how it is.'

'I have no intention of killing my cousin, as you very well know. Serena has lived all her life in exile, I would not wish that on her again. As to Jasper killing me—believe me, it will not come to that,' Nicholas said grimly.

'All the same, much better to wait.'

'But…'

'Nick, think about it. If you go there tonight, Serena's bound to find out that you called Jasper out. Any other female would swoon and feel flattered, but Serena—there's no knowing what she would do.'

'She would probably offer to take my place,' Nicholas said with a smile. 'You're right. At the very least she would try to stop me. She is un-accountably keen not to allow me to fight her battles for her.'

'Well, then. Best thing you can do is go home and rest. See Serena in the morning, after you've seen to Jasper. That way it will all be over before she's even had breakfast.'

'After I've seen to Jasper,' Nicholas repeated

thoughtfully. 'You are quite right, I must get Jasper out of the way first.'

He found Georgie waiting with Edwin outside the door of the card room.

'Did you call him out?' she asked excitedly.

'Mind your own business,' Nicholas replied shortly. 'Did Serena take the carriage?'

'I procured a chair for her, she insisted,' Edwin said stiffly. 'She said she wouldn't use your carriage.'

'I see.'

'I feel obliged to tell you, sir, that you have treated my cousin abominably,' Edwin continued nervously. 'She was most upset. Were it not for the fact that I understand you now have a prior engagement, I would feel it incumbent upon myself to call you out on her behalf.'

Nicholas looked startled. 'There is no need, I assure you. Despite appearances, I have your cousin's honour very much at heart.'

'Oh, Nicholas, I knew it,' Georgie said, jumping up and squealing excitedly. 'You're in love with her.'

'Be quiet, Georgiana,' her brother replied repressively. 'I am taking you home now. And if you know what's good for you, you won't breathe a word of tonight's events to your mother.'

'Oh, no, I would not. I promise you.'

'May we offer you a ride home?' Nicholas asked Edwin.

'No, I thank you. I must see my cousin. I have something of a personal nature to impart to her.'

'You never mentioned it to me,' Georgie said, looking miffed.

'That is because it is personal,' Edwin said pompously. 'Family business.'

'Fine, keep your stuffy secrets,' Georgie replied, turning her back on Edwin and marching off on her brother's arm in high dudgeon without saying goodnight.

'Edwin, please don't mention my meeting,' Nicholas called.

But Edwin, in discussion with Lord Avesbury, did not hear him. He took a chair the short distance to Upper Brook Street, unwilling to risk the possibility of mud, horse manure or worse marring the perfection of his evening attire.

Serena answered the door herself, having dismissed her footman. Fully expecting Nicholas intent on continuing their argument, she was as astonished to see her cousin as he was to see her opening the door clad in such a revealing gown.

'Edwin!'

'Cousin Serena!'

She ushered him into the ground-floor parlour. 'What on earth brings you here at this time of night?'

'Are you all right?'

'I'm fine, Edwin. If you are referring to my disagreement with Mr Lytton…'

'Mr Lytton has another dispute to settle now,' Edwin blurted out.

'What do you mean?'

'I should not have said, I mean…'

But Edwin was no match for Serena. Pretty soon she was in full possession of the story. 'They are to fight a duel tomorrow morning,' Edwin said.

Serena was outraged. 'How dare they!'

'But, Cousin Serena, it is only right that he defend your honour if you are to be married,' Edwin protested.

Serena stamped her foot. 'We are not to be married.'

Edwin was shocked. 'But, Cousin, they say

you are—that is, they say—I mean, if you are not to be married…'

'Edwin, it is none of your business. What is it you want?'

He handed her a letter. 'From my father—he said to give it to you and you would understand.'

She took the missive curiously and broke open the seal. Inside was a brief note from her uncle enclosing another letter written in a faded, spidery hand.

'The other night, when you were so upset about your papa being a murderer, I realised I didn't actually know the whole story,' Edwin explained. 'I asked my father about it. Told him what you said, *that's a fine thing coming from him*. Didn't know what you meant—still don't know—but he got very upset. Said he was sorry. Said to tell you he never meant any harm.'

'He said nothing else?' Serena asked, anxious to hear that Edwin remained in ignorance of Mathew's murderous intentions.

'No. Just gave me this letter, told me it was important you received it as soon as possible. Said to tell you he hoped it would make things right between you.'

Serena stared at the letter, a strange excitement rising in her breast. 'Thank you, Edwin. I think I'd like to be alone to read this now, if you don't mind.'

Her cousin was only too relieved to be on his way. He was halfway to the door when Serena called him back.

'Where is the duel going to be fought?'

'Tothill Fields, so Avesbury said.' He shuddered. 'Why? You're not thinking of calling the magistrates, are you? Affair of honour, you know, cousin.'

'I promise I won't call the magistrates, you may set your mind at rest on that score. Goodnight, Edwin. Thank you again.'

Serena closed the door on her cousin. She lit a branch of candles on the mantel and sat down to read. The covering note from her uncle was brief and to the point.

I surmise from something my son let slip that you are aware of my foolish behaviour with regards to yourself. I am deeply sorry for behaving so very badly and can only hope that in time you will forgive me. I feel that I owe it to you to atone with something more meaningful than my apologies, however, and hope that the enclosed missive will serve that purpose. It was sent to me almost twenty years ago, but I did not act upon it. At the time your father was settled on the Continent and I was settled in managing his estates. I saw no reason to disturb that equilibrium, and informed the author of the enclosed letter that your father was dead. Do not judge me too harshly, my motives were for the best. You may decide for yourself whether or not to use the letter to obtain justice for your father. In the light of the rumours I have heard regarding your personal preferences for a certain gentleman, I expect it is more likely that you will not. I leave the matter entirely in your hands. With all respect, I hope to continue your loving uncle.

With a shaking hand, Serena turned to the second letter. *Dear Mathew*, it began. *What I have to disclose is of a shocking nature, but I find myself, on the eve of my second marriage, unable to continue to live a lie.* She read to the end, a smile slowly suffusing her face.

Nicholas must see this. It would be a fitting note on which to say goodbye. She would take it with her to Tothill Fields, for she was determined to prevent him fighting his cousin. No one had the right to fight her battles, especially not if by doing so he took on responsibility for her ruin, which she was determined he would not bear. She would be gone from London soon enough, but it was his home. She would not have people think ill of him.

Looking at the clock on the mantel, Serena cudgelled her brain in an effort to recall what Papa had told her about the conducting of affairs of honour. Daybreak, that is when they were held. Daybreak at Tothill Fields. About four hours away. Time enough to snatch some sleep.

Nicholas was denied the luxury of any such respite. His nerves were strung tight as a bow as he lay wide awake in bed. While the clock moved painfully slowly towards the appointed hour, a cold rage possessed him. He would not kill his cousin—he had no wish to grant Jasper the pleasure of condemning him to a life of exile from beyond the grave—but he determined to make it so close a thing as to strike the fear of death into him.

In any case, darker forces already had Jasper in their grip. If he was in the hands of a cent-per-cent, as Charles had hinted, he was in deep trouble. Moneylenders, especially the type who lent funds to desperate men, had no compunction in murdering defaulting clients. With any luck, Nicholas consoled himself, one of them would rid the world of Jasper, saving him the bother. He could not find it in him to pity Jasper such a fate. As far as he was concerned, his cousin was beyond the pale.

Dressing himself carefully in a plain dark waistcoat and coat in the early dawn light, Nicholas tried to quell the rising panic that arose every time he thought about Serena. After last night's débâcle, and the terrible, terrible mess he had made of his declaration, there was a strong chance she would have nothing more to do with him.

He must not think such thoughts. That way

madness lay. For too long now he had been buffeted, first this way, then that, by fate and the whims of others. His father. His cousin. Even Serena's papa. It was a feeling he neither liked nor was familiar with. Now he was determined to wrest control back, to dominate rather than be dominated, beginning in the most elemental, brutal way possible. Winning the duel would make reparation, and assuage some of the guilt consuming him.

Then he could turn his attention with a clearer conscience to Serena. By noon his fate would be decided one way or another. If she wouldn't have him… No! He halted the thought in its track. He would make her, even if it took him the rest of his life. With grim determination, Nicholas made his way down the dark staircase and unbolted the front door.

Charles and Lord Cheadle arrived promptly with the apothecary in Lord Cheadle's town coach. 'Lovely morning for it,' Lord Cheadle said bracingly. 'Haven't acted for anyone in a long time, duelling seems to have gone somewhat out of fashion. Glad to see someone keeping the tradition going,' he added with a nod in Nicholas's direction.

They made their way through the empty streets, the clatter of the horses' hooves on the cobblestones the only sound to break the early morning silence.

Arriving at the duelling ground, they found Jasper already present. The two sets of seconds conferred, selected a suitable flat piece of ground and carefully tested the length of the pair of wicked-looking foils that Jasper had provided.

Nicholas stripped off his coat and waistcoat, rolling up the ruffled sleeves of his shirt. His boots were next, leaving him in his stockinged feet on the early morning dew. Jasper did not strip to advantage beside his cousin. Though of similar build, what had been muscle in his salad days was now running to fat. Dissipation showed in the deep grooves that ran from his nose to his mouth. Though he had exercised some caution in the amount he had drunk the previous night, his grey eyes were dull and red-rimmed from lack of sleep.

None the less, Nicholas knew he would be foolish to underestimate the effect of desperation on his cousin's fighting prowess. Jasper was no novice. He looked his cousin over with contempt, his eyes glinting steel grey, colder and more dangerous than the foils with which they were now arming themselves. Even such a hardened one as Jasper quailed before such a look.

The seconds called time. The opponents stood face to face. They shook hands curtly. Sunlight winked on the lethal steel as they assumed the *en garde* position. The seconds stood to on either side of the duellists. To Lord Cheadle fell the honour of calling a start. *'Allez'*, he enunciated clearly, and the duel began with a hiss of tempered steel in the crisp morning air.

Chapter Twelve

She had overslept. Too much champagne cup
had given her an aching head. Too much champagne cup had made her act stupidly beyond
measure. In the grey light of dawn, Serena was
mortified. She had behaved appallingly. One
thing for she and Nicholas to be the subject of
gossip following that night at Almack's. That had
been both their doing, and she still could not
bring herself to regret it. But for last night there
was no excuse. She had been angry and intent on
revenge. Nicholas did not deserve such treatment.
His only crime had been a failure to love her, and
she had degraded him in front of his friends.
Worse. He had tried to stop her folly, but she had
merely made it worse. True, he had been angry,
but she had made him so. She deserved every

harsh word he threw at her. She could only be thankful to have hung on to the tiny scrap of dignity left to her, in refusing to admit her love for him. But he must not be allowed to fight another of her battles. He must not come to any harm.

Because of the difficulty of first locating a hackney carriage, then persuading the driver to take her to so remote a location as the Tothill Fields at such an early hour, Serena arrived late on the scene. As she paid off the cab, she could see the two swordsmen facing each other in the distance. Clutching her heavy woollen cloak about her, the precious letter safe in her reticule, and running as fast as her kid boots would carry her through the long grass heavy with dew, she reached the scene just as Lord Cheadle gave the command to start.

She heard the clash of steel on steel, and had the presence of mind to come to a halt on the periphery of the ground marked for the duel. It was too late to intervene. All she could do was try to avoid distracting Nicholas. With her heart in her mouth, she watched as the contest raged.

They were almost equal in height and reach,

but it was immediately obvious to Serena that Nicholas had the lead. His finely muscled body was in perfect shape, and he carried himself with the balance and control of an athlete. But it was his keen eye, his steady hand and total focus that gave him the real advantage over Jasper, whose late nights, compounded with the imminent threat of debtors' prison, made his eye bleary, his hand shaky and his concentration patchy.

Bare knuckles and not foils were Nicholas's preferred sport, but he had been schooled well enough. Jasper, who fenced regularly, had the better skill, though not sufficient to compensate for his body's shortcomings. A few years ago they would have been very evenly matched.

Serena watched with bated breath, aware of the tense silence surrounding them, save for the hiss of the blades, the pad of feet on soft ground, the harsh breathing of the duellists as they thrust, parried, and thrust again. The seconds watched with almost as much concentration as the fighters, unconsciously swaying back and forth, their actions mimicking that of the combatants. Their own swords pointed downwards, ready to intervene in the event of foul play. Stockinged feet shuffled lightly across the grass as Jasper and Nicholas danced forwards, then back, with each lunge and retreat.

Jasper breathed heavily, his skin a waxen pallor, his cheeks stained with the red flush of exertion. Nicholas was coping better with the fast pace of the fight, his shirt clinging with sweat to his muscled torso, but his face still grimly focused, his breathing even, his piercing eyes never wavering from his opponent. Relentlessly he fought, patiently waiting for the mistake that would allow him to breach Jasper's defence.

Jasper's wrist began to ache. The attacking moves had all been his, but now he was blown, all his energy focused on avoiding a hit. Nicholas was toying with him. Several times he could have inflicted a fatal wound, but on each occasion he feinted back at the last minute. On the sidelines, caught up in the visceral thrill of the battle, certain of Nicholas's victory, Serena had to repress the urge to shout encouragement.

Jasper, becoming desperate, thrust wildly at Nicholas's shoulder. The counter-riposte was lightning quick, the foil touching Jasper's chest, pulling back at the last minute. 'What is this truly about? What is it you want, Cousin?' he gasped.

'The truth,' Nicholas replied, easily deflecting the next thrust with another counter-riposte, touching Jasper's shoulder with the point of his foil, withdrawing. 'I know all about your evil plot.'

'I don't know what you're talking about. I—' Jasper broke off as Nicholas's foil sliced into his left arm with a surface cut.

'Tie it up,' Nicholas commanded.

'But surely honour is satisfied,' Charles intervened.

'Tie it up,' Nicholas repeated harshly, 'my honour is very far from satisfied.' Roughly, he pushed away Charles's restraining arm. 'Damn it, leave me alone. I have not finished with him yet.'

'Nicholas! Nicholas, stop this.'

'Serena!'

She threw herself at him. 'Enough, you must stop. I'm sorry. I'm so sorry for last night. Whatever he said, your cousin, I probably deserved it. I won't have you risk your life for me.'

'You have nothing to be sorry for, you had provocation enough. And in any case you are mistaken, Serena,' Nicholas said, looking contemptuously at his cousin, 'this does not concern last night.'

Jasper sneered. 'Would you have me dead, Nick, is that it? Why not, for I'm as good as, anyway.' With a careless shrug and a strange smile Jasper resumed the *en garde* position.

Nicholas pushed Serena to the sidelines. 'Wait there. Trust me,' he said.

She had no option. The seconds stood back. The swordplay resumed.

Jasper fought with a new wildness, sweat pouring down his face. Nicholas parried, broke through his guard, touched his chest, retreated again. Like a cat playing with a mouse, Serena thought, caught up anew in the exhilaration of the fight.

'Let us cut to the chase,' Nicholas said, his own breathing annoyingly even as he shortened his sword arm, lunged, touched, retreated. 'My man of business spoke to your latest employee yesterday. One "Fingers" Harry, currently awaiting trial in Newgate.'

Jasper struggled for breath. His mouth thinned in an evil smile. 'So that's what this is all about.'

'It was you,' Serena gasped from the sidelines

For a split second, Nicholas shifted his attention from his opponent. Jasper capitalised, breaking through his guard, his near-fatal lunge deflected only at the last moment. Serena watched in terror, her hand covering her mouth, but Nicholas was safe. 'Well,' he demanded, 'do you admit it?'

'Yes, damn you to hell, and damn that bitch over there with you.' Sweat clouded Jasper's eyes. He blinked, shook his head in an effort to clear his vision, thought he saw an opening, and thrust. He felt rather than saw the lightning *redoublement* thrust that Nicholas made into his right shoulder. The foil clattered from his twitching fingers. Blood spurted from the wound.

For a few long moments no one moved. Jasper stood looking uncomprehendingly at his foil, the wicked blade glinting on the ground, the first bright red drops of his own blood spattering the grass beside it. Then the seconds rushed forwards. The doctor hurried from the carriage.

'One moment.' Nicholas pushed the apothecary away. 'I want to know the whole,' he said, staring down at Jasper, whose wound was now bleeding copiously. 'Were the highwaymen your doing too?'

Jasper silently nodded his assent.

'Once could be construed the impulsive act of a desperate man,' Nicholas said contemptuously, 'but to plot twice to kill an innocent girl is the act of a cold-blooded evil one.'

'In that case, I wish you had finished him off.' Serena said, surveying Jasper distastefully. 'In fact, if you give me your sword, I will run him through myself.' She reached imperiously for the foil.

Jasper recoiled. 'Keep her away from me.'

'Did the *bon papa* teach you swordsmanship as well as how to handle a gun, then? Really, Serena, much as I wish to oblige you in all things, I cannot agree to your murdering my cousin, especially in front of witnesses,' Nicholas said with a sardonic grin, handing his sword to Charles.

She stilled, caught in his gaze, momentarily forgetting everything save his presence and her overwhelming love for him.

'Lady Serena, you should not be here. Nick, I take it honour is satisfied now?' Charles waited for his friend's nod before pushing the doctor forwards. 'Let this man through before the blighter bleeds to death.'

'One last thing.' Nicholas leaned over his cousin's prone body. Jasper's face had assumed a waxen pallor. His wound bled sluggishly, bright blood spilling crimson on the dewy green grass. 'You sought twice to secure my inheritance for yourself by having my potential bride killed. Why Serena? Why not me?'

Jasper snorted. 'I wish I had. She has more lives than a cat, that one, you would have been easier prey. You think me beyond redemption, but I found the idea strangely repugnant. Much as I despise you, you are, after all, the only family I have.'

'Preferred to murder a defenceless female instead,' Charles said contemptuously.

'Not so defenceless,' Jasper wheezed.

'Man deserves to be hanged,' Charles exclaimed.

'If his creditors get hold of him, he will wish he had been,' Nicholas replied.

Beside them on the grass, Jasper fainted. The

doctor ripped open his shirt and exposed the wound. Charles turned green. Nicholas tugged Serena over to the shelter of a copse of trees, out of earshot of the rest of the duelling party.

'When did you find out about Jasper?' she asked.

'Yesterday.'

'So you weren't defending my honour after all,' she said with a wry smile.

'I was trying to atone. Between my father and my cousin, we've treated you abominably,' Nicholas explained.

Serena returned his gaze, a frown marring the perfect alabaster of her brow. 'Let us not forget my own family's role in this. Edwin did not come to visit me last night in order to inform me of your duel. He came to deliver this.'

She handed Nicholas Uncle Mathew's note and the letter that he had enclosed, watching with bated breath as Nicholas read his father's confession.

'Secrets and deceit at every turn,' she said when he had finished.

'Yet I cannot feel sorry for it now—without those secrets, we would not have met.' Nicholas handed her back the letter. 'So this is why you came. I had supposed you wanted to stop the fight.'

'Yes. No. I came for both those reasons. And one other.' She smiled bravely, blinking away the tears that welled up as she looked at his beloved countenance. 'I came to say goodbye. Our acquaintance started with a fight. I thought it only fitting,' she said with an attempt to smile, 'that it should be ended by one.'

Nicholas took her hand, pulling her close. 'Not goodbye, Serena,' he said urgently. 'Never that.'

She laid her cheek on his chest. In his shirt sleeves and stockings, with the sweat from the fight cooling on his heated body, he was just as he had been that first day. For a moment she allowed herself to be held. To experience for one last time all the coiled power and reckless-ness and overwhelming maleness of him. To breathe in the essence of him. Then she pushed herself away. 'Nicholas, I—'

'I'm sorry for last night,' he interrupted tersely. 'I was inept.'

'*Inept!* It is I who was inept.'

'No, you were merely overwrought and rather intoxicated. Much as it pains me to admit it, I was the inept one. My only excuse is that I've never actually said the words before. I found myself apprehensive, unsure of your reaction. That is why I tried to make you say it first. A mistake, I realised straight away, but by then it was too late.'

Serena felt as if her heart had suddenly decided to take up residence in her throat, and it was severely impairing her breathing. 'I'm not altogether sure I understand you. What words?'

Nicholas smiled down at her, a strange, tender look in his eye she had never seen before. 'Dearest Serena, I love you. I'm in love with you. I think I have been in love with you from the very start, but was too blind to see it. I finally realised yesterday that it was the only explanation for this unshakeable feeling I've had from the very first day we met. That you were mine and only mine.'

She heard the words through a haze, a shimmering, mesmerising haze of pure joy and unbridled happiness. 'Oh,' was all she managed to say.

A clearing of the throat startled them both. 'Your servant, Lady Serena,' Charles said diffidently. 'Sorry to interrupt, but we're ready to leave.' He nodded at one of the departing coaches. 'Doctor's gone off with your cousin. You'll be relieved to know he thinks he'll make a very slow and painful, but full, recovery. We're off in the other coach for breakfast.'

'I think we'll pass on that, thank you, Charles. Serena and I have some rather important things to discuss.'

'Oh, right. Arrangements.' Charles nodded knowingly. 'Take my advice, make it a special licence, Nick. Happy to stand beside you if you need support.' With this, he left them to rejoin Lord Cheadle.

'We are not getting married,' Serena said rather uncertainly.

Nicholas smiled. 'You may not think so, but we are.' The slam of a door made him look in the direction of the departing carriage. 'I would very much like to discuss it with you—in fact, I'm looking forward immensely to persuading you—but right now we seem to have a transportation problem.'

'I noticed there was an inn not far from where the hackney dropped me,' Serena suggested helpfully.

Nicholas raised an eyebrow. 'It is hardly likely to be respectable.'

She giggled. 'Nor are we. As you have informed me many times, I am a ruined woman, and you, Mr Lytton, are a rake. I think it will suit us very well.'

Nicholas drew her a long look. That strange smile again. The new light in his eyes that made her quite light-headed. 'Why not? We have business to finish, Lady Serena, and I have no desire to finish it in the open.'

Serena eyed him blatantly as he donned his jacket and boots. 'That is the second time I have watched you fight,' she said, tucking her arm into his as they walked across the fields towards the smoking chimney of the thatched inn. 'I must confess, I enjoyed it even more than the first. Once I knew you were going to win, that is.'

'Most women would have had hysterics, fainted at the very least.'

'I considered that, of course, but I realised it would have been a distraction. And I do so very much want you to stay alive.'

They continued in silence until they reached the

inn. A startled landlady showed them to the taproom, looking at them dubiously, but promising they would not be disturbed, telling them to ring the bell if they wished to partake of breakfast.

'She thinks we are up to no good,' Serena said.

'I hope to prove her right.'

She felt the familiar tingle in response.

'Come here, Serena.'

She walked into his arms. She belonged there, it was obvious. Nicholas shook his head at his own stupidity. 'Before Charles interrupted us, I told you I love you. Just in case you think you may have misheard me, I think I should tell you again. I love you, Serena, I love you with all my heart.'

'Oh, Nicholas,' Serena said, bursting into tears.

'I don't like to be too dictatorial at this early stage in our relationship, but I'd really rather you didn't cry whenever I tell you I love you. Especially since I aim to tell you every day for the rest of our lives.' Giving her no time to answer, however, Nicholas kissed her.

His mouth was warm, his lips gentle. It was a new kind of kiss. Serena felt her heart soar as if it had grown wings. Tenderly, Nicholas licked away the tears that glittered on her cheeks, touched her brow, her neck, kissed the lobe of her ear, her eyelids, murmuring her name over and over, holding her as if she was the most precious thing in all the world.

Somehow, she could not have said how, Serena was on his lap on the settle, her arm around his neck, her head resting on his shoulder, her bonnet discarded. 'Are you sure?' she whispered tremulously.

'I've told you before, I don't make false promises. I love you. I think I've loved you from the moment I set eyes on your beautiful face in the stable yard at Knightswood Hall, but I was too foolish to understand. I blamed it on your irresistible body. I blamed it on our isolation. I blamed it on—oh, everything I could think of. When Charles suggested I marry you to protect my inheritance I leapt at the idea, because it gave me an excuse to call you my own without admitting what I felt. When you turned me down, I realised my life had lost its meaning. That's when I finally admitted to myself that I wanted you for no other reason than that I couldn't live without you. I can't be sure, but I'm willing to take the chance if you are.'

'Oh, Nicholas, I love you so very much,' Serena said, wrapping her arms around his neck. 'I'm afraid I'll wake up to find this is all a dream.'

His arm snaked round her waist to pull her closer against the heat of his body. He smiled, that smile of his that always made her wish to throw caution to the winds. 'If it's a dream, it's a wonderful one,' he murmured, kissing the corners of her mouth. 'Quite the most wonderful one I have ever had,' he continued, licking along her full bottom lip, pulling her astride his lap.

Serena wriggled deliberately. She felt him harden against her. Shivering with pleasure, she wriggled again. 'Why, Mr Lytton, I do believe this morning's duel has left you a trifle overexcited,' she said wickedly.

Nicholas shifted to lift her up, slipping his hand up her thigh under her dress, closing into the heat between her legs. 'Lady Serena,' he said, his breathing becoming ragged, 'I regret to inform you that it has had the same effect on you.'

His touch lit the torchpaper of passion, setting them both aflame in an instant. Blue eyes met grey for one long slumberous moment, then they were kissing wildly, devouring each other with their mouths, their tongues, their hands, clothing pushed frantically aside, buttons torn, ruffles ripped in their haste to be one.

'Oh God, Serena, I've missed you so much,' Nicholas said, tugging at her dress and touching her with a stunning certainty, just exactly where she needed to be touched.

Serena moaned, fumbling with the fastenings of his breeches, shuddering with need as she wrapped her hand round his length. Digging her hands into his shoulders, she braced herself, pulling him deep inside her with one long luxurious thrust, relishing the feel of him hard against her muscles. Gripped in the vice of a passion almost painful in its need for release she thrust again, then again, slow and hard, pressing her weight on to him and against him, clenching her muscles to feel every inch of him as she moved, her arms entwined around his neck, kissing him feverishly.

His hands were on her waist, steadying her, pulling her to him. Her name was whispered over and over again in her ear, against her mouth,

in a voice hoarse with passion, becoming inar-
ticulate as he thrust with her, into her, higher,
deeper, harder, faster until the world exploded,
a million pieces shattered and reformed as one.
For long moments afterwards they lay spent in
one another's arms. One body. One mind.
Utterly and completely content.

'I don't know how you do that,' Nicholas said
huskily some time later, stroking Serena's hair
tenderly back from her brow. 'One minute I'm
a perfectly sane and rational person, the next
I'm a seething cauldron of need and cannot think
of aught save you, and this.' He laughed softly.
'You know, if the landlady chooses to come in
at the moment, she's going to get the shock of
her life.'

She gave a muffled giggle. 'My reputation will
be in tatters.'

He kissed her gently before lifting her from his
lap and standing up to tidy himself. 'Your reputation is almost beyond recovery.'

Serene straightened out her skirts as best she
could. 'Almost!' Catching a glimpse of herself in
the spotted glass above the fire, she laughed. 'My
hair. Oh dear, I see what you mean. I look—'

'You look absolutely beautiful,' he interrupted, turning her away from the mirror and pressing a kiss into the warm centre of her palm.

'Despite my ruined reputation,' Serena reminded him.

'About that.'

She caught her breath as she met his gaze, such a blazing look of love as was writ there.

'Actually,' Nicholas said with a smile, 'it's not about that at all. I don't want you to marry me to retrieve your reputation. I don't want you to marry me in order to secure my inheritance. I don't want you to marry me to ease my guilt. I don't even want to marry you because it means I have the right to do as I will with this delicious body of yours—though that is, of course, an added attraction. I want you to marry me because I love you, and because I can't live without you, and because now that I've found you I realise I've been waiting for you all my life.' He pulled her close, gazing deep into her eyes. 'So I most humbly beg you, Lady Serena, to be my wife, because you want me as I want you, and for no other reason.'

'I wouldn't have it any other way,' Serena replied, her face flushed with love. She curtsied.

'And therefore, Mr Nicholas Lytton, I thank you most kindly for your very beautiful proposal and I say yes, yes, yes, with all my heart.'

The kiss that sealed their pledge was tender and would have become passionate were it not for the sharp *'ahem'* that announced the land lady's presence.

'Begging your pardon, I'm sure,' she said with a reproving look. 'But would you be re-quiring breakfast? Only this *is* the taproom, and we have other customers who was wishful to share it.'

'Breakfast is an excellent idea' Nicholas said. 'I don't know about you,' he continued, grinning at Serena, 'but I find I am unaccountably famished.'

She giggled. 'I find I am also rather hungry,' she agreed. 'The fresh air, you know.'

'And the exercise,' he concurred, causing his affianced bride to blush wildly.

'So is that a yes?' the landlady asked impatiently.

'It is a yes,' Nicholas said.

'It is a very, very definite yes,' Serena said.

'About time,' the landlady snorted, slamming the door.

'Indeed,' Nicholas said, 'I think that will be the opinion of most of our acquaintance.'

'Do we have to face them?' Serena blushed charmingly. 'It's just—I would prefer to be alone with you. We have a nursery of brats to make, in case you had forgot.'

He laughed. 'I never thought I'd say this, but a nursery of brats is now very high on my list of wishes. In fact, I think it is so important we should give it top priority. What do you say to a special licence and an extended stay at Knightswood Hall? It is where we met, and it holds a special place in both our hearts I think.'

'That, Nicholas would be perfect.'

And so it was that the marriage of Mr Nicholas Lytton and Lady Serena Stamppe took place in private at the country home of the groom not many days later. Not long after the groom placed the ring on his bride's finger, they lay entwined in one another's arms, pressed close, heart to heart, under the vast canopy of a four-poster bed. It was a position with which they would become very familiar, so all-consuming and long-lived was their passion. And in tribute to the quest that first brought them together, the ring that Serena wore on her left hand had embellished upon it a tiny Tudor rose.

* * * * *

HISTORICAL

Large Print
THE VISCOUNT'S UNCONVENTIONAL BRIDE
Mary Nichols

As a member of the renowned Piccadilly Gentlemen's Club, Jonathan Leinster must ensure the return of a runaway. Spirited Louise has fled to her birthplace, hoping to find her family – but charming Jonathan stops her in her tracks! His task is simple: escort Louise promptly home. Yet all he wants to do is claim her as his own!

COMPROMISING MISS MILTON
Michelle Styles

Buttoned-up governess Daisy Milton buries dreams of marriage and family life in order to support her sister and orphaned niece. But Viscount Ravensworth shakes up Daisy's safe, stable existence. Could a tightly laced miss be convinced to forgo society's strict code of conduct…and come undone in the arms of a reformed rake?

FORBIDDEN LADY
Anne Herries

Sir Robert came in peace to claim his lady honourably. But Melissa denied their love and her father had him whipped from the house. Embittered, Rob sought his fortune in fighting. As the Wars of the Roses ravage England, Melissa falls into Rob's power. He should not trust her – but can he resist such vulnerable, innocent beauty?

 MILLS & BOON®

HISTORICAL

Large Print

PRACTICAL WIDOW TO PASSIONATE MISTRESS
Louise Allen

Desperate to reunite with her sisters, Meg finds passage to England as injured soldier Major Ross Brandon's temporary housekeeper. Dangerously irresistible, Ross's dark, searching eyes warn Meg that it would be wrong to fall for him… But soon sensible Meg is tempted to move from servants' quarters to the master's bedroom!

MAJOR WESTHAVEN'S UNWILLING WARD
Emily Bascom

Spirited Lily is horrified by her reaction to her new guardian, Major Daniel Westhaven. He's insufferably arrogant – yet she can't help longing for his touch! Brooding Daniel intends to swiftly fulfil his promise and find trouble-some Lily a husband. Yet she brings light into his dark life – and into his even darker heart…

HER BANISHED LORD
Carol Townend

Hugh Duclair, Count de Freyncourt, has been accused of sedition, stripped of his title and banished. Proud Hugh vows to clear his name! Childhood friend Lady Aude de Crèvecoeur offers her help – after all, turbulent times call for passionate measures…

 MILLS & BOON

HISTORICAL

Large Print

THE EARL'S RUNAWAY BRIDE
Sarah Mallory

Five years ago, Felicity's dashing husband disappeared into war-torn Spain. Discovering a dark secret, she had fled to England. Still haunted by memories of their passionate wedding night, Felicity is just about to come face to face with her commanding husband – back to claim his runaway bride!

THE WAYWARD DEBUTANTE
Sarah Elliott

Eleanor Sinclair loathes stuffy ballrooms packed with fretful mothers and husband-hunting girls. Craving escape, she dons a wig and disappears – *unchaperoned!* – to the theatre. There she catches the eye of James Bentley, a handsome devil. His game of seduction imperils Eleanor's disguise – and tempts her to forsake all honour…

THE LAIRD'S CAPTIVE WIFE
Joanna Fulford

Taken prisoner by Norman invaders, Lady Ashlynn's salvation takes an unexpected form. Scottish warlord Black Iain may be fierce, yet Ashlynn feels strangely safe in his arms… Iain wants only to be free of the rebellious, enticing Ashlynn. But then a decree from the King commands Iain to make his beautiful captive his *wife*!

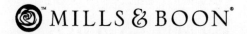

MILLS & BOON

HISTORICAL

Large Print
RAKE BEYOND REDEMPTION
Anne O'Brien

Alexander Ellerdine is instantly captivated by Marie-Claude's dauntless spirit – but, as a smuggler, Zan has nothing to offer such a woman. Marie-Claude is determined to unravel the mystery of her brooding rescuer. The integrity in his eyes indicates he's a gentleman…but the secrets and rumours say that he's a rake beyond redemption…

A THOROUGHLY COMPROMISED LADY
Bronwyn Scott

Has Incomparable Dulci Wycroft finally met her match? Jack, Viscount Wainsbridge, is an irresistible mystery. His dangerous work leaves no space for love – yet Dulci's sinfully innocent curves are impossibly tempting. Then Dulci and Jack are thrown together on a journey far from Society's whispers – and free of all constraints…

IN THE MASTER'S BED
Blythe Gifford

To live the life of independence she craves, Jane de Weston disguises herself as a young man. When Duncan discovers the truth he knows he should send her away – but Jane brings light into the dark corners of his heart. Instead, he decides to teach his willing pupil the exquisite pleasures of being a woman…

MILLS & BOON